GUESTS AND GUILT

An Isle of Man Ghostly Cozy

DIANA XARISSA

Text Copyright © 2018 Diana Xarissa
Cover Copyright © 2018 Linda Boulanger – Tell Tale Book Covers

ISBN: 1985610728
ISBN - 13: 978-1985610729

All Rights Reserved

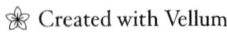 Created with Vellum

For everyone who is a little sister.

AUTHOR'S NOTE

Here we are, seven books into the series, and I thought it was high time we met some of Fenella's relatives. She does have four older brothers, after all. I'm really enjoying writing about her, and it was fun bringing James over for a visit. Hopefully, if any of her other brothers decide to visit, things will go better for them.

I believe the series is best read in (alphabetical) order, but each story should be enjoyable on its own, if you prefer. While the book is set in the Isle of Man, a UK crown dependency, Fenella grew up and lived most of her life in the US. For that reason, the book is written primarily in American English. The only exception is when UK or island-born characters are speaking. I try to make sure that they speak in British English. Fenella is trying to start to use British English, but she usually forgets.

This is a work of fiction. All of the characters are products of the author's imagination. Any resemblance to actual persons, living or dead, is entirely coincidental. The shops, restaurants, and businesses in this story are also fictional. The historical sites and other landmarks on the island are all real; however, all of the events that take place within them in this story are fictional.

You are more than welcome to get in touch to share your thoughts or just to say hello. I love hearing from readers. All of my contact details are available in the back of the book. Thanks for spending time with Fenella and her friends.

1

"Hello, baby sister," the voice on the other end of the phone said.

Fenella frowned and then forced herself to smile. "James, what a surprise. I haven't heard from you in ages."

"I'm really busy," her older brother replied. "But I've been thinking about you."

"Have you, now? How nice," Fenella replied, bracing herself for what she knew was going to follow. James always needed money. The only question was how much he was going to ask for today.

"So much so that I've decided to pay you a visit," was his unexpected reply.

"A visit?" Fenella echoed.

"Yep. I'll be there next week. You can pick me up at the airport, right? I'll send you a postcard with my flight details. I can stay in your apartment, can't I? I can just crash on the couch. That would be fine."

"I have a guest room," Fenella said as her stunned brain tried to think. As soon as the words were out of her mouth, she was sorry she'd said them. She didn't want James staying with her. She didn't even want him on the island.

"Excellent. I won't be any bother. I just need a break, you know? I've been working too hard lately."

"On what?"

"What do you mean?"

"What have you been working too hard on?" Fenella asked, wincing at the bad grammar.

"The next book, of course."

"Yes, of course," she sighed. "Send me the details, then, and I'll pick you up at the airport."

"I can only stay for three weeks," he said, "but that should be plenty of time for me to decide if I want to move there or not, shouldn't it?"

"Oh, yes, plenty of time," Fenella said. Before she could say anything else, James hung up on her.

"Plenty of time," she muttered as she banged her head against the nearest wall.

"My dear child, what are you doing?" Mona demanded.

Fenella looked over at the ghost of her dead aunt who was still staying in the fabulous apartment she'd left to Fenella. "Trying to keep from screaming," she said softly.

"What's wrong?"

"James is coming for a visit."

Mona frowned. "I never liked James. I always thought your mother spoiled him, as he was the youngest, well, until you came along, of course. But that made things worse, because suddenly, at twelve, he wasn't the baby anymore."

"Well, whatever you think of him, he's coming for a visit."

"When? I shall have to go away to the ghost hotel while he's here, I think."

"There's a ghost hotel?" Fenella asked, surprised.

Mona shook her head. "No, but perhaps I can petition for one before James arrives."

"You can petition…" Fenella began and then trailed off. Mona was always saying outrageous things about the afterlife. Fenella was usually better at just ignoring them, but clearly hearing from James had befuddled her.

"So tell me about James," Mona said. "I remember him as a child, of course, but when I used to visit your mother in the US, he was rarely there. Didn't he write a novel or something?"

"Yes, that's exactly what he did. He wrote a book, got it published, and even won an award or two. That was thirty or more years ago, though. He's been living on that one accomplishment ever since."

"I didn't realize writing paid that well."

"It doesn't. James got a healthy advance and was persuaded by my other brothers to invest it wisely. He bought himself a small house in the Poconos to serve as his retreat where he could focus on his next masterpiece. He gets enough royalties every year to just about survive, as his book keeps appearing on reading lists at various colleges and universities. As far as I know, he's never done much more on book two than make outlines and then burn them in his fireplace."

"He's not married?"

"He's too much of a free spirit to marry," Fenella sighed. "I've stopped trying to keep track of his girlfriends. They never last long. His serious lack of money seems to deter most of them and his unwillingness to commit drives away the rest."

"He sounds charming," Mona said dryly.

Fenella shrugged. "I'm sure he can be when he wants to bother. He never seems to have trouble finding women. His problem is keeping them around."

"And now he's coming here," Mona sighed.

"Yeah, hurray," Fenella sighed.

"Do you and James not get along, then?" Mona asked.

"He went and talked to a lawyer about contesting your will," Fenella replied.

Mona gasped. "You can't let him stay here, then. I won't allow it."

"He's my big brother. Of course he will stay here."

"I assume he wanted to contest my will because he wanted to get his hands on my money. As soon as he sees this flat, he's going to start demanding that you give him some."

"He can make whatever demands he wants. The money is legally mine and it's up to me how I spend it."

"Don't give in to him, even though he is your brother," Mona told her. "If I'd wanted him to have my money, I'd have left it to him."

"It's my money now," Fenella reminded her. "It may be easier to give him some just to get him to stop bothering me."

When Fenella had inherited Mona's estate, she'd quit her job, sold her house, and moved back to the Isle of Man. While she'd been born there, her family had moved to the US when she had been only two, and she hadn't even visited in the forty-plus years that had passed since then. The estate included the gorgeous luxury apartment where Fenella was now living, an expensive sports car, and several bank accounts. For some months Fenella had been living fairly frugally as she tried to work out how expensive life on the island was going to be.

A recent meeting with the lawyer who was dealing with the estate had given Fenella a much better idea of her financial position. She'd been shocked to discover that Mona had been considerably wealthier than Fenella had initially believed. Money was no longer a worry for Fenella, and the idea of sharing some of her good fortune with her brother wasn't out of the question any longer.

"I still don't like the idea of you giving him anything," Mona said. "I want to be here when he arrives, but if he's anything like you've suggested, I will probably stay elsewhere during his visit."

"I wish I could stay elsewhere during his visit."

"You can, of course. You own a number of properties around the island," Mona reminded her. "Maybe you should go and stay in one of them, rather than staying here. There are some with multiple bedrooms, so you and James could each have your own room."

"That's a tempting thought, actually. I'm not sure I want James in this apartment. It's my home and it's rather, well, personal to me."

"You haven't done one thing to personalize the space."

"No, because it's perfect just the way it is. James won't appreciate it, though. He'll just see dollar signs on every piece of furniture."

"Ring Doncan and find out which of your properties is empty," Mona suggested. "I'm sure there will be a little house somewhere on the island that you could move into before James arrives. He doesn't even have to know about this flat."

"I'd really rather be outside of the center of Douglas with him, actually. Here he can walk to dozens of pubs, and knowing James, he'll want to try them all. It would probably be better for both of us if I could keep him from drinking too much."

"Ring Doncan," Mona repeated herself.

Fenella did just that, luckily getting an appointment for the next day.

"What do you think?" she asked Katie, the small black kitten who'd walked into Fenella's apartment just after Fenella had arrived. It hadn't taken long for Katie to make herself at home.

"Merrroowww," Katie replied.

"You don't want to meet your Uncle James? No, I don't blame you. Maybe you can stay with Shelly and Smokey while he's here."

"Meerrew," was the reply.

"Go for a walk," Mona suggested a short time later as Fenella paced around the apartment. "You're making both Katie and me crazy with all your pacing."

"I'm worried about James's visit."

"Yes, I know that, but wearing a hole in the carpets isn't going to make things any better. Go walk up and down the promenade until you're too tired to walk anymore. By then it will be time for dinner and then you can watch mindless television until bedtime. Tomorrow, you and Doncan can work out how to deal with James."

Mona was right, even if Fenella hated to admit it. She ran a comb through her shoulder-length brown hair. It was probably time to get her color touched up and more highlights added, she thought. While she would be fifty in less than two years, she didn't want to look fifty. Keeping her grey hair covered up made all of the difference. She added a fresh coat of lip gloss to her lips and then shrugged. She wasn't likely to see anyone that she wanted to impress on the promenade, anyway.

She was locking her door behind her when the door to the apartment next to hers opened.

"Hello, hello," Shelly Quirk said in her typically bubbly way.

"Hello," Fenella replied. "I was just heading out for a walk. I don't suppose you'd care to join me."

Shelly grinned. "I was just going to do the very same thing," she said. "I had lunch with Gordon, and I ate far too much. I really should walk all the way to Peel or something, but I'll settle for a brisk stroll up and down the promenade."

The pair rode the elevator down to the building's lobby and then walked outside into the autumn sunshine. Fenella was glad she'd pulled on a light jacket before she'd left home. Shelly was wearing bright red pants with a red and white striped sweater on top. For Shelly, who loved colors and patterns in everything she wore, the look was almost subdued.

"How is Gordon?" Fenella asked as they began their stroll.

"He's fine," Shelly replied.

"But? I can hear a but in your tone."

Shelly shrugged. "I just can't work out what he wants, that's all. I had a hard time last month, dealing with the anniversary of John's death. Gordon was really understanding through all of that, when I didn't want to go out or see anyone. Now, though, we're back to going out once in a while, but I can't tell if he's just being friendly or if he's, well, interested in more."

Shelly had lost her husband, John, just months before Fenella had moved to the island. When Shelly sold the home the pair had shared and moved into the apartment next to Mona's, the two had become close friends. Mona had helped Shelly through the worst of her grief, encouraging the new widow to embrace life and celebrate with the bright clothes that had become Shelly's signature.

Not long after Fenella had arrived, Shelly had reconnected with an old friend, Gordon. He'd known both Shelly and John for many years and had been widowed himself some years ago. The pair were spending a great deal of time together, but Shelly kept expressing confusion as to where the relationship was going.

"Ask him," Fenella said, repeating her earlier advice. "Just flat out ask him where things are going. That's the only way you'll know for sure."

"Or I could just keep waiting," Shelly sighed. "Waiting isn't so bad. At least I don't look like an idiot, asking him where things are going when things may be exactly where the man wants them to be right now."

"Or maybe he's too shy to tell you that he'd like to take things further."

"And maybe I'm not ready for anything more than friendship, anyway."

Fenella stopped and gave her friend a hug. "Maybe the next time I see him, I should ask him what his intentions are," she said. "He should understand that I'm just worried about you."

"I'm not ready for that yet, either, but I'll keep it in mind. For now, let's talk about you. How's your love life?"

"Nonexistent," Fenella laughed, "and I'd thought things were going so well, too."

When she'd first moved to the island, it had felt like potential suitors were everywhere, but in the last month it seemed as if they'd all disappeared, leaving Fenella on her own.

"Is Donald still in New York?"

"Yes, his daughter is improving, but she'll need months of physical therapy and other treatments. He wants to bring her back to the island for those things, but she isn't stable enough to move yet."

Donald Donaldson was a very wealthy man who'd romanced Fenella whenever he'd been on the island. She's always felt as if he were simply playing with her, but he'd recently told her that he was really falling for her. She'd been trying to work out how she felt when his daughter, Phoebe, who lived in New York City, had been in a car accident. Donald had been in New York ever since, taking care of Phoebe. He called Fenella at least twice a week and had sent several bouquets of flowers to her while he'd been gone, but their relationship was on hold at the moment.

"When did you last talk to Daniel?" Shelly asked.

"He texted me a few days ago to say hi, but that was all he said, really," she sighed. Daniel Robinson was a police inspector. Fenella had first met him over a dead body, and once the case was solved, she and Daniel had begun spending some time together. While Fenella was pretty sure that they both had feelings for one another, Daniel had been off the island taking some classes for over a month now and the man's occasional texts seemed to be coming further and further apart.

Things were tense between them, as well, because Fenella had found herself caught up in a few murder investigations while he'd been away. After the last case, another inspector had casually mentioned that Daniel was involved with a woman he'd met on his course. Fenella had no way of knowing if that was true or not, but Daniel was due back in less than two weeks, so she'd probably have her answer soon.

"Have you seen Peter lately?" Shelly asked. Peter Cannell lived in the apartment on the other side of Fenella's. When she'd first arrived, he taken her out a few times, but things seemed to have settled into a comfortable friendship between them now.

"Actually, now that you mention it, I haven't seen him in ages."

"I know he's been working more, but he's out a lot of evenings as well. I wonder if he's seeing someone."

"I don't know, but we were never more than friends, really."

"Maybe you need a new man in your life," Shelly suggested.

"I don't think so," Fenella replied. "I'm enjoying being on my own, really. Katie keeps me company, anyway."

"I do love having Smokey around. She's made my apartment feel a lot less empty. I don't know that I could have made it through the anniversary of John's death without her."

"Anyway, I probably need time to get over Jack."

Shelly laughed. "Do you really, though? From everything you've told me about the man, you were over him before you dumped him."

Fenella had to smile. She had been in a relationship with Jack Dawson for over ten years, but she'd known all along that they weren't right for one another. They were both history professors at the same university, which would have made ending the relationship awkward. As soon as she'd decided to move to the island, however, Fenella had had no trouble telling the man that they were through. Jack still seemed to be having difficulty accepting that, however, and he still called Fenella occasionally to try to persuade her to move back to Buffalo, New York.

"I certainly don't miss him," she admitted, "and I truly am enjoying being on my own. After ten years with Jack, it's lovely to make all of my own decisions without having to think about another person. Katie isn't nearly as much work as Jack was."

"I know what you mean. I loved John dearly and if I could have him back, I would in a heartbeat, but Smokey is less work and I am enjoying being in charge of my life in a way that I never was when John was alive. That was one of the things I admired about Mona. She was always fiercely independent, even at a time when women weren't meant to live on their own."

Fenella often heard such things about her aunt, Mona Kelly. The woman had led a fascinating, if slightly scandalous, life. From what Fenella had heard, Mona's wealthy boyfriend, Maxwell Martin, had showered her with expensive gifts, including property and cars, but the pair had never married. Fenella wasn't sure if it was Mona or Max who'd been unwilling to make the commitment. Mona had passed away at the age of ninety-one, still happily single. The Mona who haunted Fenella's apartment looked and acted like a woman in her thirties, however, sometimes making Fenella feel old.

"Okay, what's wrong?" Shelly asked a few minutes later. The pair had walked to the end of the promenade and were turning back toward home.

"What makes you think something is wrong?"

"You've been staring at the sea and sighing deeply for the last five minutes."

"I'm sorry. My brother, James, is coming to visit."

"That's the brother who wrote the book and hasn't done anything since, right? The one who really wanted to fight over Mona's estate but couldn't afford to pay to take you to court?"

"Yep, that's the one."

"Why is he coming here?"

"He said he wants to visit to see if he wants to move here."

"Oh, no," Shelly exclaimed.

"I should be happy. I truly do miss my brothers, all of them, even James. I just can't help but feel as if the whole visit is going to be a battle. He's going to take one look at Mona's apartment and realize how much it must be worth. Then he's going to start telling me about how badly he needs money and how lucky I am to have simply been given a small fortune without having to do anything to earn it."

"And then you're going to start to believe him and give him some money," Shelly guessed.

"Probably. He really does need money. He always needs money. I'm sure he needs a new car. He's probably had his current one for ten years or more. His house probably needs a new roof or a new furnace, or more likely, both. I know my other brothers help him out once in a while, but they all have their own expenses. I am really lucky that Mona left me her estate, when you think about it."

"It would be better if he didn't know just how much you've inherited."

"Yeah, but I'm not sure how to keep that information from him. He's going to see the apartment and all of the gorgeous furniture, not to mention Mona's car."

"Maybe you should move into the building next door while he's here," Shelly suggested. "I'm sure you could afford a flat over there that would convince James that you're almost penniless."

Fenella chuckled. "I was thinking about moving into one of Mona's other properties, if I could find one that would be suitable."

"Mona had other properties?"

"Oh, yes, lots of them. Apparently I own houses all over the island."

"That doesn't mean James has any right to any of them," Shelly said quickly. "Don't let him talk you into giving him a house over here."

"He was Mona's relative, too, though. If he does want to move over here, maybe I could give him a little house, maybe somewhere quite far away from Douglas."

"I understand that you want to help him. He's your brother, after all. But don't you think it would help him more if you told him no? How old is he?"

"Sixty."

"So he should be old enough to take care of himself and stop asking his family for money, surely."

"I know that, but I also love him and worry about him. He's never been any good at being an adult."

"Or maybe he's never had to be any good at being an adult, because his family have always looked after him," Shelly suggested.

Fenella shrugged. "I'm going to go and see Doncan tomorrow. Maybe he'll have some ideas about all of this."

"If you do move out of your flat, do you want me to keep Katie for you?"

"I don't know if I can stand not having her around for three weeks, but it might be easier for her to stay with you. I don't know. Moving seems awfully drastic, but I also don't feel like I want him in my apartment."

"Maybe you could just get him a room at one of the hotels on the promenade. I'm sure you could find a good reason for having to do so, if you tried."

"I already told him that I have a guest room, otherwise I'd turn my spare bedroom into an office before he arrives."

"What if you already had a guest in the guest room? Maybe I should stay there while he's here."

"That's an idea. We could tell him that your apartment flooded or something, and you need a place to stay while it's being repaired. I'd happily pay for the man to stay in a hotel, that's for sure."

"See what Doncan says tomorrow, but at least we have one idea that might work."

Feeling better about the impending visit, Fenella enjoyed the rest of their walk in the sunshine.

"It's nearly time for dinner and I don't feel like cooking," Shelly said when they finally returned to their building. "Can I twist your arm into going out with me somewhere?"

"Sure. I don't feel like cooking, either. Just let me feed Katie, and we can go, if you're hungry now."

"I'm always hungry," Shelly laughed. "I shouldn't be, not after my huge lunch, but I am."

The pair ate at one of the nearby Chinese restaurants. "How about a trip to the pub?" Shelly asked as they left the restaurant.

"Why not?" Fenella replied.

The Tale and Tail had once been the private library in a large mansion. When the building was sold, contents and all, the new owners turned the bulk of the mansion into a luxury hotel. By adding a large bar to the center of the library, they'd turned the space into the most wonderful pub that Fenella had ever seen. The walls were still lined with books, and patrons were welcome to borrow them, one at a time. She and Shelly were regulars there. Crowd levels varied enormously, and Fenella was pleased to find the place nearly empty as she and Shelly walked inside.

"Your usual?" the bartender called.

Fenella nodded and then looked around the room. Aside from the books, the pub was also special because of its resident cats. There were half a dozen or more cat beds scattered around the room, and cats of all ages, shapes, and sizes lounged in them, on the shelves, or on the couches and chairs on the upper level. Fenella and Shelly took their glasses of wine up the narrow winding staircase and settled in at the first empty table they found. Within minutes, a pair of small cats joined them and made themselves at home on the women's laps.

"This is perfect," Shelly sighed, "and to think I didn't even know this place existed a year ago."

"I didn't, either," Fenella pointed out. "I barely knew the Isle of Man existed, really."

"Why didn't you ever visit after you moved away?"

"I'm not sure. It never seemed like a place to visit, I suppose. I didn't have any memories from here, as I'd been so young when we moved. My brothers were a lot older when we moved and they've never visited, either, though. My mother came back on her own once, but my father never returned once he was back in the US."

"That's right, he was American, wasn't he?"

"Yes, he was, and I don't think he ever really felt settled over here. From what my mother told me, he wanted to move back to the US as soon as they were married, but she wouldn't leave her own mother behind."

"Do you want to go back to Buffalo for a visit?"

"I don't know," Fenella said, feeling surprised by the question. "I've not really thought about it. I mean, once I realized how much money I actually have, I did think that I'd like to do some traveling, but I was thinking more about seeing all of Europe or maybe visiting Australia. I never even considered going back to Buffalo."

"You don't miss it?"

"I don't think I do. It's strange, being that it's September, though. This is the first September I can remember when I'm not involved in going back to school. I started kindergarten in the US at the age of four, and September has meant back to school for me ever since. Until this year, of course."

"You went straight from being a student to being a teacher?"

"I started teaching undergraduates while I was doing my PhD, so I was both a student and a teacher for a few years. I was fortunate enough to get a position in the history department at the same university as soon as I finished my doctorate and I was there right up until I moved here."

"It's odd for me, too," Shelly told her. "I did my teacher training and then got my first teaching job right out of school. Every September has meant back to school for me as well. I didn't even think about that when I retired right after John died."

"Do you miss it?"

"I'm not sure. Some days I feel as if I'm not doing enough with my life, and I do miss being around children and feeling as if I'm making a difference in their lives. But other days I'm awfully glad that I can simply do whatever I want to do with my time and that I don't have to wipe another runny nose or help a child find their missing mittens ever again."

They finished their glasses of wine and then headed for home. Fenella was feeling reflective as she walked back toward Promenade View Apartments. Perhaps it was simply the approaching autumn that made her feel slightly nostalgic for her old life. Or maybe it was James's upcoming visit that had started that train of thought. Whatever the reason, by the time Fenella had given Katie a small snack and changed into her pajamas, she was almost looking forward to seeing James again.

"Right, so we'll put the apartment on the market and split the proceeds, fifty-fifty," James said. "That seems fair, doesn't it?"

"No, not at all. It's my apartment," Fenella told him.

"Yes, but, really only on a technicality. You should be glad that John, Joseph, and Jacob didn't come as well. They'd all want a share, too, you know. This way we each get half. If they were here, we'd each get a quarter and you'd get nothing."

"It doesn't work like that. Your math is all wrong. This is my apartment."

"Sure, but only at the moment. I'm sure it will sell quickly and then you can take your share and buy yourself something else. There are apartments in the building next door, I believe. Or you can go back to Buffalo. I'm sure Jack would have you back."

"I don't want to go back to Buffalo and I don't want to sell this apartment. I want you to leave."

"Now, now, don't be silly," James said. "I'm just trying to be fair. Why should you get all of Mona's money? She was probably senile when she wrote her will. Maybe she just forgot about me and your other brothers. We want to do what's fair, don't we?"

"Then we should sell everything and split it five ways," Fenella suggested.

"Everything? Is there more than just the apartment?"

Fenella stared at her brother. "Not really," she said.

"Tell me," he demanded.

"I won't," she replied. When he grabbed at her arm, she pulled away.

"Mmmmmerrroowww," Katie complained as Fenella sat up and pulled on the bedclothes.

Fenella blinked and then rubbed her eyes. "I had the most awful nightmare," she told Katie. "James wanted to sell the apartment."

Katie shook her head and then curled back up and went back to sleep. Fenella glanced at the clock. It was only three and far too early to get up. She snuggled back down under the covers. Doncan won't let James get away with anything, she reassured herself. It's all going to be okay.

2

"Fenella, how nice to see you again," Doncan Quaye said the next morning. "What can I do for you today?"

"James is coming for a visit."

The man raised an eyebrow. "The brother who wanted to contest the will?"

"That's the one."

"Is he threatening anything or just paying a brotherly visit?"

"He claims he's just paying a brotherly visit."

Doncan nodded. "He doesn't have any legal right to anything that Mona left you. Obviously, you can give him anything you'd like, but only if you truly want to do so. The money, property, et cetera, are all yours."

"I know, but, well, I don't even know why I'm here," Fenella sighed. "I'm worried about seeing him."

"Are you worried that he'll be able to talk you into doing things that you really don't want to do?"

"Maybe. He is my big brother, though, and I do feel, well, guilty for having inherited Mona's entire estate. Perhaps we should give some money to all of my brothers."

"We can certainly do that if that's what you truly want to do. They are all very well provided for in your will, of course."

"Yes, but they only get that money if they outlive me. That might not happen. They are all quite a bit older, after all. I don't know, maybe we could give them each a lump sum. That might make me feel less guilty."

"As I said, we can certainly do that. Perhaps you could share your inheritance from Mortimer Morrison with them?"

Fenella nodded. Mortimer had been a neighbor, although Fenella had never met him. Through an odd series of events, she'd ended up looking after his dog, though. She'd attended his memorial service along with Shelly, and they'd both been surprised to learn that he'd left his estate to be divided among everyone who had done so. The amount they were each to get was still undetermined, but the estate was proving to be worth more than anyone had expected it to be.

"That might work, and it would mean I wouldn't have to touch the money from Mona."

"Do your other brothers need the money?"

"Not really. They've all done quite well for themselves. James is the only one who didn't finish college and never found a proper job."

"Is James going to be staying with you?"

"I don't know. I told him he could, because it's the right thing to do, but I'm not sure I want him in my apartment, not staying for three weeks, anyway."

"Do you want me to see what other properties you have that might be able to accommodate him? Maybe you have a little house that he might like."

"I'm just afraid he'll never leave," Fenella replied.

Doncan chuckled. "You needn't worry about that. I can make sure he has no choice but to go."

Fenella frowned. "I don't want to upset him, though."

"Let's take things one step at a time. Shall I look for a small house that he can use while he's here?"

"Yes, I think that might be best. I was thinking about putting him up in a hotel, but he might like a house better."

"And if it's your property, it won't cost you anything."

"That's true, too, aside from gas and electricity and whatever."

"All of your properties are managed by an agency that deals with all of the utility bills. You will have to cover them while your brother is staying there, but those expenses will be considerably less than what it would cost for a hotel room for three weeks."

"Okay, see what you can find. I'll start working on finding an excuse as to why he can't stay with me."

"Perhaps Shelly could have a sudden problem with her flat, flooding, maybe? If she needed to stay in your spare room, there wouldn't be any room for James."

Fenella laughed. "Shelly and I had the very same idea," she said.

Doncan turned to his computer and opened up a file. After a few minutes, he smiled at Fenella. "I see two possibilities here. Let me ring someone and check on them."

Fenella sat patiently while Doncan made his call. When he put the phone down, he made a few notes before he spoke. "Right, well, the letting agents are more efficient that I had hoped. One of the houses has already been rented back out; they simply hadn't updated the database yet. The other one is available, however. It's a little bit larger than you might have been thinking, though."

"How large?"

"It has four bedrooms and two baths. It's on a housing estate on the outskirts of Douglas. It's a great neighborhood for families. There's even a primary school nearby. It's on Poppy Drive."

Fenella nodded. "My driving instructor took me through that neighborhood a lot. It's lovely. I didn't realize that I owned a house there."

"You do. Do you want to go and have a look at it?"

"It's empty?"

"There isn't anyone living there at the moment, although it is fully furnished."

"I probably should take a look."

"Let's go now," he suggested. "I could do with a half hour away from my desk. I've been working too hard lately."

"It feels huge, even though I know it's small by American standards," Fenella said a short while later. She was standing in the small living room of the home she hadn't known she owned. The furniture was bland, but functional, and she knew it was much nicer than anything James owned.

"Do you think it will do for your brother?"

"I think it's going to have to, as I don't want him staying with me."

"I'll have the letting agent take it off the books for the time being, then," Doncan said.

"I may tell James that it belongs to a friend of mine," Fenella said thoughtfully as they locked up the house behind them. "I'd rather he didn't know that I owned it."

"You may tell him anything you like," Doncan said. "Here are the keys. You just have to let me know when you're done with it and want to start renting it out again."

Fenella shook her head. "I can't quite get my head around all of this. I didn't even know I owned this house, and now I have the keys to it and can use it whenever I want."

"I'm sure you'll get used to it all in time. Should we talk about cars next?"

"Cars?"

"Are you worried about James wanting to drive Mona's car?"

"Oh, goodness, I didn't even think of that. Once he sees it, he's going to want to drive it, and I'm not going to be able to say no. Knowing him, he'll hit a tree or back into a lamppost or something."

"Maybe you should buy yourself something a bit less exciting to drive, then," he suggested. "Something boring and practical that's older."

"You're probably right."

"Should we go car shopping, then?"

"Are you sure you have time for all of this?"

Doncan laughed. "Whenever Mona came to see me, we nearly always ended up going on an adventure together. She'd decide that she wanted to buy a flat in Peel or check on a business she had part ownership of in Port St. Mary, and somehow she always talked me into going along with her. I remember the day we bought that little red car. She

GUESTS AND GUILT

let me drive it around the car park at the car dealership while we waited for my secretary to bring the check. My life has been a lot less interesting since Mona passed away."

"If you have time, I would appreciate your help with car shopping, then. I have been thinking about getting something more practical for day-to-day use anyway."

"If you ever decide you want to get rid of Mona's car, let me know. I'd love to buy it from you, if I can afford it. My wife would probably suggest that I can't."

"I have no intention of selling Mona's car. I already love it a lot."

A short while later Fenella drove herself back to Doncan's office in a very sensible four-door car. It was only a few years old, but Fenella suspected that it hadn't been exciting even when brand new. It was exactly the sort of car a middle-aged spinster should drive, she decided. Which was perfect for when James was on the island. Its automatic transmission made it easier to drive than Mona's car, too, and Fenella felt a little bit sad as she realized that it already felt comfortable to her. No matter how much she loved Mona's car, this boring, practical car suited her much better.

"Thank you so much for all of your help," she told Doncan when they were back in his office. "I'm feeling better about James's visit now."

"I'm glad to hear that. Before you go, would you like me to start setting up a trust for Mona's estate?"

"A trust? Why?"

"Just to give you a little bit of time, really," he explained. "Once it was in place, depending on the details, you could have just as much access to the estate as you do now, but it would take about a month, maybe a bit longer, to set everything up. During that time, your access to the bulk of the estate would be severely limited."

Fenella grinned. "So I wouldn't be able to give James a big lump of money, even if I wanted to help him."

"Exactly."

She thought for a minute and then shook her head. "I don't think so. I'm going to do some serious thinking about the money over the next few days. I may well decide to share some of it with my brothers. The idea has been at the back of my mind anyway. James's impending arrival has just moved it to the forefront. I'll call you if I change my mind, though."

"You do that. You can always tell James that the trust is in progress, even before I actually start working on it, if you need to," he told her. "Don't let him talk you into anything."

"I won't," she promised, hoping she was right.

"I'd quite like to meet him, if you have time while he's here," he added.

"I suspect we'll have lots of time. I can't imagine what he's going to do on the island for three weeks. He doesn't like museums or historical sites, it's probably going to be too cold for the beach, and he's going to be staying too far from the center of Douglas to spend all of his time at a pub."

"There is a small pub near the house on Poppy Drive," Doncan warned her. "It's easy walking distance from it, actually."

"Maybe we can keep that little fact from James, at least for a while," Fenella said. She was less worried about the pub than she was the fact that the house in question was right across the street from Daniel Robinson's home. Once he was back on the island, that could be incredibly awkward.

"I think I'm all set," Fenella told Shelly a week later. "I'm awfully sorry about the flood in your apartment."

"I still don't understand how it happened," Shelly sighed. "I mean, I never imagined that a broken dishwasher could make such a mess."

"I'm just glad we could arrange things with, um, Jason, so that my brother could stay in his house while you're staying here."

Shelly laughed. "Is that what you're going to call your friend who is lending you the house?"

"Unless you have a better idea. I could pretend it's Donald's, I suppose. He probably owns lots of houses all over the island. But if he comes home while James is still here, I'd have to tell him the whole story very quickly."

"What if James wants to meet Jason?"

"Jason is away, that's why the house is empty," Fenella said. "I don't know about Jason, though. Maybe Steve or Harry or Larry or Fred."

"You really need to pick one and stick to it."

"Which one do you like?"

"I don't know. Fred? It's as good a choice as any."

"Okay. Let's go with Fred. So Fred is a friend of yours, okay?"

"Um, okay, I suppose. Although I'm not sure why, if he's my friend, I'm not simply staying in his house?"

"This is why I never lie," Fenella sighed. "It all gets too complicated. Okay, Fred is my friend, but he's gone to Australia, and he asked me to keep an eye on his house. Having James stay there is ideal, really."

"Let's hope James doesn't ask too many questions," Shelly sighed.

"When I was little, he could always tell when I was lying. I was terrible at lying when I was younger. Actually, I'm probably not any better now. This is never going to work."

"So just tell him that you didn't want him staying with you, so you made other arrangements," Shelly suggested.

"I can't tell him that. He's my brother. I don't want to upset him. It will be fine. Anyway, my friend Fred said that James could stay in his house, and you're staying with me because your dishwasher ruined your kitchen and you have to wait for new flooring and new appliances and whatever."

"All this talk about my kitchen is making me want to redo the one I have," Shelly told her. "Do you think I could actually get my dishwasher to flood my kitchen?"

"Why not just get a new kitchen installed?"

"Oh, I couldn't do that. The one I have is almost brand new. It just isn't really to my taste. I'd love a kitchen just like yours, but I can't possibly tear out the kitchen that's there, no matter how much I'd like a new one."

"Of course now that you have the money from Mortimer, a new kitchen is suddenly a lot more affordable."

Shelly put her fingers in her ears. "La, la, la, la, la. I'm not listening to you as you try to tempt me. My kitchen is fine; it's actually really nice. I just like yours better, that's all. Anyway, for the next three weeks, mine is under construction and I have to stay with you. I won't actually stay with you, though, unless you think James might find out that I'm not."

"Maybe you should stay here for at least the first night or two, just in case. I mean, I don't think he'll be checking my spare room to make sure it's been slept in, but he just might if he gets suspicious."

Shelly laughed. "I don't mind staying here for the whole three weeks if it helps you. I often slept here in the early days after John died. I couldn't face being alone and Mona was kind enough to indulge me. We just have to decide what to do with Smokey."

"Oh, bring her over. Katie loves having her around. They'll have great fun together."

"And so will we. Except when you're out showing James the island."

"Yeah, that should be interesting. He has no interest in history or culture, but I'm sure he'll be fascinated by each and every pub he sees."

"Oh, dear, that doesn't sound like fun at all."

"Do you have any ideas for things we can do, actually? I haven't spent nearly enough time exploring the island myself. I'm sure there are lots of things to do that I haven't heard anything about yet."

"Does he golf?"

"No. He doesn't like to walk."

Shelly laughed. "That leaves out a lot of hiking and glen-walking as well, then."

"I can't see him wanting to do anything like that," Fenella sighed. "Maybe I'm being unfair. I haven't really seen him in over a year, and we didn't exactly see each other regularly before I moved, either. He had his little house in Pennsylvania and I was in New York. Visiting him was pretty low on my list of priorities, and he only came to see me when he was really desperate for money."

"I thought you said he was always desperate for money."

"Well, yes, but he used to work his way through the family, starting with my oldest brother and working his way down to me. We used to discuss it amongst ourselves, actually. We always agreed that we'd only give him a set amount, but I'm sure at least one of my brothers always gave him more than the amounts we'd all agreed upon. James was the baby, you see, or at least he was nearly the baby."

"He's the youngest of the brothers, then?"

"Yes, there's almost exactly two years between each of them, starting with John, then Joseph, then Jacob, and then James. I was a surprise who came along about twelve years later. Surprise sounds better than accident, anyway."

Shelly laughed. "Tell me about the others. I know we've talked about them before, but I don't really remember what you said."

"John is retired and currently married to his third wife. He never had any children and neither does Carol. Her last husband left her millions, and she and John seem very happy together. They live well and they probably give James a lot more money than they should, but they can afford to do so, I suppose."

"And you miss him very much. I can hear it in your tone of voice."

Fenella nodded. "He was nearly eighteen when I was born and was almost like another parent to me. When our parents passed away, I leaned on him the most and he was wonderful to me. Really, every time something bad has happened in my life, John has been there to help me pick up the pieces. I really do miss him a lot. Carol has been good for him, too, and I like her. I'm hoping they might come and visit one day, but so far I haven't been able to persuade them."

"Tell me about Joseph, then."

"He retired in August after teaching high school for his entire career. His wife taught at the same school, but she's older than he is, so she's been retired for a while now. They have two girls who are in their thirties and happily single. I'd love it if any or all of them would come to visit as well."

"That leaves, wait, I'll remember, Jacob?"

"Yes, that's right. Jacob is a semi-retired dentist. He still looks after a few favorite patients, but mostly he potters around his house and annoys his wife."

"That sounds about right."

"When he isn't annoying Candy, he annoys his son, Matthew, who is just about finished with dental school and about to take over the practice."

"Candy?"

Fenella laughed. "Yes, his wife's name is Candy. She's also incredibly young, like thirty-five or something, so only ten years older than Matthew."

"Oh, dear," Shelly said.

"The thing is, she's also incredibly sweet, and she's been wonderful for both Jacob and Matthew. They've always had a difficult relationship and she's managed to get them to communicate a lot more effectively. There was a time when Jacob was ready to sell his practice and Matthew was ready to study anything other than dentistry just to annoy Jacob. Candy has managed to turn the whole situation around. I have nothing but respect for her, in spite of her age and her name."

"Would you like them to visit?"

"Oh, goodness, yes. Candy is also a lot of fun. She's been good for Jacob in that way as well. He's learned to enjoy life a lot more since she came along."

"And Matthew?"

"Matthew has always been my favorite nephew. Okay, he's my only nephew, but he's really quite wonderful. I think I like him better than Joseph's girls, but I'd never admit that to anyone else. I'd love it if Matthew wanted to come and stay for a while. Maybe I'll suggest that to him after he finishes school, before he starts working full-time. A trip to the island would be a nice break for him."

"Which brings us neatly back to James."

Fenella made a face. "We've always had a difficult relationship. I've always felt that he resented me for usurping his role as baby of the family. Obviously, it wasn't my fault, but I don't think he sees it that way."

"Is he a good writer?"

"He wrote one good book, or so I'm told. I've never read it. He actually asked all of us to not read it. I suspect it's semi-autobiographical and he's afraid we'll take offense. I've read a synopsis, so I know it's about a young man coming of age in a foreign country. I don't know if the main character has a younger sister or not, though."

"None of you have ever read it?"

"John read it, actually. He said someone from the family had to read it whether James wanted us to or not. He told me it was rather dull, but just the sort of thing that English professors like."

Shelly laughed. "Maybe I won't rush out to get a copy, then."

"I feel as if I should be more curious about it than I am," Fenella admitted. "I should want to read it, but I'm afraid it would make me angry at James. We don't really get along as it is, so I feel as if it's probably best if I leave it."

"How long ago did he write it?"

"Oh, thirty years ago, maybe. As I said, he's been working on the second one ever since."

"Maybe the island will inspire him."

"I hope not. He'll want to stay if it does. I suppose it might, though. He could write about an older man rediscovering his heritage or some such thing."

"English professors would probably love that, too."

"Yeah, they probably would."

"And now I should let you get some sleep," Shelly suggested. "I'll be over early tomorrow morning with my bags and Smokey. We'll make sure we're well and truly moved in before you leave for the airport."

"Did you want to come with me?"

"Aren't you taking Mona's car? There isn't room for more than one passenger in Mona's car."

"No, I'm taking my car," Fenella replied. "I've been driving it a lot and it's really much more convenient." She could hear the regret in her own voice as she admitted that the boring and practical car better suited her lifestyle than Mona's flashy sports car.

"In that case, maybe I will come with you. I'm really eager to meet James, after everything you've told me about him."

"I just hope he's on his best behavior, at least when he first arrives. No doubt after a short while the niceness will wear off and he'll start whining and making demands, but hopefully I'll get a few good days with him before all of that begins."

Shelly gave her hug. "I'll see you in the morning," she said. "It's going to be okay, you know."

"I know. It's only three weeks. I did check that he had round-trip tickets booked. Even if he decides to move here, he'll probably have to go back after his three weeks are up. He'll have a house to sell and whatever else back in Pennsylvania."

"We'll get through it together," Shelly told her. "You and me and Katie and Smokey. He isn't allergic to cats, is he?"

"Not that I know of."

"That's a shame," Shelly laughed.

Fenella let her friend out and then began to pace around her living room.

"Go to bed," Mona suggested as she appeared on one of the couches.

"I'm too nervous to sleep."

"You shouldn't be. Everything will work out in the end. James will be tiresome, but he'll quickly get bored, and then he'll leave and we won't see him again."

"I hope you're right. I really don't know what to do with him for three weeks."

"He'll have to find ways to entertain himself, then. Keeping him happy isn't your job."

Fenella didn't argue, even though she didn't agree. She paced for a while longer, until Mona finally stopped sighing deeply and simply faded away. Before she got ready for bed, Fenella made sure the guest room was ready for Shelly.

"You'll like having Shelly and Smokey around, won't you?" she asked Katie. The cat looked at her and then nodded before she raced off to the kitchen and began to shout.

"You've had your dinner. I suppose you think you deserve a treat because we're going to have houseguests."

Katie yowled her agreement, so Fenella gave her a few small treats before she got ready for bed. By the time Fenella's face was washed and she was in her pajamas, Katie was curled up in her usual spot in the exact center of the king-sized bed. Fenella was sure that she'd toss and turn all night, but as soon as her head hit the pillow she fell into a deep sleep.

"Argh," she said as Katie patted her nose. "It can't be morning yet. I just closed my eyes."

"Meerreew," Katie replied.

Fenella opened one eye and squinted at the clock. It was seven and she really needed to get up.

"Meerroooww," Katie said.

"Yes, okay, I'll get you some breakfast," Fenella told her.

She did that before she took her shower and then got dressed. "I want to look the way he remembers me," she told Katie as she pulled clothes out of her wardrobe. "That means jeans and a sweatshirt, rather than any of Mona's fancy clothes." Katie shrugged and then left the room.

Along with the apartment and the car, Mona had left behind an enormous wardrobe full of gorgeous and very expensive clothes. Fenella loved going through Mona's things and selecting outfits for dates or special occasions, but she often wore her old and comfortable jeans for everyday. While seeing her brother again might be considered a special occasion, looking like her old self was more important than ever today.

She combed out her hair, admiring the highlights that had been added a few days earlier, and then applied her makeup with care. While she didn't want James to think she'd changed, she did want him to think she looked good.

"Okay, I'll just spread everything out in the guest room, shall I?" Shelly asked a short time later.

"Yes, please. Try to make it look like you've been here a day or two," Fenella replied. "I'm going to try to be vague about your stay, but I want him to think you're already entrenched before he gets any ideas about suggesting you move."

A short while later, it looked as if Shelly had truly taken over the guest room. Smokey was settled on the bed, looking as if she belonged there.

"And now we have just enough time for a quick lunch before we have to get to Ronaldsway."

"Why is the airport called Ronaldsway?" Fenella asked a short time later as they dug into the large pizza they were sharing.

"I think the original name was something in Norse," Shelly told her. "It was the name of the area before the airport was built."

"I really should study some Manx history," Fenella said. "I've all the time in the world to do so, after all."

"I'm sure everyone at the Manx History Institute would love to hear you say that. You should talk to them."

"Someone suggested that I should talk to a woman called Marjorie, actually. She works at the Manx Museum, I think."

"Marjorie Stevens is the librarian and archivist there. She'd be a great person for you talk to if you're serious. Don't talk to her if you aren't sure, though. She fiercely dedicated to the island and she expects everyone else to be as well."

"Maybe I'll wait to talk to her after James has gone, then."

"That's probably wise."

The drive to the airport didn't seem to take long enough to Fenella. She was feeling increasingly nervous as she parked her car.

"It's a nice car," Shelly said. "It's just a bit dull, especially compared to Mona's."

"Yes, but I still have Mona's for when I want a bit of excitement. I'd rather James not know about Mona's car, though."

"I'll try not to mention it."

Fenella sighed. "It probably doesn't matter. It won't take him long to realize that I've inherited a good deal more than a nice apartment and a bit of furniture."

They walked into the building and headed to the small arrivals area. From there they could see the baggage claim carousels through huge windows.

"His flight is on time, anyway," Shelly said after they'd checked the arrivals screen.

"Oh, goody."

A few minutes later, Fenella found herself smiling affectionately at her brother as he strolled up to the baggage claim. "There he is," she told Shelly. "The man with the full head of badly dyed brown hair."

"Has he always dyed his hair?"

"No, actually, he went grey quite young, and he never seemed to mind. He was still grey the last time I saw him. He was about twenty pounds heavier as well."

They both watched as James pulled several bags off the baggage carousel. A moment later a woman in a tight and short dress, with badly bleached blonde hair and what appeared to be an artificially enhanced figure, walked over and said something to him. James laughed and then pulled the woman into an embrace that was far too intimate for their surroundings.

"Who is that?" Shelly hissed.

"I've no idea," Fenella said, trying to ignore the sick feeling in her stomach.

3

"Baby sister," James said loudly as pushed his luggage cart through the sliding doors into the arrivals hall. "I've missed you so much."

"It's great to see you," Fenella said as the man pulled her into a tight hug. Tears welled up in her eyes as she realized she was telling the truth. It was really great to see the man who was a link with everything she'd so impulsively left behind. While she didn't exactly miss her old life, she was suddenly nearly overwhelmed by a rush of emotions she hadn't been expecting.

"You know you can come back any time you want," James told her. "You can even come and stay with me in Pennsylvania if you don't want to go back to Buffalo."

"Thanks, but I'm really happy here. I'm just happy to see you."

"And I'm happy to see you, too. But you must meet Stephanie. Fenella Woods, this is Stephanie Arnold. Stephanie, my baby sister, Fenella."

"It's nice to meet you," the woman said. She offered her hand and squeezed a few of Fenella's fingers for a moment.

Fenella studied her curiously. She didn't look much over thirty, but

GUESTS AND GUILT

she was wearing enough makeup to make it difficult to be sure. "I didn't realize you were bringing a friend with you," she said to James.

"I wasn't planning on it, exactly, but, well, I didn't want to leave Stephanie behind. Knowing her, she'd have replaced me while I was away."

Stephanie laughed and then nodded. "I probably would have."

"This is my friend, Shelly Quirk," Fenella said quickly, pulling Shelly into the group. "She lives next door to me, but she's actually staying with me at the moment, as her kitchen flooded and it's taking ages to get everything replaced."

"I thought you said we could stay with you," James said.

"I said you could stay with me," Fenella replied, trying not to put too much emphasis on the word "you." "But that was before Shelly's emergency. I hope you won't mind that I've made other arrangements for you."

"What sort of other arrangements?" he asked.

"A friend of mine has a house in Douglas that he rents out fully furnished. It's between tenants at the moment, so he said you could use it while you're here."

"A friend? What sort of friend lets strangers stay in his house?" James asked.

"As I said, it's an income property for him, not his actual home. He was one of Mona's friends, actually. She had a lot of friends and admirers on the island," Fenella replied, improvising wildly.

"I came over to spend time with you," James frowned. "I was looking forward to having lots of late-night chats about things."

"And if it were just you, maybe you could crash on a couch or something, but the house will give you and Stephanie a lot more privacy," Fenella said, suddenly quite happy that he'd brought his unsuitable girlfriend with him.

"She's right. I don't want to sleep on a couch," Stephanie said with a giggle. "I'm too old to try making out on one, too."

James laughed. "Yes, okay. We'll stay in your friend's house. I hope it's nice, though. Stephanie has very high standards."

What exactly does she see in you, then, Fenella stopped herself from asking. She glanced over at Shelly and could almost see the same question on her friend's face.

"Let's go and take a look at the house," Fenella suggested. "If you don't like it, we can talk about finding you a hotel or something."

"I suppose that's fair enough," James agreed.

Fenella led them all out to her car. "Here we are," she said, opening the back. "I hope everything fits."

"It's a good thing you didn't bring Mona's car," Shelly whispered as James struggled to load their many bags into the car.

"I probably brought too much stuff," Stephanie said with another giggle, "but I wanted to be ready for anything. I'm going to be seeing a lot of old friends and I want them to see how happy and successful I am."

"Old friends?" Fenella echoed.

"Oh, yes. Like James, I grew up on the island," Stephanie told her. "I left not long after I finished school, and I haven't been back since. I'm really happy that I'm getting this chance to reconnect with the girls I was best friends with back then. It's going to be wonderful."

It took a minute to get everyone into the car. Stephanie wanted to sit in the front and James wanted to drive.

"I'm sorry, but you aren't driving my car," Fenella said firmly. "You weren't driving yet when we left the island, were you? Have you ever driven on the other side of the road?"

"No, but how hard can it be? You manage it, right?" He laughed loudly.

"You and Stephanie can fight over the front seat," Shelly said. "I'm happy in the back." She climbed in while Stephanie and James had a whispered conversation.

When it ended, Stephanie laughed and then climbed in next to Shelly. "I'm going to hold you to that," she told James after they were all in the car. "And a few other kinky things, too."

"Right, so how did you two meet?" Shelly asked quickly.

"I'm a huge fan of his writing," Stephanie said. "I'd just recently gone back to school, and when we read his book, I was sure I recognized the Isle of Man as the protagonist's original home. I loved the

GUESTS AND GUILT

story and I think I started falling in love with James before I even met him."

Fenella rolled her eyes and then started the car's engine. She loved a lot of books, but she'd never felt attracted to their authors simply based on what they'd written.

"Did you meet at a book signing, then?" Shelly wondered.

"No, not at all. James doesn't do book signings. No, I wrote him a long letter, telling him how much I loved his work. He sent it back with a bunch of corrections, telling me where I'd misunderstood things and also correcting my grammar, punctuation, and spelling."

"Oh, that's, um, interesting," Shelly said.

Fenella would have rolled her eyes again, but she was busy driving.

"It was amazing. I couldn't believe he'd taken the time to respond. Of course I had to send him another letter and this time he actually wrote a reply. The rest is history."

"How long have you been seeing each other, then?" Shelly asked.

"Only a few months," James said, "but they've been some of the best months of my life. Stephanie inspires me in a way I've not felt in a great many years. I've been working incredibly hard on my new book ever since I met her."

"How much have you written, then?" Fenella asked.

"Oh, you can't measure art in those sorts of terms," James replied airily. "Actually writing the book is the easy part, anyway. I'll get to that. What matters now is that I'm feeling the book. It's all coming together in my head."

"Too bad you can't sell your thoughts until you put them on paper," Fenella said dryly.

"Oh, they'll get to paper eventually," James told her. "For now I'm just so exhilarated that I can't be bothered to sit down and type."

"How nice," Fenella said.

"And I'm crazy about your brother," Stephanie added. "When I found out he was coming to the island, I simply had to come along. It's the place that we both sprang from, after all. It seemed the perfect place to celebrate our love."

This time Fenella did roll her eyes, in spite of the traffic. She simply couldn't stop herself.

33

"What do you do?" she asked the woman.

"I've done just about everything in the course of my life so far," Stephanie replied. "I'm a free spirit. I travel and I experience the world. Sometimes I have to take a job in order to pay for food or clothing, but mostly I survive due to the generosity of both friends and strangers."

Fenella could only imagine that most of her generous friends were men. "But you said you went back to school. What are you studying?"

"Everything," Stephanie sighed. "There's so much knowledge in the universe. I simply want to absorb all of it."

Shelly began to cough violently. Fenella looked at her. "Are you okay?"

"Yeah, sorry, just a little tickle," she said. Fenella could see repressed laughter in the woman's eyes.

"Where are you studying?" she asked Stephanie.

"Wherever the wind takes me," was the reply that Fenella didn't find unexpected. "I was in LA when I took the class that led me to James. Now I'm learning from him."

"And I am learning from you," James said.

Stephanie laughed. "I doubt that, but you're kind to say so. I mean, I do know a few tricks in some areas, but, well, beyond that I'm simply an eager student."

"I'm sure you're both tired from the trip," Fenella said. "I thought it might be best to drop you off at the house and let you get some rest for today."

"I'm energized by travel," Stephanie said. "Moving from one place to another ignites my spirit."

Fenella glanced at James. He looked completely exhausted. "James, are you feeling ignited?" she asked.

He shook his head. "I'm a bit tired, but if Stephanie wants to do something, we can. I'll manage for a short while, anyway."

"Oh, no," Stephanie said quickly. "You need your rest. I'd forgotten how difficult traveling must be for you. As a writer, you're constantly watching and soaking in everything that is new and different. I'm just floating through life, but you are experiencing it with a writer's eye. You must rest."

"Maybe just a short nap would be good," James agreed.

"I must start making phone calls, anyway," Stephanie said. "I want to see my old friends as soon as possible. Perhaps they'll be able to meet us all for dinner tonight."

"I don't want to be in the way of your reunion," Fenella said quickly.

"Oh, no, you're more than welcome. Everyone on the planet is part of the same family, anyway. I want you to experience knowing the people from my past, as James is part of my present and you are his sister. It will be a very special meeting of minds, personalities, and spirits."

"I'm afraid I'm going to have to give it a miss," Shelly said.

"But you are Fenella's partner, are you not? You are part of her life now and should be part of James's life as a consequence," Stephanie argued.

"I'm Fenella's friend," Shelly replied. "She's being kind enough to let me stay in her flat while my kitchen is being remodeled. Even if I didn't feel as if I would be in the way at your reunion, I have other plans for tonight."

"I thought you and Fenella were a couple," Stephanie said. "You seem perfectly suited for one another."

"We may be, but unfortunately we're both attracted to men and not one another," Shelly replied. Fenella could tell that her friend was trying not to laugh again.

"This is the house," Fenella said a moment later as she pulled into the driveway. "I hope you like it."

"It's huge," Stephanie exclaimed. "I wasn't expecting anything this large. I grew up in a tiny cottage in Ramsey. I just assumed that was what most of the houses on the island were like. All of my childhood friends had the same sort of cottages, anyway."

"This is a fairly modern development," Shelly told her. "As more and more people in banking and insurance moved over here in the late nineties, housing estates like this one started appearing everywhere."

"It looks nice," James said.

Everyone climbed out of the car, and then James and Fenella unloaded the suitcases. Shelly offered to help, but James insisted that they could manage. Stephanie stood off to the side, staring at the house.

"The energy is good," she announced as Fenella headed for the front door. "It would be better if the door were more central, but it isn't too bad. Is the house usually rented out? It feels slightly sad, as if it feels as if it isn't properly loved."

"It is a rental unit," Fenella told her, "but it's very well looked after."

"It wants a family," Stephanie told her.

Fenella didn't bother to reply. She unlocked the door and then stepped back to let James and Stephanie go in first. Shelly winked at her as they followed the couple into the house.

"It's the nicest place I've ever stayed," Stephanie announced, "or maybe not the absolute nicest, but it's very nice."

"I'm glad you like it. I'm sure you'll be more comfortable here than you would have been in my spare bedroom," Fenella replied.

"I just hope we have enough time to get to know one another," Stephanie said. "That's very important to me."

"You're here for three weeks. I'm sure we'll have plenty of time," Fenella replied, feeling as if she already knew the woman quite well enough. "There's bread, milk, coffee, and a few other things in the kitchen, just in case you need a snack. I can take you grocery shopping tomorrow, once you're over your jet lag."

"Thanks for finding this for us," James said. "It's really nice. Now I think it's time for my nap. Maybe you could meet us back here around six and we could go and get dinner somewhere?"

"That sounds good," Fenella told him. She gave him a hug and then she and Shelly headed for the door.

"What about a hug for me?" Stephanie asked.

Fenella forced herself to smile at the woman. "Sure," she muttered.

Stephanie hugged her tightly. "We're going to be like sisters, I can tell," she said happily. "I'll see you later."

As Fenella slowly reversed out of the driveway, Shelly began to laugh. By the time they'd reached the corner, Fenella was laughing with her.

"I take it he never mentioned he was bringing his girlfriend," Shelly said when she finally stopped.

"Never mentioned bringing her, never even mentioned that she existed."

"I can't imagine how he could have forgotten about her. She's incredible."

"That's one word for her."

Shelly chuckled. "You didn't like her? I thought she was great."

"I don't know what I thought of her, really," Fenella said. "She seems to truly think that James is a good writer, though. I'm sure he loves that."

"She does look a little young for him."

"She looks a lot young for him, but she was wearing too much makeup for me to be sure. She could be anywhere from twenty-five to fifty."

"I'd put her at thirty-five, if I had to guess."

"And she's a free spirit who relies on the generosity of others to survive. She and James have a lot in common."

"I suspect these three weeks are going to be expensive for you," Shelly said.

"Yeah. I'm sure James maxed out his credit cards to pay for the flights, so he probably won't have any money for food or anything while they're here. I'm surprised how happy I am to see him, though. I won't complain about treating him while he's here."

"Too bad Stephanie is part of the deal, too."

"If she makes James happy, I can put up with her, too," Fenella said firmly, trying to convince herself as much as Shelly. "Are you sure you can't join us for dinner, though?"

"I'm sorry. I would, but I truly do have other plans. Gordon is going away for a week for work, so we're having dinner together tonight before he leaves."

"I suppose I can't argue with that," Fenella sighed.

Back at home, Fenella curled up with a good book and tried to forget all about James and Stephanie. When Mona appeared a short time later, Fenella was happy to be interrupted.

"Not enjoying the book?" Mona asked as Fenella put it on the table next to her.

"I can't concentrate. James is very much on my mind."

"I thought you might bring him here for a short while."

"He was tired and wanted a nap," Fenella explained. "I'll have to bring him and Stephanie here soon, though, whether I want to or not."

"Stephanie?"

"Oh, yes, he brought his girlfriend with him. He forgot to mention her in any phone calls or emails, but her name is Stephanie Arnold."

"Tell me about her."

"She's somewhere between thirty and fifty, although she dresses as if she were twenty-five. Her hair is bleached blonde and I'm pretty sure she's had her figure artificially, um, inflated. She took a class where they read James's book, and she started writing to him. That's how they met."

"How romantic. Or odd."

"It is a bit odd, but they seem weirdly happy together. Maybe they just haven't known each other for very long."

"Is she a writer?"

"She's a free spirit who travels wherever the wind takes her."

"Really? And how does she fund her travels?"

"The generosity of friends and strangers."

Mona laughed. "I'm looking forward to meeting her."

"Since you owned the house they're staying in, can't you go over there and check her out?" Fenella asked. "I mean, you can appear in the car when I'm driving it."

Mona shook her head. "There are limits to where I can go. It's complicated, but it's basically to do with places that had significant meaning in my life. I can go just about anywhere in this building, therefore, and into my car, but I can't simply go to a house that I used to own but never even visited when I was alive."

"You never even visited?"

"No. Max often gave me properties. I rarely visited any of them. Doncan took care of making sure they were well managed. As I didn't have any intention of ever using any of them myself, there was no need for me to visit them."

"It's a very nice house, actually. If I hadn't already fallen in love with the views and the location here, I might be tempted to move into it after James is gone."

"It's far too big for one person. Are you sure you aren't just tempted because it is across from Daniel's home? It would be a good place to be to keep an eye on him."

"I don't need to keep an eye on him. He can do whatever he likes."

"No need to use that tone with me," Mona said. "Anyway, you'd miss me if you moved there. And Katie would miss me, too."

"Merrooww," Katie said.

Fenella laughed. "That didn't sound like agreement."

"You should work on your cat language skills. Katie definitely agreed with me."

"Meerrrrrreeeeeewwwww," Katie said loudly.

Mona shook her head. "I don't know why I bother." She sighed and then faded from view.

Fenella went back to her book and managed to read a few chapters before she needed to get ready to pick up James and Stephanie for dinner. Not being sure what Stephanie would be wearing, Fenella opted to change into one of Mona's casual dresses. It was a pretty autumnal shade of red that suited the weather and Fenella's mood.

As she drove back toward the rental house, Fenella found herself wondering why James had brought Stephanie along. The extra airfare wouldn't have been cheap, and it wasn't like James to do anything that cost money without a very good reason. Perhaps Stephanie had paid her own way. That made more sense.

"Fenella, darling, do come in," Stephanie said when she answered Fenella's knock. "James is still sleeping, but I know he set an alarm, so he should be up soon. Come in and sit down. We can get better acquainted while we wait for James."

They sat in the living room on opposite ends of the couch. "James told me that you've never been married," Stephanie began.

"That's right, I haven't."

"I've been married four times, but you mustn't let that worry you. I've never met a man as wonderful as James before."

Four times? Fenella wondered if she should doubt the woman's sanity or admire her optimism. "I'm not worried. James can take care of himself."

"Do you think so? I find him endearingly incapable. He's just on a higher plane, mentally, than the rest of us, so things like laundry and cooking are mundane challenges that are beyond him."

"He's lived on his own for a great many years," Fenella pointed out.

"Yes, but he wasn't truly living, was he? He was so consumed by his day-to-day chores that he wasn't actually able to create. Now I take care of the cooking and the cleaning, and his mind is free to take its flights of fancy and imagine the people who will populate his next masterpiece."

"Great," Fenella muttered.

"Oh, and excellent news. I've spoken to one of my friends and they're all going to meet us for drinks later. There's a pub right around the corner from here, apparently. That's what Annie told me, anyway."

"Yes, there is a pub nearby. I've never been there, but I've been told it's nice."

"It's within walking distance, that's what really matters," Stephanie laughed. "We can have dinner and then park here and walk to the pub. It won't matter how much we drink, then."

"Except I'll have to drive home eventually."

"You're welcome to stay here. I mean, you found us the house, of course you can stay here. There are four bedrooms and James and I are only using one of them, after all."

"Yes, well, we'll see. I'm more interested in dinner than anything else right now. I'm starving."

Stephanie glanced at the stairs. "It doesn't sound as if James is awake yet. Maybe I should go and check on him."

"That would probably be a good idea."

"Yeah, it would, wouldn't it?" The woman stood up and then sat back down. "Maybe we should give him another half hour. He was really tired."

"Maybe you should wake him and see what he wants to do," Fenella suggested. "If he wants another half hour of sleep, I can go and get something from a takeaway and bring it back here. Then he can eat as soon as he gets up."

"The thing is, he gets really grumpy when he's woken up. I try really hard not to wake him unless it's an emergency. He does so much of his writing when he's dreaming, you see. I don't want to interrupt his next great idea."

"Whereas I'm happy to interrupt. That sounds better than sitting here and starving. Do you want me to wake him?"

"Would you? I mean, I don't want him angry at you, either, but maybe he won't get angry with you. You're his sister, after all."

Fenella nodded and then reluctantly got up and climbed the stairs. Before she'd even reached the top, she could hear her brother snoring away in the master bedroom.

"James," she called loudly. "James, it's time to wake up." She stopped outside the door and knocked loudly on its frame. "James, come on, big brother, rise and shine."

The snoring stopped and then James rolled over, his eyes still firmly shut.

"James, wake up," Fenella nearly shouted. "Come on. It's time for some dinner and then drinks at the pub." It was the word drinks that made him open his eyes, Fenella noticed.

"Ah, baby sister, did Stephanie send you to wake me? She hasn't left me already, has she?"

"Left you? She sent me up because she didn't want you to get angry at her. She said you don't like to be woken up," Fenella replied, surprised at how articulate the man was on first waking.

"I don't, but we're on vacation. I couldn't possibly have become angry with her under the circumstances."

"Yes, well, whatever. It's time for dinner. Stephanie and I will be downstairs when you're ready."

James nodded. "I won't be long. I must say, I'm feeling a good deal better. That nap was exactly what I needed."

Stephanie was right where Fenella had left her, sitting in the living room, watching the traffic outside. "Was he very angry?" she asked as Fenella walked back into the room.

"Not at all. He'll be down shortly."

Stephanie blew out a breath. "Oh, thank goodness for that," she exclaimed.

"Is everything okay?" Fenella had to ask.

"It's fine. Why wouldn't it be fine?"

"You seemed awfully worried about upsetting James, that's all. You mustn't let him yell at you, you know."

"He doesn't, not really. It's all fine. Truly it is."

Fenella wanted to ask her more questions, but she could already hear James coming down the stairs.

"Where are we going for dinner, then?" he asked when he reached the living room.

"What sounds good?" Fenella asked him.

"Oh, my, what about fish and chips or a good steak and kidney pie? I remember them from my childhood, but I haven't had them since. Mum used to make cottage pie, but that was about the only traditional British thing she ever made."

"There's a pub just around the corner that does food," Stephanie said. "We're going to be meeting my friends there later. Maybe we could just go there."

"I don't know anything about the food there, but I'm willing to try it," Fenella said.

"You can't imagine I'd say no to a pub," James laughed.

As the pub was so close by, Fenella left her car at the house and the trio walked over.

The building was larger than she'd been expecting, with a separate dining room.

"It's dark," she remarked as they were led to a table in the dining room.

"Pubs are supposed to be dark. It makes the women more attractive," James told her with a laugh.

He went and got them drinks from the bar while they looked over the menus. After they'd ordered, Stephanie took James's hand. "I should tell you about my friends," she said. "You should know what to expect."

"Should I? Why?" he replied.

"You told me so much about Fenella before I met her that I felt as if I were meeting an old and dear friend as soon as I saw her. I want you to feel the same about my friends. We were all inseparable once and they're really the closest thing I have to a family anymore, even if I haven't seen them in twenty years or more."

"Go on, then. Tell me about your friends," James said.

"I spoke to Annie Lawrence. She's always been sort of the leader of our little group. She promised to call all of the others and make them come tonight. I met Annie when I was two and she and her parents moved into the cottage next door to ours. She was nearly three and I've been told that I idolized her from the moment I met her. We were both thrilled when we ended up in school together. We were more like sisters than friends, really, as we spent nearly all of our time together, in school and out of it."

"What is she doing now?" Fenella asked.

"I'm not really sure. We didn't talk for long, just long enough to arrange tonight. I'm really looking forward to getting caught up, though."

"Is she married?" James wondered.

"She said she wasn't. Neither is Maureen. That's Maureen Rhodes. We met her in school when we were all around five or six. Her parents fought a lot, so Maureen used to stay over at my house whenever she could once she got into her teens. My mother used to joke that she never could remember how many children she had because Maureen and Annie were both usually staying with us."

"What a fun way to grow up, though," Fenella remarked. "Do you have any siblings?"

"No, which is probably why I bonded so tightly with Annie and Maureen. They were my substitute sisters."

"Is that it?" James asked.

"Oh, no. Courtney Bridges will be here, too. Courtney's family didn't move to the island until she was around fourteen, so she arrived at school when we were in the middle of exams and everything. It was just her and her mum that moved here, actually. Her dad stayed in London and her mum filed for divorce once they were settled here. Annie and Maureen and I took Courtney under our wings and helped her find her way on the island. It was such a big change for her, moving here, but we were happy to help her."

"That was kind of you. Children aren't always that understanding when someone new moves into their neighborhood," Fenella said.

Stephanie shrugged. "Courtney was cool. Her mum got a big divorce settlement. I think her father cheated. Anyway, Courtney had the nicest clothes and things and her father even bought her a car when she passed her driving test. She was a good person to be friends with."

"Is that everyone, then?" James asked.

"That's everyone. As I said, we were inseparable. We called ourselves Annie's gang or sometimes CAMS, using each of our initials. Annie didn't like that one, though, because it gave Courtney top billing, as it were."

"When did you move to the US?" Fenella asked.

"Oh, after school, about twenty years ago or so," Stephanie replied vaguely. "I didn't intend to stay there. It was just meant to be a vacation, but then I fell in love with an American man and ended up marrying him and staying."

"So you haven't seen your friends in over twenty years?" James asked. "I hope you recognize them."

"Oh, I'm sure I will," Stephanie said as the food was delivered. "Our spirits are still intertwined, even if our lives have drifted apart."

4

The food was better than Fenella had expected from a pub. The chocolate gateau was even better and the perfect end to the meal.

"We should probably move over to the pub itself while we wait," Stephanie suggested after Fenella had paid the bill. "The girls won't know to look for us over here."

They moved over to a large table near the back of the main room of the pub. "I'm not sure I should stay," Fenella said as James and Stephanie settled into their seats.

"Please stay," Stephanie replied. "I really want you to meet my friends. And once we start talking, I'll probably be so busy with them that James will feel quite left out. If you're here, you two can chat and he won't even notice that I'm ignoring him."

Fenella laughed. She had to admire the woman's honesty, at least.

"Let's get a couple of bottles of wine," Stephanie suggested. "We should have done that with dinner, really."

"I'm driving, so I won't be drinking," Fenella said.

"But I'm not, so I shall be drinking enough for two," James told Stephanie. "Go and order two bottles to start with. Will your friends be driving?"

"I suspect one of them will be, but unless they've changed a lot, they'll all be drinking anyway," Stephanie replied.

Fenella frowned. When the other women arrived, she'd have to find out about the driving arrangements. She didn't approve of anyone drinking and driving.

"It looks like they're late," James said a few minutes later. He and Stephanie had already finished half of the first bottle of wine. He refilled their glasses as Stephanie jumped to her feet.

"They're here," she squealed and then dashed to the door. Loud happy screams filled the pub as the foursome hugged one another in a flurry of excitement. A moment later Stephanie was back, dragging her friends along behind her.

"Okay, okay, sorry, I'm crying," she said when she reached the table. "Okay, these are my amazing best friends, slash sisters who I love dearly," she said. "And this is James, who is an amazing author and a wonderful person, and his dear sister, Fenella, who is my dear friend."

Fenella smiled at the hyperbole. The pair had only met six hours earlier. "Hello," she said.

"Okay, I've done this all wrong," Stephanie laughed. "Let me introduce everyone properly. James and Fenella, this is Annie," she said, waving at one of the women.

Annie took a step forward and then bowed. "It's a real pleasure to meet you both," she said.

Fenella's initial thought was that Annie looked a good deal older than Stephanie. Even though the woman was wearing a thick layer of makeup, there was no doubt in Fenella's mind that Annie was over forty. Her dress was a bit tight in spots, as if Annie had gained ten or fifteen pounds since she'd bought it. Her short hair was streaked with grey, and Fenella thought she looked tired.

"This is Maureen," Stephanie continued.

Maureen giggled and then waved at everyone. "Hello, hello," she said.

Again, Fenella was certain the woman was over forty. Her dress seemed too large for her very slender frame and Fenella wondered if Maureen had been ill. The fact that her dark brown hair looked like a wig made Fenella even more concerned about the other woman's health.

"And this is Courtney," Stephanie conclude.

Courtney took a step forward and then threw her arms up over her head. "Ta-da," she said.

Fenella laughed. "Hello, Courtney," she said as she admired the woman's perfectly tailored dress. Courtney's hair was medium brown, with some darker lowlights scattered through it so perfectly that they had to have been put there by an expensive hairdresser. Her makeup had been expertly applied and her jewelry, while low-key, looked valuable.

"Everyone sit," Stephanie said, "and have wine."

"I'm driving," Annie told her. "I can't have more than one glass."

"We'll be here for hours," Stephanie objected. "Just stick to one an hour and you'll be fine."

"Well, I'll have one, anyway," Annie laughed.

The woman took seats around the table. James moved over to sit next to Fenella, leaving the seat next to Stephanie available for one of her friends. Annie quickly claimed it.

"So, tell me what you've all been doing since I moved away," Stephanie said, looking around the table.

"If you were on social media, we wouldn't need to have this conversation," Annie said.

"I don't have a computer," Stephanie replied. "They bring too much negative energy into my life."

Annie laughed. "Only you would worry about such things. Computers are essential for work and for play now."

Stephanie shrugged. "What do you do on your computer at work, then?" she asked.

"I work at the hospital in the records department," Annie told her. "I sit for hours upon hours typing up reports and sending out appointment letters. Computers make it all easier, although that doesn't make the job any more fun or interesting."

"I can't imagine it," Stephanie sighed. "I'd hate being stuck in an office all day, every day. I need sunshine and fresh air in order to function properly."

"Yes, well, if I didn't have a mortgage maybe I could have more fun," Annie snapped, "but I like having a place to live that's all mine."

"Is that why you've never married?" Stephanie asked.

Maureen took a sharp breath. When everyone looked at her, she shrugged. "I forgot that Stephanie doesn't know anything about our lives for the last twenty years. If she did, she wouldn't have asked that question."

"I don't mean to upset anyone," Stephanie said quickly. "Why don't you each tell me what you want me to know? I won't ask any more questions."

Annie downed the rest of her drink in a single swallow and then refilled her glass. "No, it's okay. You were my closest friend once upon a time. Maybe you should know what happened after you left."

"Only what you want to tell me," Stephanie said.

"It wasn't even long after you left," Annie said. "You probably remember Scott Lang. He was in our class at school."

"I do remember him. He was gorgeous. I always wanted him to notice me," Stephanie sighed.

"Yeah, well, be glad he didn't," Annie told her. "Not long after you left, he noticed me, and I still have the scars to prove it."

"Really?" Stephanie gasped. "He hit you?"

"Oh, yeah, he used to hit me, and you know what? I kept going back for more, because the physical pain was nothing compared to how I felt when I thought about leaving him. He made sure I was well and truly madly in love with him before he started anything."

"You should have left him the first time he hit you," Maureen said in a tone that suggested she'd said that same thing many times before.

"Yeah, I know that now, but then, well, I was crazy in love with the man. He was gorgeous, and most people didn't believe me when I told them that he hit me, either. He was very clever about doing things that wouldn't leave marks, too."

"I'm so sorry," Stephanie said, putting her hand on Annie's arm.

Annie shook it off and guzzled down her second glass of wine. "Wasn't your fault, though. I just couldn't seem to break his hold on me. We were together for three years and every time he hit me, things got a little bit worse. He was living with me, not working, spending all of my money, and then one day I came home from work early and caught him in our bed with a man. I never found out who the man was or where he'd come from, but I suspect he saved my life. That was probably just about the only thing that could have snapped me out of my obsession with Scott."

"Wow," Stephanie said.

"Yeah, wow," Annie replied with a bitter laugh. "I threw them both out of the flat and had the locks changed that afternoon. Scott left the island a few weeks later, and as far as I know he hasn't been back since."

"And Annie hasn't looked at another man since he left," Maureen added.

Annie shrugged. "I can't see the point. With my luck, whoever I meet will turn out just like Scott. It's not a chance I'm prepared to take, anyway."

"There are lots of great guys out there," Stephanie said. She looked over at James. "I found a pretty good one."

"Yeah, tell me that again in six months," Annie laughed. "I don't know anyone who's actually happily married."

"I am," Courtney said quietly.

"But you're still newlyweds. Wait," Annie replied darkly.

Courtney flushed but didn't reply. After an awkward moment, Stephanie spoke again. "Your turn, Maureen. What have you been doing for the past twenty years?"

Maureen giggled and then drank some wine. "You know me. I'm always an optimist. I've been engaged six times, but still haven't actually made it down the aisle. One of these days, maybe."

"Ha, you're better off on your own," Annie scoffed.

Maureen shrugged. "I like having a man in my life, but then, I always did. Maybe that's because my dad was never around much. Whatever. I'm currently between men, but I'm sure someone else will come along before too much longer."

"I hope so, if that's what will make you happy," Stephanie said.

"I always wanted children," Maureen told her. "And now I'm starting to worry that I'm getting too old. My last boyfriend took off when I started talking about kids, though, so I'm trying not to think about them."

"I can't imagine having children," Stephanie told her. "I'm far too selfish."

"I adore them. I work at a nursery, taking care of the littlest babies, and it's the best job ever," Maureen replied. "I get paid to sit and cuddle babies all day long."

"When you're working," Annie said.

Maureen nodded. "I've been sick for a lot of this year," she said. "I'm not really meant to drink, actually, but sometimes you just have to have some fun. A few drinks won't kill me, and if they do, at least it was them and not the cancer. Cheers." The woman emptied her glass and then refilled it.

Fenella frowned. It seemed as if Stephanie and all of her friends were determined to get quite drunk. As Annie refilled her glass again, Fenella couldn't keep quiet. "I thought you were driving," she said.

Annie shot her an angry look. "Yeah? So?"

"I'll pay for a taxi for all of us," Courtney said, "and I'll have Annie's car driven back to her house as well. It will be fine. You should give me your keys," she added, looking at Annie.

Annie glared at Fenella for another minute and then switched her glare to Courtney. "That's our good friend Courtney for you," she sneered. "Always throwing money at every problem."

"I'm not getting into a car with you, not when you've already had three glasses of wine. We've not even been here an hour yet," Courtney said. "As I need a taxi, it won't cost much more to take you and Maureen home as well. We can leave your car here if you're not happy with me paying to have it driven home for you."

"Oh, no, I'm quite happy for you to pay for anything and everything," Annie laughed. "You can keep buying drinks, as long as no one is driving." She handed her ring of keys to Courtney and then emptied her glass again.

"Drinks are on me," Stephanie said. "It's the least I can do after all these years."

"You can say that again," Annie told her.

Stephanie turned red. "What's that supposed to mean?" she demanded.

"Don't pay any attention to Annie," Courtney told her. "She's had a difficult time of it since you left. I think she missed you more than anyone."

"Of course I did. Stephanie was my baby sister, or very nearly," Annie said, wiping angrily at her eyes as a few tears fell.

"I'm sorry," Stephanie said, her own eyes filling with tears. "I needed to get away. I needed to see the world. I needed to find myself."

"Looks like you found a pretty good plastic surgeon while you were at it," Annie replied.

Stephanie shrugged. "I'm not ashamed to admit that I've had work done. I was insecure, and I thought that bigger boobs and fuller lips and whatever would make me happier. I spent a lot of time chasing happiness in all of the wrong places."

"Haven't we all?" Annie said with a sigh. "Eventually, though, we learn to give up on happiness and just settle for being miserable."

"Oh, Annie, don't say that," Stephanie exclaimed. "Happiness is within your grasp. I can help you find your way."

"You haven't heard Courtney's life story yet," Maureen interrupted. "She's probably the happiest one of the three of us."

Courtney shrugged. "I'm not unhappy, at least. Things didn't exactly go the way that I'd planned with my life, but I can't complain, I suppose."

"When I left, you were planning to go to university," Stephanie said. "Didn't you want to study English literature, or something like that?"

"I had all sorts of grand plans, but in the end I did a degree in accounting and came back here to work for one of the local banks. I've been there ever since," Courtney told her.

"Making more money than Maureen and I put together," Annie said, pouring herself another drink. "You need to see her house. You could fit three of mine inside hers."

Courtney frowned. "I work very hard for everything I have," she said.

"And she married well," Maureen giggled, "really, really well."

"I married the man I love," Courtney said tightly. "That he has money is completely irrelevant."

"She married one of the bank's best customers," Annie said. "She probably won his heart by helping him hide all of his assets from the tax man."

Courtney turned bright red. She opened her mouth and then snapped it shut again. After a few slow breaths, she took a sip of wine and then smiled a fake-looking smile. "I know you're only teasing, Annie, but you really shouldn't say such things. You could get me fired if anyone believed them."

"Sorry, Courtney. You know I'm just desperately jealous of your lovely life. Your husband is pretty incredible, too."

"Sam is a very special man," Courtney agreed. "I'm very fortunate to have found him."

"How long have you been married?" Stephanie asked.

"Not terribly long. Just over a year, actually," Courtney replied.

"Ah, I wish I'd have known. I'd have sent a gift," Stephanie told her.

"We had a very simple ceremony at Sam's estate in the south of France," Courtney told her. "We didn't tell anyone about it until after the ceremony."

"And they didn't need any gifts, anyway," Annie said. "Besides, if they'd had the ceremony on the island, Sam's kids would have made things difficult."

Courtney took another sip of her wine as an angry look flashed over her face.

"So you're a stepmum?" Stephanie asked. "How exciting."

"It really isn't," Courtney replied. "Sam does have two children from his first marriage, but they are in their twenties and certainly don't consider me their stepmother."

"She was having an affair with Sam when he was still married to his first wife," Annie said loudly.

"That isn't strictly true," Courtney snapped, "and I'd greatly appreciate it if you'd not spread rumors about my private life."

Annie looked at Stephanie and giggled. "It's something of a sore subject with Courtney. We should talk about something else."

GUESTS AND GUILT

"Let's talk about you," Courtney suggested. "What did you do after you left the island?"

"I expanded my mind," Stephanie replied. "I traveled all around England, Wales, and Scotland and immersed myself in the culture and heritage of those wonderful and historical places."

"You should have taken me with you," Annie said. "It would have been fun."

"It would have," Stephanie agreed, "but I was mourning the deaths of my parents and trying to escape from my past. Having them both pass so suddenly and so quickly nearly made me crazy. I wanted to get away from anything that might remind me of them, and sadly, that included my friends on the island."

"It was a very difficult time for you," Maureen said. "We all understood why you wanted to get away."

"I'd have done the same, if I'd suddenly inherited all that money," Annie said. "I'd have brought a friend along, though."

Stephanie nodded. "I'd do things differently if I could do them over again, but at the time, I wanted to cut all of my ties and make a fresh start. When I met new people, I never told them about my parents. Not talking about them helped me to not think about them, as well. It wasn't a healthy way to deal with the grief, but it was what I did."

"So you traveled all over the UK," Maureen said. "Then what?"

"Then I decided to see more of the world. I went to Canada for a few years, but it never felt quite right to me. While I was there, I met an American who persuaded me to move to California with him. We got married eventually and it was good for the first year or two. Eventually, I realized that he was keeping me from meeting my full potential, so I left him."

"Was this before or after all of the plastic surgery?" Maureen asked. As soon as the question was out of her mouth, she flushed and then laughed. "Sorry, that sounded really rude, didn't it?"

Stephanie shrugged. "You guys are my best friends in the world. I don't have any secrets from you, just stories you haven't heard yet. It was before the surgeries. My next husband was a plastic surgeon, actually. I went to him to talk about my boobs and he ended up telling me he wouldn't operate on me because he wanted to, er, um, sleep with me too much. He sent me to his friend, who did the surgery just before Stanley and I got married."

"So you've been married twice?" Courtney asked, her tone laced with disapproval.

"Oh, no, I've been married four times," Stephanie replied cheerfully. "Stanley was too demanding. We were only together for a year or so before I'd had enough. After I left him, I had some more work done, because I was feeling so insecure after the way that he'd treated me. Never get involved with a man who tries to create physical perfection for a living. He'll never be satisfied with anything less than what he can create himself."

"I don't think any of us have to worry about that. There aren't a lot of single plastic surgeons on the island, as far as I know," Maureen told her.

"Anyway, after Stanley, I decided that I'd had enough of men and I joined a sort of commune. The money from my parents had run out by that time, and Stanley had a much better lawyer than I did, so I didn't get much from him. The commune was great. I lived and worked there for a few years. We were aiming for self-sufficiency, but if I'm honest, we had no idea what we were doing, so we never even got close."

"I saw a television program about communes once," Maureen said. "At the one they talked about everyone was sleeping with the commune's leader. He told them all he was like a god or something and he took turns with all of the women and men. It was terrible."

"I believe that's more like a cult than a commune," Stephanie said. "After a few years, mine started to get that way, though. It had been started by these four guys, and after a couple of them left, the other two started getting stranger and stranger. Eventually, I'd had enough and I ran away with the son of one of the founders. We got married in Las Vegas and both got jobs there in the casinos."

"Vegas always looks so glamorous when I see it on television," Maureen sighed.

"It isn't, though. When you work there you see the ugly side of it. You meet the people who come and spend money they don't have. The addicts always think they're going to win big with the next deal or the next throw of the dice. I hated it there. It was full of nothing but negative energy and greed."

"So what happened to husband number three?" Courtney asked, sounding bored.

"Oh, his father came and dragged him back to the commune. I'm pretty sure it's truly a cult now. I was lucky to get away when I did."

"And you stayed in Vegas?" Maureen asked.

"No. Like I said, it was too full of negative energy. I went back to California and reconnected with some old friends. I stayed there until recently, actually, working when I needed to and enjoying the company of friends."

"I thought you said you'd had four husbands?" Courtney said.

"Oh, I always forget about Chuck. He wanted to be an actor, but he didn't have any talent. He came out to LA to try his luck and ended up staying with one of my friends. Don't get me wrong, he was gorgeous, but he didn't want to be a model, he wanted to be a star."

Stephanie stopped and took a drink of wine before topping up her glass. Fenella looked around the table. Annie looked almost too drunk to move. Maureen appeared to be half-asleep and Courtney looked bored. No one asked Stephanie to continue as the silence dragged on.

"Oh, sorry, I left you hanging, didn't I?" she said after a few minutes. "Chuck and I started going out and having fun together, and one night we were both really drunk, and he decided we should get married. It sounded like fun, really, so we did. Three weeks later, he moved back to Milwaukee or Minnesota or wherever he was from and that was the end of that."

After another short pause, she spoke again. "Ever since I left the island, I've been trying to better myself. I tried to do it with surgery, with men, and with special diets, but none of those things made me happy. Now I'm working on improving my mind. I started taking classes and it's changed my life."

"What sort of classes?" Maureen asked.

"I took one on quilt making and another on creative writing. Those were just community education courses. Then I decided to get more serious and I took a class at the college near my apartment. It was on great American literature, and one of the books that we read was the one that James wrote. I fell in love with him as I read his incredible prose."

"He could have been a ninety-year-old woman or gay," Courtney said. "You can't possibly fall in love with someone based on a book they wrote."

"You should read James's book," Stephanie countered. "You'd fall in love with him, too. He's just such an amazing author."

"I doubt that very much," Courtney replied.

"Just in case, maybe I won't read it," Maureen said with a giggle. "I mean, I never could compete with you when it came to men."

Stephanie laughed. "None of you could compete with me when it came to men," she said. "I was always the most popular of the CAMS."

"We all did okay, though, back in the day," Annie said.

"Yeah, that's true," Stephanie replied. "But I was always the most popular."

"Did you want an award for that or something?" Courtney snapped.

"Oh, no, not at all," Stephanie said with a light laugh, "and I don't mean to sound as if I'm bragging. It's just that seeing you all again has brought back so many memories. I don't believe in having regrets, but I have truly missed you all."

"No regrets?" Annie repeated. "None at all?" she asked.

"No, none at all. Life is too short to waste time with regrets," Stephanie replied.

"I have a few, well, one, really," Maureen said, "but we don't need to talk about that."

"No regrets, no lies, and no secrets," Stephanie said. "That's how I live my life now."

"No secrets?" Maureen asked.

"None. Not from the people that matter to me. I've told James every single thing there is to know about me," Stephanie replied.

"Everything?" Courtney asked, raising an eyebrow.

"Everything," Stephanie replied. Then she laughed. "Well, everything I can remember, anyway. I'm sure I've forgotten one or two things after all these years. Having said that, do you remember the time we broke into the school with a bottle of wine and a bunch of plastic cups?"

"We thought we were so cool," Maureen laughed, "right up until the police came."

"We got away with it, though, thanks to Courtney," Annie said.

Courtney nodded. "It was a good thing I knew about the back staircase to the back exit from the building. I still can't believe that we all managed to get out before the police found us."

Half an hour later, Fenella yawned for the tenth time in five minutes. The four women were busy reminiscing about their childhood and Fenella was tired of the stories.

James leaned over and whispered in her ear. "Do you think they'd notice if we left?"

Fenella sighed. "Probably, but I want to leave anyway," she whispered back.

"Yeah, this is dumb. I've heard enough of these stories from Stephanie already to know how they all end." He cleared his throat loudly. When everyone at the table was looking at him, he gave Stephanie a sheepish grin. "I'm sorry, darling, but jet lag is getting the better of me. I really need to get back to the house and get some sleep."

"I guess that's the end of the party, then," Stephanie said.

"It doesn't have to be. You can stay and have fun with your friends until the pub closes, if you want," James told her. "I'm just falling asleep sitting here."

"Fenella, you'll stay with us, won't you?" Stephanie asked.

"I wish I could," Fenella lied politely, "but I have a cat who needs her last meal of the day. I should have left hours ago." Fenella knew that Shelly would have taken care of both Katie and Smokey, but there was no way that Stephanie knew that.

"I'll leave the key under the doormat," James said as he stood up. "You can let yourself in when you get back."

"I'm not sure I remember where the house is," Stephanie laughed. "I may have had a few drinks too many."

Fenella found a scrap of paper in her handbag and wrote the house's address on it. "Here you are. Have a taxi take you there."

Stephanie nodded and slipped the paper in her pocket. "I didn't bring any money, though," she said. "How much will a taxi cost?"

"You can ride in ours," Courtney told her. "The driver can drop each of us at our own homes. I'll pay for it."

"And my car," Annie said.

"Yes, and we'll get your car driven home for you," Courtney agreed.

"Oh, James, are you sure you have to go?" Stephanie asked. "I mean, I'll miss you so much."

"But you've missed your friends for years. This is your time together. Enjoy it," James replied.

Stephanie looked uncertain for a minute, and then Annie lifted her glass. "To Annie's gang, the CAMS," she said. "Life was so much simpler twenty years ago."

"It wasn't so simple that time you and Harry Henderson decided to climb up Tynwald Hill stark naked," Maureen laughed.

Fenella stood up and grabbed her handbag. She really didn't want to hear any more of the CAMS's stories. She and James made their way out of the pub and into the crisp autumn evening.

"I'm sorry about that," James said as they began the short walk back to the house. "Stephanie is great, but when she starts drinking, she loves to talk about the past. I don't drink too much anymore, mostly, but sometimes, when I'm with her, I try to keep up."

Fenella swallowed a dozen replies. The man didn't need a lecture from her tonight. He was jet lagged and a little bit drunk. He probably wouldn't remember anything she said, anyway.

"Are you sure you're okay to drive?" he asked her when they'd reached the house.

"I didn't actually drink anything other than soda," Fenella replied.

"Really? I didn't notice. You're smarter than I am, then."

"I always was."

James laughed. "I'm sure you think I'm only here to ask you for money, but I'm really glad to see you, you know."

"I'm glad to see you, too," Fenella told him. "It's been too long."

"It has. And once I'm recovered from my jet lag, we'll get properly caught up."

Fenella got into the car and pulled out of the driveway slowly. James stood on the steps and waved at her as she went. When she opened her apartment door a short while later, she was startled to see lights on in the living room.

"Did you forget I was staying here?" Shelly asked with a laugh.

Fenella nodded. "I did, but I'm glad you are," she replied. She gave Shelly a hug, and then they sat down together while Fenella told her friend all about her evening.

"I'm almost sorry I missed it," Shelly said when Fenella was done. "But not really."

"I wish I'd missed it," Fenella yawned.

After making sure that Katie and Smokey were happy, the women headed for bed. Fenella fell asleep wondering what Mona was doing. The loud ringing noise made both cats shout loudly. Fenella sat up in bed and looked at the clock. It was five in the morning and far too early for anyone to be calling.

"Hello?"

"Fen? It's James. Stephanie never came home last night."

5

Fenella sat up in bed and rubbed her eyes. "Maybe she went home with one of her friends," she suggested.

"Yeah, maybe, but she never called me, either. She would have called or texted me if she wasn't come back here."

"Give me a few minutes to wake up and I'll come over," Fenella said. "She'll probably turn up before I get there, though."

"Yeah, I sure hope so," James replied.

Fenella got out of bed and then shook her head at Katie. "That's it, you just keep on sleeping."

Katie opened one eye and then squeezed it shut again. Fenella headed for the shower. It was only five o'clock and it had already been a long day. A quick but very hot shower helped a little bit, but the coffee she made as soon as she was out of the shower helped more. Not wanting to wake Shelly, Fenella left her a note.

Had to go to see James. Hopefully I'll be back soon, but don't worry if I'm not. I filled both cat bowls with breakfast and gave them fresh water. Don't let them try to tell you otherwise. Call me if you need me.

She was in her car and on the way to the house on the outskirts of town not much more than half an hour after James had rung.

GUESTS AND GUILT

"Oh, it's you," James said when he answered her knock. His face fell and he shuffled back into the house looking old and tired.

"I take it she isn't back yet, then," Fenella said.

"No, and she isn't answering her phone, either. I've sent her a dozen text messages, but she hasn't responded."

"Maybe she forgot to charge it."

James frowned and then nodded. "You could be right about that. She always forgets to charge it, actually. Maybe she decided to stay with one of the others and then couldn't call me because her phone was dead."

"That's certainly one possibility. Is the key still under the mat?"

James frowned. "I didn't check."

Fenella swallowed a sigh as she turned back around and opened the front door. She'd helped James tuck the key underneath the mat last night before she'd left. As far as she could tell, it hadn't been touched. She picked it up and then shut the door.

"You should have left it there. How will Stephanie get in now?"

"She can knock and we'll let her in," Fenella suggested.

"Oh, yeah," James flushed. "I'm not thinking very clearly, really. I didn't sleep very well when I first got back here last night and then I fell into a really deep sleep for a few hours. When I woke up, I didn't know where I was or what time it was or anything. It took me a while to remember where I am and why I'm here. And then I remembered that Stephanie was with me, but she wasn't here."

"Do you have any way to contact her friends from last night?"

"No. I mean, I don't have their numbers. They might be in the phone book, though, I suppose."

A quick search of the house didn't turn up a phone book, however. "We could call directory assistance, couldn't we?" James asked.

"What's the number?"

"How should I know? Assuming it isn't the same as the one in the US, it could be anything."

"Exactly. I can go home and get my phone book or we can wait a few hours until my friend Shelly will be awake and ask her to check for us," Fenella suggested. "We wouldn't want to start calling Stephanie's friends this early in the morning, anyway. No doubt they're all quite hung over."

"They aren't the only ones," James groaned.

"I have painkillers."

"You're my favorite sister."

"I'm your only sister," Fenella pointed out as she shook a couple of pills into her hand. She handed them to James, who swallowed them immediately.

"They'll work better if you drink some water with them," she told him.

He shrugged. "Too much like work," he said.

Fenella wanted to argue, but she settled for sighing deeply instead.

"She's probably with another man," James said gloomily.

"Stephanie? What makes you think that?"

"She's too young for me, for a start. And she's, well, she's a flirt. And once she starts flirting, well, she behaves badly."

"Do you really think she would have gone off with another man while she's here on vacation with you?"

"She's been staying with me at my cottage and that hasn't stopped her."

Fenella stared at him for a minute. "She's been cheating on you, and you still let her stay with you and brought her on vacation with you?"

"She'll tell you it isn't cheating," James sighed. "She's just so full of life and energy that she can't stop herself from wanting to share her love with everyone."

"Everyone?"

"Not everyone," James said hastily, "but sometimes, especially when she's drinking, she forgets how much she cares about me, that's all. I can't keep up with her, you know. We'll go out, and then after a few drinks, I need to go home to bed. She won't be tired, so she'll stay and have a few more drinks. Sometimes she comes home to me and sometimes she doesn't."

"And you dragged me over here to get stuck in the middle of all of this, why exactly?"

"I don't know. When I first realized she wasn't here, I was worried. That's why I called you. Now that I'm waking up, though, well, it seems likely that she simply went home with another man. No doubt she'll turn up here in a day or two."

"In a day or two?" Fenella demanded.

"Or maybe later today. She'll turn up when she's ready to return."

"And she'll have a lot of explaining to do to me."

"You won't understand, though. You're a different type of person."

"Yeah, that's true. I'm the type of person who stays faithful when I'm in a relationship. I'm the type of person who quit drinking to excess when I grew up a little bit. I'm the type of person who worries about my big brother when I think someone is taking advantage of him." She would have continued, but James held up a hand.

"Maybe that's why I called you," he said. "Maybe, subconsciously, I was hoping that you'd be able to convince me to break up with her."

"I don't even know what you see in her in the first place."

James shrugged. "Can we talk over coffee?" he asked.

"Sure," Fenella replied. "Did you make any?"

"I couldn't work out the coffee maker works. It isn't like my one at home."

Fenella swallowed a sigh as she walked into the kitchen. At least there were signs that the man had tried, she thought as she filled the coffee maker and switched it on.

"Toast?" she asked.

"Sure."

Feeling as if she should tell him to make it himself, she slid slices of bread into the toaster on the counter. When they popped, she put them on a plate and handed it to James. "There's butter in the refrigerator and jam in the cupboard," she told him as she put more bread into the toaster. Shelly had suggested that they do some basic grocery shopping for James, and Fenella had gone along somewhat reluctantly. Now she was grateful for everything they'd bought as she buttered her own toast and then poured cups of coffee for both of them.

"That's better," James said after he'd finished his toast and his first cup of coffee. He refilled his cup and then sat back in his seat and smiled at Fenella. "You wanted to know what I see in Stephanie. That isn't an easy question, really. I'm not sure I'm ready to tell my baby sister some cold and hard truths about my life."

Fenella shrugged. "You don't have to tell me anything. I just want you to be happy, and it doesn't sound as if Stephanie is making you happy."

"It isn't that simple. I don't know if I've ever been happy. Maybe it just isn't possible for me to be happy. Maybe happiness is overrated, anyway."

Fenella sipped her coffee and tried to work out an appropriate reply. In some ways she could understand what James meant. There had been more than a few years in her life where happiness had seemed impossible. She hadn't been unhappy, exactly, more like she'd just been keeping her head down and surviving. It was only now that she'd made such a dramatic change to her life that she'd started to find happiness.

"I hated college," James said, "and I hated feeling as if whatever I did I was never going to be as successful as our older brothers. They all went to college, did really well, started careers, made our parents proud. I went to college and it was really hard work. I did try, you know, even though I pretended that I didn't. I studied and I wrote long boring papers about subjects I didn't understand and I tried to do calculus and learn Spanish, and I couldn't do any of it, not well. So I quit."

"Do you want more toast?" Fenella asked, feeling uncomfortable with the way the conversation was going.

"No, not really. I'm not much of a breakfast person. Maybe college would have been easier if I hadn't had all of these voices in my head. I would sit in class and these ideas would start flowing and the imaginary people in my head would start talking to one another. I simply couldn't focus on what the professors were saying. I thought I was either crazy or that I was meant to be a writer, but I wasn't sure which."

"Did you talk to our parents about it?"

"No, not really. I didn't want to admit that I was struggling. I started drinking to try to stop the voices from bothering me. It seemed to help for a little while, and then it stopped helping and things got worse. I finally dropped out of school and shut myself up in a room with a typewriter and a load of paper and typed out everything that was in my head."

"I remember when that happened. You disappeared and no one knew where you'd gone. Mom and Dad were really worried about you."

"I didn't mean to worry anyone. I just needed to be alone to get everything out of my head. It took me about two weeks of almost nonstop typing, but when I was done, the voices stopped. I gave the stack of paper to Mum and then went traveling."

"Yeah, I remember that, too. Mom lost a lot of sleep while you were traveling. She used to sit by the phone every Sunday night, waiting for it to ring."

"And I usually forgot all about calling her," James sighed. "I was a terrible son. I was so caught up in my own life, I never even thought about the people I'd left behind."

"But the voices had stopped?"

"Yes, the voices had stopped. I felt like a huge weight had been lifted off my shoulders. I suppose I was happy for that year when I was traveling. I didn't have much money, but I had enough to get by and I made a lot of friends on the road."

"Like Stephanie, relying on the kindness of friends and strangers."

"Yeah, like that, but probably with a lot less sex," he said wryly. "Anyway, when I got back home, I started working odd jobs. I was starting to think about going back to school when Mum told me that she'd sent my book to an agent who was the friend of a friend of hers."

"That sounds like Mom. Always trying to find ways to help us, even if we didn't want any help," Fenella laughed.

James nodded. "Yeah, I was furious with her. I'd never intended for anyone to see what I'd written, but I suppose I'd never really made that clear to her. I told her that I wasn't interested in publishing anything and that she should tell the agent that if he ever called. Six months later, Mum called me and said that the agent had four different offers from publishers if I wanted to reconsider."

"Four? Wow. I'm impressed. I never knew any of this at the time."

"You were still a kid. It didn't concern you."

"I wish you would have told me all of this years ago, though. It's fascinating."

James sighed. "That isn't the word I would use, but it's my life story, for better or worse."

"So what happened when Mom told you about the offers?"

"Dad and I went to New York and met with the agent. He told me about all of the offers and I picked one. Dad and I didn't agree, and the agent was on Dad's side, but I know for sure that I made the right choice."

"Why? What did you turn down?"

"The offer I took was for a good deal of money. I've been living off that money, plus what I inherited when Mum and Dad died, for thirty-five years. But there was a better offer. One of the publishers offered me nearly double the advance that I ended up taking."

"Double?"

"Yeah, but it was a two-book deal," James explained. "They wanted me to produce a second book in twelve months. I would get all of the money up front, but I'd have to pay back half of it if I didn't write the second book in time."

"And you didn't think you could manage it?"

"I knew I couldn't manage it. I told you, the voices had stopped. There was no way I could write a second book in a year. I didn't have anything else to say. Dad and my agent both thought I should try, that the words would come if I pushed myself, but I knew better. And I stuck to my guns and refused to agree. Eventually I signed the single-book deal."

"And got a nice big advance."

"Yes, I did. And then Dad and John and Joseph all sat me down and insisted that I invest nearly every penny in complicated funds that I couldn't touch but that would generate an income for me. They left me just enough money to buy my little house, and then found a way to tie up my royalties as well so that they go straight into my investment portfolio. I was furious at the time, because I wanted to take all of the money and blow it on a fancy car and maybe a cruise around the world or something."

"They were right, though," Fenella suggested.

James shrugged. "I suppose so. I would have fought them harder, but I really thought that I'd eventually write another book. I knew I couldn't have another one done in a year, but I assumed it would happen eventually. I mean, the first one had written itself, in my head, without me even wanting it in there. How hard could it be to write another one, if I actually tried?"

"I assume it was harder than you'd expected."

James chuckled. "Harder isn't the word. Impossible is the word. I used to drink to silence the voices, I now began to drink to try to get them back. Sometimes, when I was almost too drunk to think, I would hear hints of ideas, but they always vanished when I sobered up again."

"I'm sorry."

"Yeah, me, too. I thought maybe I needed to travel again, but now I wasn't just some guy who'd dropped out of college and wanted to crash on odd couches. Now I was an author who'd had a big advance. No one wanted to let me sleep on the couch for free anymore. I was supposed to be staying in five-star hotels and dining on caviar and lobster. That I sometimes couldn't even afford bread and milk didn't enter into anyone's mind."

Fenella topped up both of their coffee cups and then got up and refilled the coffee maker. It was still only seven o'clock and far too early to be worried about not being to sleep later, even if she'd already drunk more caffeine that she usually did in a day.

"Anyway, then it was time for the book tour, which was a nightmare in its own special way."

"Why?"

"People wanted to talk about the themes in my work and the hidden symbolism in what I'd written, stuff like that. I didn't know there was any hidden symbolism. I'd never been any good in English classes when we'd been asked to identify all of that junk. I either liked a book because it told a good story or I didn't like a book. Now everyone wanted to know why my main character called his dog "Paw-Feet," and I had to tell them that it was simply the first name that popped into my head when I was writing. It wasn't a popular answer."

"Paw-Feet?"

James laughed. "You really have never read my book, have you?"

"No, I haven't. You said you didn't want us to read it."

"Yeah, and I meant it. Especially you, with your doctorate and your lifetime spent teaching college kids. You'd easily see that my book is just a bunch of words strung together in a mostly incoherent fashion by someone who had no idea what he was doing."

"You're being too hard on yourself," Fenella said, surprising herself. She'd never been very complimentary about James's writing, but he seemed to have forgotten how successful he'd been. "Tens of thousands of college kids read your book every year. It's one of the most successful books of its type in the past fifty years. Even if you didn't know what you were doing, you clearly did something right."

"Yeah, and after everything I've just said, you can imagine how happy I am to have thousands of English majors analyzing my every word," he laughed.

Fenella grinned. "The very definition of irony, I believe."

"Yeah, but the thing was, I didn't know how else to make money. I couldn't go back to doing odd jobs, mostly because I felt as if they were beneath me." He blushed and shrugged. "Yeah, I was an idiot, but for the first few years, I really did believe everything my agent told me. I was a genius with my finger on the pulse of modern society or something like that. And I was going to make millions, I just needed to write the next book."

"And you couldn't."

"It was impossible," James said flatly. "Drinking wasn't helping, so I tried other things, um, illegal substances. They didn't help make the voices come back, but they made me forget why I cared about them in the first place. I suppose it was good that I couldn't afford to fund a serious drug habit. I quit before I let myself get hooked. With drugs and alcohol off the table, I turned to women to help distract me. I felt as if I needed someone new nearly every night, and I'm sure I hurt a lot of very nice women along the way. None of them managed to inspire me, though."

Fenella sipped her coffee. She'd never really given much thought to how James lived his life. It all seemed terribly sad, really.

"Anyway, after a while I gave up on women as well. I mean, I didn't become a monk or anything, but I stopped hoping they'd be the solution to my problems. Instead, I settled into my little house and began trying to live as frugally as I could. I still wrote, nearly every day, but it was hard work. I couldn't seem to tell a story. Everything was just words piled on top of one another. I sent a few things to my agent over the years, but after a while he simply stopped returning my calls. Money is always tight, but I don't have any marketable skills and I haven't held down a job in over thirty years. You can imagine how many people are beating down my door to hire me."

"Maybe you could go back to school?"

James laughed. "I hated it the first time. I can't imagine it would be any better now, when I'd be much older than everyone else. I'd probably be the only one who couldn't even work out how to turn on the computers, too. No, it's too late for me to go back to school. What I want to do is write another book. That's where Stephanie comes into the story."

"Stephanie is inspiring you?"

"Not exactly. She's just full of ideas. She wants to write, but she can't turn her ideas into stories. I haven't even had any ideas in too many years. We're going to work together on a book once we get back home. She's writing an outline now and I really think it's going to work for us. I can almost hear her characters talking to me. If it's any good at all, she has more ideas for more books. We could make a fortune together."

"So you're prepared to let her cheat on you, as long as she keeps working on the book," Fenella concluded.

James flushed. "It sounds terrible when you put it that way, but yes, I'm willing to put up with just about anything from her, really, as long as she keeps working on the book. Our relationship is all about the book, at least for me. I don't even like her all that much, but after thirty-five years of trying, I'm prepared to do just about anything to get another book written."

"Does she know how you feel about her?"

"She's not really interested in how I feel about her. She enjoys telling people that she's involved with a famous writer. She's been with actors and models and millionaires. Now she's with me. No doubt she'll soon move on to someone else. As long as she leaves a few story ideas behind, I'll be happy to see her go."

"Will she be credited as an author on the book when it's done?"

"We haven't worked that out yet," James replied. "We'll have to see how much of it she actually writes, I suppose. I think it would sell better if it only had my name on the cover, but she doesn't agree."

Fenella had a lot more questions about his collaboration with Stephanie, but she wasn't sure James had any more answers.

"Do you really think that she went home with another man last night?" she asked instead.

"I don't know. It's one possibility. Or maybe she went home with one of her friends, or all of them. Maybe they wanted to keep talking after the pub closed so they went back to someone's house. Knowing Stephanie, she lost the slip of paper with the address on it. She might just be wandering around the streets, looking for the house."

"Maybe we should walk over to the pub and back, just in case she is lost somewhere," Fenella suggested.

"Yeah, that's a good idea. Let me find some shoes."

Fenella sat in the kitchen sipping more coffee while James made a tremendous racket above her. He'd only been in the house for a day. How could he have possibly lost his shoes already?

"If we don't find her, when we get back, I'll ring Shelly and see if she can find any of Stephanie's friends in the phone book," Fenella said when James finally rejoined her.

"Yeah, that would be good. I have my phone with me, in case Stephanie tries calling. I'm pretty sure her battery is dead, though."

They walked directly to the pub, which was locked up tightly. The parking lot in front of it was completely empty. A single car was parked in the back, but it looked as if it had been there for more than a few days.

"Let's walk around a little bit, just in case she is lost," Fenella suggested as they turned toward home.

"I don't think this is helping," James said a few minutes later, as they found themselves unexpectedly at a dead end. "We should just go home and wait for her there."

They retraced their steps back to the pub and walked back to the house. James picked up the key from under the mat and unlocked the door.

"I never lock my door at home," he told Fenella.

"I did, in Buffalo, and I would never have left the key under the mat, either, but the island is pretty safe."

"And it isn't our house to worry about," James laughed.

Fenella bit her tongue. While the furniture in the house wasn't exactly to her taste, she didn't want to have to pay to replace it, either. Perhaps leaving the key under the mat wasn't the best idea. They went back into the kitchen, and Fenella picked up the phone on the wall and called her own apartment.

"Shelly? It's Fenella. I wasn't sure if you'd be there or at home. I need a favor, please."

"No problem. I thought I'd wait here until you got home so that I could find out what's going on. Is everything okay?"

"Yes, at least, I hope so. Stephanie didn't come back to the house last night. We assume she stayed with one of her friends, but we don't have any phone numbers for them. Can you check the phone book and see if any of them are listed? It's in the top desk drawer in my bedroom."

"Hold on a minute and I'll get it."

"She's going to get the book," Fenella told James. He nodded and then slumped back into his chair, a coffee mug tightly in his grip.

"Who am I looking for, then?" Shelly asked.

"Annie Lawrence," Fenella replied. "I think she lives in Douglas, but I'm not sure."

"I'm pretty sure that's what Stephanie said," James told her.

"Lawrence? There are two, a Matthew and an R.T. Lawrence. Is that any good?" Shelly asked.

"R.T? I can't imagine any name starting with R that would have the nickname Annie, can you?" Fenella replied.

"Not really, but I can give you the number if you want it," Shelly said.

"I'll take it. Whoever it is might know Annie, I suppose." Fenella wrote down the number that Shelly read out. "What about Maureen Rhodes?" she asked.

"Give me a second," Shelly said.

Fenella could hear the pages turning as she waited.

"There are a few more of them than there were Lawrences, but no

Maureen or even any with initials. You can have Mark, Donald, Peter, or Susan, if you'd like."

"I don't know. Maybe she uses Mark in the phone book to hide the fact that she's a single woman? Or maybe her real name is Susan. I'm not ready to start ringing all over the island just yet. Let's leave Maureen. Maybe you'll have better luck with Courtney Bridges."

"Bridges? Let me see. There's one listing for Bridges, and it's Mr. and Mrs. Charles and Elizabeth," Shelly told her.

"That might be Courtney's parents. I don't want to call them, not unless we get desperate. Stephanie did say that Courtney was married now, but I don't think she mentioned her married name."

"I wish I could help more," Shelly said. "Is James very worried?"

Fenella glanced over at her brother, who was sitting back with his eyes shut. "Yes and no," she said. "There are a dozen possible explanations. It will be interesting to see which one is the right one when she turns up."

"If I can do anything else to help, just ask."

"I can't imagine what else you could do, but I appreciate the offer."

"Ring me back when she turns up. I'm curious now as to what's happened to her."

Fenella promised to do just that and then put the phone down. "We don't have any definite results, but I have a number that could be Annie. Should I try or should we wait a while longer?"

A knock on the door interrupted them.

"That's will be Stephanie," James said happily. He started to his feet, but Fenella was already on her way to the door. She waved James back into his chair.

She wanted to have a word with Stephanie, and there was no time like the present. Whatever the nature of her relationship with James, simply not coming home at night and worrying both James and Fenella was unacceptable. Fenella opened the door and then gasped.

The man on the doorstep frowned. "I don't know why I'm even the slightest bit surprised to see you here," Mark Hammersmith said, shaking his head.

6

Fenella glanced back into the house. James had stayed in the kitchen. She stepped out the front door and pulled it shut behind her.

"I'm going to guess that you're here because something has happened to Stephanie," she told the police inspector. "I know you'll want to talk to my brother about her, but maybe I could break the news to him?"

The handsome man, who was in his mid-thirties, shrugged. His brown hair flopped over one of his green eyes and Fenella felt an irrational urge to tell him to get a haircut. Maybe she was getting old, or maybe she was just worried because whatever had brought Mark to her door wasn't going to be good news.

"Let's back up a little bit," Mark said. "Why are you here?"

Fenella sighed. She really wanted to know what had happened to Stephanie, but she didn't dare argue with a police officer. "My brother and his girlfriend are staying here," she explained. "They're visiting from the US and I arranged for them to stay here because I thought it would be more comfortable for them than staying in my apartment with me." If she could, Fenella thought, she'd prefer to keep Shelly out of the story.

"Whose house is it?" Mark asked.

Fenella blushed. "Technically, it's mine, but I really don't want my brother to know that," she said quickly.

Mark raised an eyebrow. "Do I want to know why?"

"James wanted to contest Mona's will. I didn't realize, when I first arrived here, just how much I'd actually inherited. I'd rather James not find out, not until I've decided what I want to do with everything." Fenella spoke as rapidly as she could, expecting her brother to come looking for her at any moment.

"So the house is yours, and you're letting your brother and his girlfriend stay here," Mark checked. He typed a few things into his phone before he looked up at her. "Tell me about the girlfriend."

"Her name is Stephanie Arnold. She's somewhere near forty, and blonde with, um, some cosmetic enhancements, if you know what I mean."

"Let's say I don't. Can you elaborate?"

"She's had her breasts enlarged," Fenella blurted out. "I believe she's had other work done, too, but that's the most noticeable, um, enhancement."

"Tell me about your brother."

"James? He's sixty and he's an author. What do you want to know about him?"

"Where was he last night?"

Fenella shivered. "James, Stephanie, and I went to the pub around the corner for dinner and then met some of Stephanie's friends for drinks."

"I thought you said she was visiting here from the US?"

"She is, but she grew up on the island and still has some friends here. Last night was all about reconnecting with them."

"Names?" he asked.

Fenella supplied them, guessing at the spellings. The man typed them all into his phone, a frown on his face.

"How much did everyone drink?"

"Annie and Maureen seemed to drink the most. I saw Courtney sipping her drink throughout the evening, but I don't know how much she actually drank. My brother had more than he should have, but then he got tired and we came back here."

"And how much did you drink?"

"I stuck to soda. I had to drive home at the end of the evening."

"What happened after you left the pub?"

"As I said, James and I came back here. Stephanie stayed because she wanted to spend more time with her friends."

"Why did you assume that something had happened to her when you saw me?"

"She never came back to the house last night. James called me at five this morning, and I came right over. We've been trying to work out what might have happened to her ever since."

"Did you try ringing the police or Noble's?" he asked.

Fenella frowned. Noble's was the island's main hospital. She should have thought to call there to inquire about Stephanie. "No, I didn't try calling anyone," she said. "It felt too early to start making phone calls when I first got here. Then James and I took a walk around the neighborhood, hoping she might simply have forgotten which house was theirs. When we got back here, I rang Shelly, my neighbor, to see if any of Stephanie's friends were in the telephone book. They weren't. James and I were just talking about what to do next when you knocked."

Mark nodded. "What time did you leave here last night?"

Fenella shrugged. "It was before midnight, maybe even before eleven. I gave Katie a snack, and I was in bed before midnight."

"And Katie is the only witness to that?"

"Actually, Shelly is staying with me at the moment," Fenella said, feeling her cheeks turning red. "She can confirm what I told you."

"And you didn't go back out after you'd arrived home?"

"Not until around five, when James called."

"And Shelly can confirm that?"

"I don't know," Fenella frowned. "She didn't wake up when I did go out, so she probably wouldn't have woken up if I'd gone out again in the middle of the night. When are you going to tell me what's going on?"

"Did your brother say anything about going back out last night?" Mark asked, clearly ignoring Fenella's question.

"No, he told me that he went straight to bed and slept soundly until around five. That's when he realized that Stephanie hadn't come back."

"Is there any sort of alarm system on the house?"

"I don't think so," Fenella said in surprise.

Mark made a few more notes on his phone and then slid the device into his pocket. "At around three o'clock this morning a woman's body was found," he said in a dull monotone. "The initial reports suggest that she was around forty and had had some cosmetic enhancements done over the years. She did not have any identification or money on her. The only thing that was found with the body was a slip of paper in her pocket with this address on it."

Fenella felt her knees give way. She sat down on the step and took a few slow and steady breaths.

Mark bent down. "Are you okay?" he asked.

"Not really," Fenella said flatly. "I knew when I saw you that it was going to be bad news, but I was really hoping that she'd just been injured or arrested or something. James is going to be really upset."

"It was a serious relationship?"

Fenella shook her head. "You'll have to ask James about that, but even if they were just friends, the news is upsetting. I just met her yesterday, after all, and I'm, well, upset."

Mark nodded. "I'm sorry to have to break it to you like this, but it's part of my job."

"What happened to her? You said the body was found? How did she die?"

"She was hit by a car, not far from here."

"It was an accident?" Fenella checked.

Mark frowned. "Do you have any reason to believe that it was anything other than an accident?"

"No, not at all," Fenella said hastily. "She'd been drinking heavily. She must have forgotten which way to look when she was crossing the road or something."

"Or something," Mark echoed. "We still need someone to make a formal identification of the body."

"I just met her yesterday," Fenella protested.

"Perhaps your brother could do it?"

"Maybe. He should have her passport and things, as well. Can't you simply use them?"

"It would be best if he identified her for us. Of course, I'll want the passport, and any other identification she had with her as well."

"What did the driver say when he or she reported the accident?" Fenella asked.

"The driver didn't report the accident. The body was found by a man returning home from his late shift."

"It was a hit and run?" Fenella asked. Tears filled her eyes. "I don't know why, but that seems to make it worse. Any leads on the car involved?"

"I probably shouldn't tell you this, but we've already found the car. It was parked in front of the pub. We have reason to believe that it was stolen from the owner's drive."

"But you aren't sure?"

"We're sure the owner didn't have anything to do with the accident," Mark told her. "She's in hospital at the moment, recovering from an emergency appendectomy. She's a single mother with two kids who are currently unhappily staying with their father and his second wife. They were all tucked up in bed when all of this happened, and that's been confirmed by their home security system."

"Home security system?"

"Yeah, it seems the father had it put in fairly recently because the older child, a boy of fourteen, had started sneaking out of the house. Now if he tries it, an alarm goes off and wakes up not just his father but everyone on the street. So far it seems to be keeping the boy where he belongs."

"Unless he found a way around it and snuck out, took his mother's car, and accidently killed Stephanie," Fenella suggested.

"It's a possibility we are considering, but I suspect it's more likely the car was stolen from the drive. There are quite a few teens in this area who like to take cars and go for rides around the island in the middle of the night. Usually they just hit stone walls or road signs, though, not people."

"We should go and tell James. He's been so worried." Fenella got to her feet.

"You may tell him, if you think that will be easier for him," Mark said.

"It might, although it still isn't going to be easy."

Fenella opened the door and led the man into the kitchen. James was sitting at the table with his head tipped backwards. He was fast asleep and snoring loudly.

"He looks really worried," Mark said wryly.

"James," Fenella said. She put a hand on his arm. "James, wake up."

James jumped and then looked around, blinking. "Where am I? What's going on? Fenella? What's happened? Where's Stephanie? I thought she was at the door?"

Fenella shook her head and then sat down next to James at the table. "This is Mark Hammersmith. He's a police inspector."

"Police? Has Stephanie managed to get arrested? I'm sure she was drunk and she was probably disorderly, too, but she isn't a bad person, really."

"There's been an accident," Fenella said as gently as she could. She took James's hand. "Stephanie was hit by a car."

"I never should have left her to walk home alone," James said as his eyes filled with tears. "The other three, they were going to make sure she got home safely. I'll never forgive them if she doesn't recover. How bad is it?" he asked.

Fenella glanced over at Mark. He raised an eyebrow. Fenella wasn't sure if he was offering to take over or not, but she didn't want James to hear the news from a stranger. "I'm afraid she didn't survive," she told James in a low voice.

James stared at her and then shook his head. "You're wrong. She's tough and she's strong. She'll be fine. I'm sure of it. The doctors will be able to patch her up. That's what they do, doctors, they fix people. As soon as she gets to the hospital, they'll fix her right up."

Fenella sighed. "I'm sorry, but it's too late for that." She squeezed James's hand tightly.

"Her passport is here. How did the police even identify her? They've probably simply mixed her up with someone else," James said desperately.

"Mark would like you to go with him to identify the body," Fenella said. "She had the address for this house in her pocket."

"That doesn't prove anything," James yelled. "Anyone could have this address in their pocket. Maybe one of her friends took down the address from her so that they could visit. Or maybe whoever it is knew the previous residents. That body doesn't have anything to do with me or with Stephanie. Wait until she gets home. She's going to laugh when she hears about all of this."

"Maybe we should go with Mark," Fenella suggested. "Then we can find out for sure if it is Stephanie or not."

"It isn't," James insisted. "She's fine. She's just with her friends. If the police want to do something useful, they can call Stephanie's friends and track her down. Then they'll have to find out who the body really belongs to, though. It's easier for them to just assume it's Stephanie, I suppose."

"Mr. Woods, we aren't looking for easy answers," Mark said stiffly. "We're looking for the truth. I would be grateful if you would come with me and see if you can identify the body or not. If you choose not to do so, perhaps your sister would be willing to make a preliminary identification for us."

"Maybe we could both go," Fenella said. "Then if you don't want to do it, I'll do it."

"I don't want to leave here. Stephanie won't know what to do if she gets here and we aren't here," James protested.

"I can leave a constable here," Mark offered. "He can sit outside, and if your friend returns, he can let me know."

James stared at the man for a minute. "You really think she's dead, don't you? She can't be dead. We have so much more work to do."

Mark shot Fenella a questioning look. "They were working on a book together," she explained.

"I don't want to see her," James said. "Not if she's, not if she's, I mean, I want to remember her as she was, vibrant and full of life. I can't stand the thought of seeing her, um, not at her best."

"But you're the only one on the island who knew her," Fenella said.

"Her friends knew her better than I did," James shot back. "I mean, they know her better than I do. I won't talk about her in the past tense, and I won't go and see the wrong body. Your police inspector friend can get Annie or Courtney to take a look at her. They'll tell him how wrong he is."

"I've sent their names to the office," Mark replied. "We're working on locating all three women. We're going to have them brought in for conversations once they've been found."

"While you're conversing, you can have them look at the body," James said. "Except Stephanie will probably turn up by that time. She'll be here any minute, I'm sure."

"Fenella, perhaps you'd be willing to come and have a look at the body," Mark said.

"Of course," Fenella replied. "Can you wait for a few minutes? I'd like to have Shelly come over here."

James looked at her and then started to laugh. "You don't want to leave me on my own, do you? You're worried that I'll realize Stephanie truly is dead and then what? Are you afraid I might take my own life? My dear baby sister, you must know I have far too much ego for that. And I checked last night. There isn't any alcohol in the house, so I can't even try to drown my sorrows. You go with your policeman friend. I'll just wait here for Stephanie to return."

"If you don't mind, I'd like to have a constable sit with you while Fenella is gone," Mark said. "If Stephanie does return, I've quite a few questions for her."

James shrugged. "I can't stop you, can I?"

"Technically, maybe," Mark replied, "but then I could simply arrest you and take you down to the station to wait for your sister."

"Bring on your constable," James laughed.

Mark nodded and left the room. Fenella patted James's arm, but he didn't say anything to her as they waited. As she couldn't think of anything to say, Fenella was silent as well.

"Mr. Woods, this is Constable Corlett," Mark said a few minutes later as he walked back into the kitchen. "Constable, Mr. Woods is waiting for his girlfriend to return. I'd appreciate it if you'd wait with him."

"Yes, sir," the constable said.

"It's nice to see you again," Fenella told the young uniformed officer. "I'm sure that baby of yours is getting big."

"He is, aye," the man replied. "He has three teeth now and he likes nothing better than biting my finger every chance he gets."

Fenella laughed. "Let's hope he outgrows it."

The constable grinned. "I'm sure once he's allowed solid food, he won't want to bite me anymore."

"Shall we?" Mark asked Fenella.

She nodded and got to her feet. After giving James one more reassuring pat, she followed the police inspector out of the room.

"I'll drive," he said as they walked out of the house.

Fenella climbed into the passenger seat of the man's car and fastened her seatbelt. Once they were underway, she sighed. "You're pretty sure it's Stephanie, aren't you?"

"Based on your description, yes. Her clothes were American brands that aren't readily available on the island, although these days anyone can get anything if they put their mind to it, I suppose. Still, everything points to her being exactly who you said she was."

"Can you take my word for it?"

"I believe the coroner would rather hear from someone who'd known her for longer than a single day, but your identification is enough for me, anyway. It's crucial to my investigation, and once you've given it, I can get properly started."

"I can't imagine what happened to her. Her friends were going to make sure she got home safely."

"Maybe they had a disagreement," Mark suggested. "I'll be talking to them as soon as we find them."

"I hope you find the driver soon. I can't imagine hitting someone and then just driving away."

"They didn't go far, just around the corner, really. If you were driving a stolen car, you probably wouldn't want to risk getting stopped."

"Can you get fingerprints from car interiors?"

"Sometimes, if we're lucky, but in this case it seems the car was wiped clean."

"Wiped clean? Someone stole a car, ran over Stephanie, and then wiped the car clean? That sounds like a planned attack. It sounds like murder."

"Try this instead," Mark suggested. "Someone, probably a drunk teen, steals a car. He or she accidently runs someone over. He or she then panics, parks the car in the nearest car park and runs a cloth over everything to try to remove fingerprints. That seems like a more likely scenario, doesn't it?"

"Yes," Fenella said quickly. She much preferred that version to murder. The last thing she wanted was to find herself caught up in another murder investigation.

Mark chuckled. "I thought you'd like that better. Especially as your brother would have to be top of the suspect list if it were murder."

"James? Why would James want to kill Stephanie?"

"I don't know, but I can tell you that we always start with spouses or significant others when we investigate murders."

"Well, even if it was murder, James didn't have anything to do with it," Fenella said firmly. "He cared for Stephanie a lot and she was helping him write his next book. He, maybe more than anyone, wanted her alive."

"I thought you said he was an author?" Mark asked.

"He is an author, but he only wrote one book. Stephanie was helping him with the next one."

"When did the first one come out?"

"Oh, a while ago," Fenella said lightly.

"How long ago?" Mark pressed her.

"Thirty-odd years ago," she said softly.

"I see," Mark said. "And here we are." He parked the car in front of a building that could have been just about anything. Mostly it looked like an office building. He turned and faced her. "This isn't going to be easy. We've done our best to make her look presentable, but there's only so much we can do, especially under the circumstances. In some ways it might be easier for you, as you only met the woman yesterday."

"Is it too late to change my mind?" Fenella muttered as she climbed out of the car.

"It isn't, but you'll be helping Stephanie by doing this. Surely that's what you want to do."

Fenella sighed. "Yes, of course it is."

She followed the man into the anonymous building. He stopped at the desk and said something to the woman behind it. She gave Fenella a sympathetic look and then picked up the phone on the desk next to her. She said a few words into the receiver and then a loud buzzer sounded behind her.

"Here we go," Mark said, offering Fenella his arm.

She took it and let him lead her through a series of doors and then down a long corridor. At the end of the hallway, a man who was holding a clipboard met them.

"We need to talk," he said sharply to Mark.

"Let me get the body identified first," Mark replied.

"Okay, but it's urgent," the man said.

Mark raised an eyebrow and then nodded. "Give me five minutes," he told the man.

The man nodded, but he didn't look happy. Mark took Fenella's arm as he pushed a buzzer on the frame of the door at the end of the corridor. A moment later the door swung open.

"Ah, yes, Inspector Hammersmith. Come in," the man who'd opened the door said. "Have you brought someone to identify the body?"

"I certainly hope so," Mark replied. He didn't introduce Fenella, which made her feel as if she ought to introduce herself. She knew she was just stalling for time. She really didn't want to see a dead body, whether it was Stephanie's or not.

"It isn't too bad," the man told Fenella. "I've seen much worse. You probably haven't, though. Sorry about that."

He moved over to a long table that was covered with a sheet and pulled the sheet down. Fenella swallowed hard as she saw the blonde hair.

"Take a deep breath," Mark told her. "If you feel sick, run out of here as fast as you can. We don't want you compromising any evidence."

Fenella nodded and then took several breaths before she took a few hesitant steps forward. It only took her a moment to recognize the woman on the table. She knew Mona would have lots of questions for her later, but she simply couldn't bring herself to study what she could see of the body.

She turned and took a few steps away before she tried to speak. "It's the woman I met yesterday who called herself Stephanie Arnold," she said. "That's all I can tell you for sure."

"Do you have any reason to believe that she might not have been who she claimed to be?" Mark barked at her.

"No, none at all. Quite the opposite, really, as I met several of her friends from the island last night. I was just being extra careful."

Mark nodded. "I suppose, with your history, that makes sense. Let's get out of here." He took her arm and escorted her out of the room. The man with the clipboard was still waiting in the hallway.

"Now?" he asked Mark.

"Sure, why not," Mark muttered. "Wait here," he told Fenella. "Don't talk to anyone. Don't call anyone, and if your phone rings, don't answer it."

Fenella nodded and then leaned against the wall. It felt cool, which made her feel slightly better. She watched as Mark and the other man walked a short distance away and began an intense conversation. Mark shook his head several times, and Fenella was sure that he glanced over at her at least twice during the ten-minute conversation. When he walked back over to her, he looked angry.

"What's wrong?" she asked.

"Nothing," he snapped. "Let's get you back to the house. I'm going to need an official statement from you and one from your brother."

"Official statement? You didn't mention that earlier."

"No, well, I should have. I should have insisted on it the moment you opened that door. Nothing is ever straightforward when you're involved."

"It wasn't an accident?" Fenella guessed.

Mark shrugged. "I'm not at liberty to say."

"Which means I'm right," Fenella sighed. "Someone murdered Stephanie. It must have been one of her friends from her past, but I can't imagine why."

"Let's leave speculation out of this," Mark said. "Let's not even talk about it until we get back to the house, actually. I'll take a formal statement from you there. I'd rather you didn't even think about the case until then."

Of course there was no way Mark could keep her from thinking about Stephanie and her untimely death. Fenella sat in silence with her mind racing all the way back to the house on the outskirts of Douglas. The only people who might have murdered the woman were her three friends from the previous evening. But which one of them had a motive for murder?

Mark parked in the driveway behind Fenella's car. "When we get inside, I don't want you to speak to your brother at all. I'll do all of the talking."

"Okay," Fenella replied, as she knew she had no choice in the matter.

"I'll take your statement first," he said as they walked up to the house.

Fenella knocked on the door, wishing she'd thought to take the key with her when they'd left. Constable Corlett opened it a moment later.

"Mr. Woods has fallen back to sleep," he told them in a whisper. "I didn't know whether I should wake him or not."

"Better not, actually," Mark replied. "You can sit with him while I talk to Ms. Woods. We can wake him when I'm ready to talk to him."

"Yes, sir," the constable replied. He left them in the living room and returned to the kitchen.

Fenella sank onto the couch and sighed. It had already been a very long day and it wasn't even noon yet. Mark sat down on a chair opposite her.

"I'm going to be taking notes on my phone, if you don't mind," he told her.

"Whatever," she replied.

He raised an eyebrow but didn't respond. After typing on his phone for a minute or two, he looked up at her. "Start with what your brother said about Stephanie before they arrived," he told her.

"He didn't say anything about her before they arrived," she replied.

"Nothing? You mean nothing except that he was bringing her on his visit?"

"No, I mean nothing, as in he never mentioned her existence, never said he was bringing her, nothing. Shelly will tell you that I was as surprised as she was to see the woman when they arrived together yesterday."

"Okay, then, start with their arrival. Walk me through everything that you can remember from the airport."

Fenella took a deep breath and then did her best to comply. Mark tapped on his phone the entire time, until the noise began to annoy Fenella. She tried slowing down or speeding up her words, but the rate at which he tapped seemed constant, no matter what she did. She recounted what she could remember up to their arrival at the house and then stopped.

"I'm going to have to talk to Shelly, too," the man told her.

"She might be at home or she could be at my apartment," Fenella replied. "I told you that she's staying with me at the moment."

"You did. Remind me of why?"

Fenella sighed and then glanced toward the kitchen. There was no sign of James, at least. "I didn't want James staying with me," she said in a low voice. "Shelly agreed to pretend that her dishwasher had flooded her apartment so that she needed a new kitchen. Obviously, she couldn't stay in her apartment while all of the work was being done, so she moved over to stay with me."

"Her dishwasher flooded her kitchen?" Mark asked.

"No, not at all. We just told James that as an excuse for why Shelly was staying with me."

"So her kitchen is fine?"

"Yes, as far as I know."

"So why is she really staying with you? Surely it would have been just as effective to tell James she was there but not really have her move in?"

"James will be visiting my apartment as some point. I wanted it to look genuine," Fenella explained, feeling foolish.

Mark nodded and then tapped on his phone a bit more. "Okay, let's keep going. What happened when you got here?"

Fenella told him about showing James and Stephanie around the house. "And then I left and went home for a while," she concluded.

"I may want to hear about what you did at home later, but for now tell me when you next saw James and Stephanie."

She told him about their dinner together at the pub, repeating everything that Stephanie had said about her friends. "And then they arrived," she added.

Mark nodded at her. "Tell me everything you can remember from the evening," he instructed her.

Fenella did her best, but she knew she'd forgotten things. "I hope I haven't forgotten anything important," she said when she was finished.

"We can go back over it all later, after I've compared your version of events with everyone else's," he told her. "You didn't see Stephanie again after you and James left the pub?"

"No, I walked back here with James and then I went home to bed. James called me at five and woke me."

The inevitable tap, tap, tap followed Fenella's words. "Okay, then, I suppose it's time to wake your brother," Mark said after a minute. "Do you want to do it or shall I?"

"Are you going to tell him that the body is Stephanie's?" she asked.

"I'd rather he didn't know until after he's given me his version of events, but I suspect the identity of the body will be his first question."

"I'm sure."

"Do you want to be the one to tell him, then?"

Fenella started to nod and then shook her head. "I don't know. He's going to be upset."

"Thinking about it, I'd rather he not talk to you. Maybe you could wait here and I'll talk to him in the kitchen."

"If that's what you want," Fenella agreed, feeling both relieved and disappointed at the same time.

"Fenella? What is going on? Where's Stephanie?" James's voice seemed to echo all around the house.

Fenella exchanged glances with Mark as James stomped into the room with Constable Corlett on his heels.

7

"Mr. Woods, I'd like to speak to you privately," Mark said, getting to his feet.

"I'm not really interested in what you want," James snapped. "Fen, what's going on?"

Fenella opened her mouth, but Mark held up a hand. "Ms. Woods isn't able to answer your question right now," he said firmly. "We should move this conversation elsewhere."

"I'm not going anywhere," James said. He dropped onto the couch next to Fenella and took her hand. "If she can't speak to me, she can at least hold my hand. Should I guess from your attitude that the body truly is Stephanie's?"

Mark hesitated and then nodded. James stared at him for a minute and then started to cry. Fenella let go of his hand and started digging around in her handbag for tissues. She handed one to James, who wiped his eyes.

"Thanks," he said gruffly. "I didn't think I would cry. While you were gone, I started thinking, and the more I thought about it, the more likely it seemed that the body was going to be Stephanie's. I thought I was ready to hear the news, but clearly I was wrong."

"I'd rather you and your sister didn't talk right now," Mark said.

"I won't talk to her," James promised, "but please let her stay with me. I'm not sure what to think or feel right now."

"She can stay until she opens her mouth," Mark replied, giving Fenella a warning look. "Constable, have a seat," he told Constable Corlett. The man glanced around and then settled into a chair next to the inspector.

"Mr. Woods, I'd like you to tell me everything you can about Stephanie Arnold. How did you meet?"

"She sent me a letter," James replied.

"An email?"

"No, a real letter on real paper in a real envelope with a proper stamp," James replied. "I get about a dozen every year from people who either loved or hated my book. It usually runs about fifty-fifty, but in the last few years I've had more hate mail than fan mail."

"Do you get emails from fans as well?" Mark asked.

James shrugged. "I don't have email. My publisher might get some, I suppose, but we haven't really spoken in years."

"What about threatening letters?"

"I've had a few over the years, but none recently. There was nothing threatening about Stephanie's letter, anyway."

"What did it say?"

"It was long, but otherwise fairly typical of the sort of thing I get. She talked about how brilliant I was and told me which passages meant the most to her. It went on and on for about four or five pages."

"And you replied?"

"And I photocopied it and sent it back to her with proofreading marks all over it. She couldn't spell to save her life and her punctuation was all over the place. I'm a college dropout, but I know when to use a semicolon."

Mark raised an eyebrow and then added something to his phone notes. "What happened next?"

"She sent me another letter. This one had clearly been much more carefully written. Maybe she had a friend go over it for her or something, I don't know. It was less fan mail and more like a letter to a friend. I found myself intrigued."

"Really?"

James flushed. "She also included a few photos," he said quietly.

"What sort of photos?"

"Just a few pictures of herself," James said. He glanced over at Fenella. "She was, um, naked in one of them."

"That's one way to get your attention, I assume."

"It wasn't the first time I'd been sent such things," James replied, "but it was the first time in a long time. If she'd been less interesting in her letter, I wouldn't have replied anyway, but as I said, I found her intriguing."

And naked, Fenella thought to herself.

"So you wrote back?"

"Yeah, and then she wrote back, and after a while she decided to come and visit me."

"She knew where you live?"

"I get my mail at a post office box. My house is a little bit remote, and I don't want fans or disgruntled undergraduates turning up there. I agreed to meet her at the café in the nearest town."

"How long ago did you actually meet?"

"Oh, goodness, two, maybe three months ago? I don't pay that much attention to the passing of time, especially when I'm working, and Stephanie and I were working on a book together. Time lost its meaning."

"Presumably that changed when you decided to visit your sister?"

"Not really. I suppose I had to pay more attention to the date, if that's what you mean."

"What did Stephanie tell you about her past?"

"One of the first things she told me was that she'd grown up on the island here. It was another point of connection in our early days together. We talked about the things I could remember about the island. I was only twelve or thirteen when we left, but Stephanie hadn't left until she was older, maybe twenty. She had better memories of the place than I do as a consequence."

"What did she tell you about her family?"

"Not much. She was an only child and her parents both died within a fairly short space of time not long after she'd left school. That was why she decided to leave the island. She wanted to get away from the memories."

"What did she tell you about her friends here?"

"Not much, not until last night, anyway," James replied. "Last night over dinner she gave Fenella and me a quick history of them."

"Whose idea was the trip to the island, then?"

"Mine," James replied. "I've been wanting to come and see Fenella since she moved here. Stephanie wasn't even going to come with me until the last minute."

"What changed her mind?"

James shrugged. "I'm not sure. I was thinking about that earlier. It sort of seems as if one day I was planning to come to see Fen and then the next day we were both coming. I don't think I even told Fen anything about Stephanie. I probably should have warned her."

Fenella gave his hand a squeeze. Now wasn't the time to worry about such things.

"Did Stephanie have any particular reasons for wanting to come with you?"

"She just said the more she thought about it, the more fun it sounded. She emptied one of her savings accounts to pay for her plane tickets."

"So she really wanted to come back to the island."

"I suppose so."

"And what did she want to do here?"

"The only thing she ever mentioned to me was looking up her old friends," James told him. "She was really eager to see Annie and the others from their little group back in the day. She called them the CAMS."

"CAMS?"

"From all of their first initials," James explained. "Courtney, Annie, Maureen, and Stephanie."

Mark spent a minute typing into his phone before looking up at James again. "And did she have other friends she wanted to see?"

"Oh, yeah, loads of them," James replied. "She had a list of former boyfriends she wanted to look up, a handful of former coworkers she planned to see, and one or two distant relatives she thought she might try to find as well."

"I'll need all of their names," Mark said, sounding tired.

"I don't have the lists. She kept them in her phone, though. If you have that, I can tell you the passcode." He gave Mark a short string of numbers and Mark typed them into his phone.

"I'm going to want to know more about the lists of people she wanted to see, but first I'd like you to take me through your trip, starting with when you left home."

"Really? I'm still feeling jet lagged and I didn't get much sleep last night. I'm not sure I can remember much of anything."

"Do your best," Mark urged him.

Fenella had to work hard not to yawn too many times as James talked them through the series of flights he and Stephanie had taken, starting from the tiny airport near his home until finally landing at Ronaldsway. "And then Fenella was there," he said, squeezing her hand.

"Keep going," Mark told him. "Tell me about the conversation in the car on the way here."

James did his best to oblige but his memory was spotty. Eventually he sighed. "And then, when we got here, I collapsed into the bed and slept like a rock for a few hours. While I was asleep, Stephanie called Annie. That much I know for sure. She may have called half the people on the island for all that I know. By the time I woke up, it was time to leave for dinner. I never really had a private talk with her again."

Mark frowned and added something to his notes. "Take me through the conversation at dinner."

Again James tried hard, but he didn't seem to remember much. "I'm sorry," he said at the end of the recitation. "I was jet lagged and tired and then I started drinking. I also didn't think any of it mattered at all. We were just having dinner with Fen and chatting about nothing and everything. It was the first day of our vacation and we had three weeks to spend here. I didn't know, I couldn't have imagined, I didn't realize..." he trailed off and another tear slid down his cheek.

Fenella handed him another tissue. "I'm so sorry," she said softly.

Mark cleared his throat. "Tell me what you can remember from when Stephanie's friends arrived," he said.

It quickly became clear that James hadn't been paying much attention to the conversation once Stephanie's friends had joined them. He couldn't remember much of anything from the conversations that had taken place between the women. "As I said, at the time it didn't seem to matter. I'm not used to social situations like that one. I tend to lose myself in my thoughts when I'm confronted by large numbers of people. It's easier than trying to follow the conversation."

"When did you decide to leave?"

"It must have been close to eleven," James said, looking at Fenella. She avoided meeting his eyes.

"Why do you say that?"

"Because I looked at my watch as I crawled into bed and it wasn't quite midnight yet. I'd only been here for a short while and I couldn't resist doing the math to work out what time it was at home, you see. I told myself I shouldn't have been tired because it wasn't even seven o'clock yet, but as I'd missed an entire night's sleep due to traveling, it felt like midnight for sure."

"What time did you go back out?" Mark asked.

"Fenella and I walked back over to the pub around seven or eight. I woke up at five to, um, use the bathroom. That was when I realized that Stephanie wasn't here. I rang Fenella right away and she came over."

"You were worried about Stephanie?"

"Of course I was worried about her. She was in a strange place and she'd gone out without any identification or any money. She never carried money, actually. She always relied on the kindness of others. I was worried that she'd forgotten where the house was and was just wandering around the streets somewhere."

"But you waited until seven to start looking for her?"

"I didn't want to go out without Fenella. I was worried I might get lost as well."

"And Fenella didn't get here until seven?"

"No, she got here not long after I called her, but by that time I'd started to think that maybe Stephanie had simply gone home with one of her friends. They'd promised to look out for her, you see. I started thinking that I was overreacting."

"So you waited for some time, and then went out and started looking for her?"

"I felt so helpless sitting here," James sighed. "We really wanted to call Stephanie's friends, but none of them are in the phone book."

Mark made a few more notes. "And you didn't go out from the time you and Fenella returned here after the pub until the pair of you went out to look for Stephanie around seven?"

"I didn't. I was too drunk and too tired to do anything other than sleep."

Mark nodded and added something else to his phone. "I'm going to leave things there for right now," he said. "I'd like to go through Stephanie's things before I go, though."

"Sure, why not. Most of them are still packed, actually. She just dropped them in the bedroom and left them there while I was napping. I don't know if she even opened the bags after she arrived."

James and Mark left the room. They were back a short time later.

"I appreciate you letting me take everything," Mark said. "We'll return it all to you after we've gone through it."

"I don't know that I want them," James told him. "I mean, they belong to her next of kin, not me."

"Do you know who that person might be?"

"As I said, I believe she had some distant relatives on the island, but I don't know for sure. She did have a will, though. She had it made up before we left."

"Did she now? Did she say why she felt she needed to write her will at that point?"

"She just said something about wanting to have everything in place in case the plane crashed or whatever. I never actually saw it, but I know she got it done. She was going to have me witness it, but her lawyers took care of it. She told me that it was okay if I'd had to do it, because I wasn't getting anything,"

"Were you disappointed by that?"

"Not at all. As far as I know, she didn't have anything to leave anyone anyway, or nothing with much value, I should say. She had a few nice pieces of jewelry, I suppose. Anyway, as far as I was concerned, she could leave her things to whomever she wanted. She isn't named in my will, either, for what it's worth."

"Do you know who I should contact to get a copy of the will?"

"She used the same lawyer that I do," James told him. "I have his address and phone number in my address book. It's upstairs. It will just take a minute to get it for you."

While he was gone, Fenella looked at Mark. "So what now? One of her friends must have killed her, surely."

"Now, I'm doing my best not to jump to any rash conclusions," Mark told her. "It's far too early to start narrowing down the list of suspects. At the moment, just about everyone on the island is on the list."

Fenella nodded. "But her friends are at the top," she said.

Mark chuckled. "You may believe that if you choose. If you speak to any of them, I'd appreciate it if you didn't mention the word murder. I may not share that little detail with them, at least not initially."

James was back before Fenella could reply. He handed the inspector a slip of paper. "Here's the man's name and address. It's just remotely possible that Stephanie had a copy of the will in her bag, though. She was weirdly obsessed with it once it was done."

"I'm hoping to find all sorts of interesting things in the bags you've given me," Mark told him. "I appreciate your cooperation to this point."

"I'm always happy to cooperate with the police," James replied. "Especially on something like this. I want to know what happened to Stephanie, and if she was murdered, I want to know that her killer is behind bars."

"I'm going to do my best to get you some answers," Mark told him. "I'll be in touch again soon. I assume you'll be staying here?"

"Yes, I suppose so."

"And Ms. Woods, will you be staying here or at your flat in Douglas?"

"I'm not sure," Fenella replied. "I don't really want to leave James alone right now."

"Don't be silly, little sis," James scoffed. "I'll be fine on my own. All

I need is a bottle of wine and the phone number for a pizza delivery place."

Fenella nodded. "Try my apartment first if you're looking for me," she told Mark, not wanting to start an argument with James in front of the inspector. She had no intention of leaving her brother on his own, though, at least for the moment.

Mark nodded and then he and Constable Corlett left. Fenella shut the door behind them and then walked back into the living room. James was sitting on the couch, sobbing.

"It's okay," Fenella said soothingly as she sat down next to him and began to rub his back. "I'm so sorry."

"Are you completely sure it was her?" he demanded.

Fenella wanted more than anything to lie to her brother, but she couldn't do it. "I'm sure," she said softly.

James nodded and then pressed his lips together and swallowed hard. After a moment he wiped his eyes and then stared at Fenella. "One of those three women killed her. Which one?"

"You can't be sure about that. The police haven't even said that she was murdered. It might just have been an accident."

"It's the only thing that makes sense," James argued. "She must have said or done something last night that upset one of them. Do you think the others will cover for their friend?"

"I don't know. Let's not talk about it, even. Let's let Mark do his job."

"Mark?"

"Sorry, Inspector Hammersmith. He and I have met before."

"You have? When?"

Fenella sighed. "I haven't told you a lot about the things that have happened since I've been here, have I?" It was a rhetorical question. She and James hadn't spoken since she'd moved, aside from when he'd rung to tell her that he was coming to visit. She hadn't told her other brothers much, either, not wanting any of them to worry. Now she took a deep breath and began.

"I went grocery shopping right after I arrived," she began, "and on the way home, I tripped over a dead body." It took her over an hour to tell James about all of the unfortunate things that had happened since she'd been on the island. The job was made more difficult because she couldn't include Mona in the story, even when Mona had played a part in solving a case. When she was done, he was staring at her, open-mouthed.

"I'm surprised Inspector Hammersmith didn't just arrest you when you opened the door," he said after a long moment. "I mean, I know you didn't kill Stephanie, but with that sort of history, you must be a suspect. How did you go from being a boring old history professor to getting tangled up in murder investigations every time you turn around?"

"I'm certainly not doing it on purpose," Fenella replied. "I just seem to have developed a knack for being in the wrong place at the wrong time."

"At least you didn't find Stephanie's body. I suppose we should be thankful for that. But now I'm surprised that your police inspector friend didn't arrest both of us."

"He isn't my friend."

"No, you sounded much more fond of the other one, Daniel, was it? Why isn't he investigating Stephanie's death?"

"He's away on a course and has been for months. He's supposed to be back soon, though."

"Will he take over the case, then? Everything you said about him sounded better than this other guy."

"I don't know if he will take over or not, but Mark is a good investigator, anyway. He'll find out what happened to Stephanie, with or without Daniel's help."

"He only has three suspects to choose from, how difficult can it be? He really should be able to work out what happened as soon as he talks to Annie and the others. One of them must have left with Stephanie and killed her."

"It probably won't be that simple," Fenella warned him. "Remember that they might all lie to protect one another, as well. We'll just have to wait and see."

"Who would lie to protect a killer?" James demanded. As soon as the words were out of his mouth, he sat back in his seat and looked startled.

"What's wrong?"

"Oh, um, nothing, really. I just remembered something that Stephanie said about something. It doesn't matter. Anyway, what do we do now?"

"What do you mean?"

"I mean, Stephanie is gone. I don't know anything about her family or friends back home, but I feel as if they need to be notified."

"I'm sure the police will take care of that job."

"That's good. I don't really want to have to tell anyone about it. Her lawyer will have the list of people named in her will, anyway. That should be everyone who matters, I suppose."

"We just have to sit back and wait while the police conduct their investigation."

"How did she look?" James asked.

Fenella frowned. "I don't know how to answer that. It was clearly her, if that's what you mean."

"No, I mean, did she look, I don't know, startled or scared or like she'd suffered any before she died?"

Fenella patted his hand. "No, none of those. I don't think she knew she'd been hit, if that makes sense."

"It does. Thank you. I hate the thought of her suffering in any way. She was so full of life. If she had to die, I just hope it was quick and painless."

"Yes, let's hope so."

"But I still don't know what to do now."

"I'm not sure what you mean?"

"I mean, it's only just noon on the first full day of my three-week vacation and I've no idea what to do with myself. I'm also starving, although it seems odd to be thinking about food at a time like this."

"You have to eat. You have to take care of yourself. We should go out and get some lunch somewhere."

"It seems wrong to go out," James argued, "but we don't have any food in the house, either, aside from bread and milk."

"We can go grocery shopping, if you'd prefer. Then you can come home and cook your own lunch."

James made a face. "I hate cooking, and I'm not very good at it, even with all the years of practice that I've had. Let's find a pub or something and have some lunch. We can work out what to do with the rest of the day after that."

"I assume you'd rather not go back to the pub around the corner."

"I don't want to go in there ever again," James said firmly, "but I'm acting as if you have all the time in the world to take me places. I've no idea what your life on the island is like. What do you do all day?"

"I've been working on a book, actually," Fenella told him. When she'd first arrived, she been passionate about her book, but lately she'd found that she'd lost interest in it. She wasn't going to share that with James, however.

"What sort of book?"

"A fictional autobiography of Anne Boleyn."

James raised an eyebrow. "That sounds difficult, but fascinating."

"Yes, it's both of those. Anyway, as I'm only doing it for my own satisfaction, I can certainly take a few days off and spend them with my big brother. Let's go and get some lunch."

"Did Mona leave you a lot of money, then?" James asked the question that Fenella had been dreading.

"She left me enough, with my pension, that I don't have to work. My advocate and I are still working through settling the estate."

"Advocate?"

"It's what they call lawyers over here," Fenella explained. "Mine is excellent, but everything seems to take a very long time."

James nodded. "I'll buy lunch, then, if you are watching your pennies."

"Oh, no, lunch is on me," Fenella insisted. "It cost you a lot to fly over here to see me. I'll pay for your meals and entertainment while you're here."

"Are you sure? I'd really appreciate it. I had to remortgage again to pay for my flights. If I can work with Stephanie's notes, I may still be able to write that second book, at least."

"I'm quite sure. Now let me call Shelly and have her feed Katie and we'll be away."

It only took a minute to get Shelly to agree to make sure that Katie got both lunch and dinner. That gave Fenella the rest of the day to spend with James. Once they were in Fenella's car, she looked over at him.

"Anywhere in particular you wanted to go?" she asked.

James shrugged. "When I was a kid, one of my friends lived in Laxey. Do you remember Henry Clucas?"

Fenella shook her head. "I was only two when we moved," she reminded him.

He laughed. "I forgot. Okay, well, Henry moved to London and then to Birmingham. We still send each other Christmas cards every few years. Anyway, when I used to visit him on a weekend, sometimes his mum would take us to the local pub there for fish and chips. I don't even know if the pub is still around, but if it is, I'd love to go there."

"What was it called?" Fenella asked as she backed the car out of the driveway.

"The Cat and Longtail," he replied. "It wasn't like the pub we were at last night, all modern and fancy. This was a real pub, and I'm not sure why his mum took us there, except the food was good. There were always a few drunks at the bar and you could barely see because of all the cigarette smoke, but we used to sit at a table in the back and feast."

"I haven't been to Laxey yet, but I'm sure we can find it," Fenella said, mentally crossing her fingers. "I've seen loads of signs for it."

"It's just up the coast from here," James told her. "I can't imagine the roads have changed much since I was a kid."

Between James's somewhat spotty memory and some helpful road signs, the pair arrived in Laxey only a short while later.

"It's still there," James said happily, pointing to the pub near the center of town.

"It doesn't look as if it's changed in the last fifty years, either," Fenella remarked.

"They probably don't allow smoking anymore."

"You sound disappointed. You don't smoke."

"I know, but the smoke was part of the atmosphere."

They walked into the pub and Fenella immediately felt the smells of many years of cigarette smoke and spilled drinks filling her nostrils. James took a deep breath and then smiled happily at her.

"It's exactly as I remember it," he said.

"Oh, great," Fenella muttered.

They ordered soft drinks at the bar and then carried them to a table near the back. James sat down and ran his hands over the sticky table. "I'm sure I carved my initials into a table just like this when I was ten or eleven," he told Fenella.

"Maybe you should check the other tables. Maybe your initials are still on one of them," she suggested, only half joking.

James looked around and then shrugged. "I think the tables have all been replaced since then. They used to be more rectangular, I think."

Fenella read through the menu and finally decided on cottage pie. "It's one of my favorite things to get on the island," she told James. "Mom used to make it at least once a week."

"Yeah, and I haven't had it since I moved out. It's tempting, but I'm going to have the fish and chips. That's what I remember most about this place. I can't have anything else."

James went back to the bar to order, with a pair of twenty-pound notes supplied by Fenella. She noticed but didn't comment when he simply pocketed the change.

"It really does feel like old times," James sighed as he sat back down. "I don't have that many memories of the island, really, but I do remember this pub. Have you been back to the old house yet?"

"The old house? You mean the house that used to belong to our parents?"

"Yeah, the house I grew up in, in other words. I know, you were only two when you moved, but for me that was my first home."

"Well, I'm sorry to disappoint you, but it isn't there anymore," Fenella said. "They tore down a load of old houses and built a large grocery store on the site."

"That's a shame," James sighed. "I was hoping to knock on the door and see if the current owners would let me have a poke around for old times' sake. Walking around a grocery store won't be nearly as much fun."

Fenella couldn't argue with that. She'd been disappointed herself when she'd found out that her first childhood home had been torn down, but she did love the modern grocery store that now occupied the space. As she had no recollection at all of the house, she didn't really miss it.

"Here we are," the bartender said as he put their plates of food on the table. "Enjoy."

Fenella picked up her fork as her mouth began to water. Her lunch looked and smelled delicious.

James grabbed his fork and grinned. "This looks exactly like I remember it. Maybe after lunch we can go and check out my other favorite place in Laxey."

8

Fenella ate a few bites before she asked. "What's your other favorite place in Laxey, then?"

"The Laxey Wheel," James told her. "It's a giant water wheel from the days when the island had a mining industry. It was closed, and so was the mine, back before I was born. Henry and I used to sneak around the site, trying to imagine how the wheel had looked in its heyday. We went down into the mine once, too, but it was too dark and scary for Henry. Don't tell me they've torn it down now, too?"

"No, not at all. It's a historical site now. You can climb up to the top of the wheel and you can walk a short distance into the mine. I've not actually been yet, so it will be interesting for me, too."

"Excellent," James smiled and then immediately frowned. "Are we being disrespectful to Stephanie, going out and enjoying ourselves like this?" he asked.

"I don't think so. You have a limited amount of time on the island and there is a lot to see and do. A little sightseeing to help take your mind off your grief seems reasonable."

James didn't reply. He ate his lunch and drank the last of his soda before he spoke again. "That was really good. Almost exactly the way I remembered it, except when we used to come with Henry's mum she used to give me little sips of her lager while we ate. I didn't even remember that until I started eating."

"She'd get herself arrested for that sort of thing these days."

"Yeah, but it didn't do me any harm." James laughed. "Or maybe it did. Maybe that's the reason I've turned out the way I have."

"I love you, just the way you are," Fenella told him firmly.

James stared at her for a minute and then grinned. "Gee, thanks, baby sister. I love you, too."

Fenella nodded. They weren't really a family for saying such things, but sometimes they needed saying.

"How was your food?" James asked after an awkward silence.

"Really good, thanks. I don't know if I'll make the trip back up here again in a hurry, but if I'm in the area, I'd eat here again."

"Maybe we can come again just before I leave. I'd like to have fish and chips here again, just one more time."

"We can certainly try. Did you want dessert?"

"We used to get a sticky toffee pudding to share," James remembered, "and Henry's mum used to get jam roly-poly. Sometimes she'd let me have a bite or two from hers if Henry ate more than his fair share of the sticky toffee pud."

"Is that what you want, then?"

James shrugged. "Let's take a look at the menu," he suggested.

There were only a few options, but Fenella happily ordered the chocolate gateau. James did get the sticky toffee pudding. When they'd both scraped up their very last bites, they headed back outside.

"I'm not sure I know where the Laxey Wheel is from here," Fenella said as they got into the car. "I mean, it must be further along this road, as we didn't pass it coming in, but I'm not sure where exactly."

"It isn't far, but I've no idea where you park for it."

They only had to go around the next corner to find both the wheel and its parking area.

"I'm not sure what I was expecting, but that isn't it," Fenella said as they walked toward the wheel that was turning slowly in the autumn sunshine.

"It looks a lot better than I how I remember it," James laughed. "She's called the Lady Isabella and she's really pretty, isn't she?"

GUESTS AND GUILT

They paid the admission fee and then slowly climbed the steps to the top.

"It was a long climb, but the views are worth it," James said as they stood and caught their breath.

"Laxey is lovely," Fenella replied. As she looked down at the village below them, she couldn't help but wonder if she actually owned any of the tiny properties she could see. She was going to have to make a point of visiting every single place on the list that Doncan had given her, but not until after James had gone home.

"It is lovely, and I have very fond memories of it, maybe more so than of anywhere else in the world. Henry and his mum lived very differently to us, and I think I was jealous of their lives."

"What was so different?"

"It was just the two of them. His mum had a job, too, which was unusual in those days. During the week he usually stayed with his grandparents, which is why he was at school with me, but he always spent the weekends and school holidays with his mum in Laxey. She had a little cottage and the two of them always seemed to have great adventures. I always felt stuck at home with three older brothers and a baby sister."

"Sorry about that."

James laughed. "Oh, I resented the older brothers much more than you. You didn't do much of anything, really. They were always banging in and out of the house, dragging in friends and making noise. There was never any peace or quiet in our house. Henry's mum's house felt completely different."

"Did you want to try to find her house after we're done here?" Fenella asked.

"Could we? I remember exactly where it was. It was just a little cottage on the beach. It's probably long gone, though."

"We can certainly go and look for it."

"Thank you. I'm really glad that I decided to come and visit you. I'd always wanted to come back to the island, but I could never find the strength to do it. I just wish Stephanie were here to enjoy it with me."

Fenella reached over and patted his back. "I know."

They took their time admiring the view from every side of the platform before making their way back down the stairs. From there, they walked over to the old mine shaft.

James put on a hard hat and walked into the mine while Fenella stood outside, trying to convince herself that it wouldn't be too claustrophobic for her.

"You may as well come in," James said from the entrance a moment later. "You can only walk a short distance. You won't have time to get claustrophobic."

Fenella dropped the unflattering hat onto her head and followed her brother into the dark mine. He was right. The public was only allowed very limited access. "It's creepy in here," she told James.

"Not really. Not with the artificial lighting and all of the signs detailing the history of the place. It was properly creepy when I was a kid, though."

Back outside, they walked around the tiled washing floors where the ore and waste had been separated after being brought out of the mines. Fenella stopped to read every sign, enjoying learning the history of the site and of mining on the island. James walked ahead of her, stopping to stare into the distance from time to time, but not speaking. When they'd had their fill of the site, they headed back to the car.

"Can you find Laxey Beach from here?" James asked as Fenella started the engine.

"If there are signs, I can."

James laughed. "I didn't see any on the way in, but I'm sure we'll find it. I might even remember the way, if you drive really slowly through Laxey."

Fenella did her best, no doubt annoying the row of cars behind them as they went. They were nearly out of Laxey when James shouted.

"That's it," he said, pointing to a small road that seemed to go almost straight down from the main road they were traveling along.

"You want me to drive down there?"

"Yeah. It's fine. Henry's mum never had a problem."

Henry's mum sounded like a crazy woman, Fenella thought but

didn't say. She made the tight turn onto the road and was immediately sorry.

"There's only room for one car. What happens if someone is coming the other way?" she demanded.

"There are some wider bits," James pointed out. "I guess we'll have to pull over into one of them."

"It's also incredibly steep. I hope the brakes on my car are solid."

"It is steep. That was always part of the excitement. It felt like we were descending into the great unknown or something."

At the bottom of the hill, James directed her to turn right. "The beach is just around the corner," he promised.

There was a small parking area as soon as they'd turned. "Just park here," James suggested. "We can walk from here."

The beach itself was only a few steps away. When they reached it, Fenella's eyes were drawn to a small cottage that looked as if it had been there for over a hundred years.

"That's Aunt Bessie's cottage," James told her.

"Aunt Bessie?"

"She was an old spinster woman who lived there her whole life. She'll have passed away now, of course, but she used to give me and Henry cake or biscuits when she saw us on the beach. She was nice, but she had very definite opinions about the proper way to do things. I wonder if anyone still lives there?"

They approached the cottage. It looked empty, but when Fenella looked in the window, she could see signs of recent renovations. "It seems as if someone is putting in a new kitchen," she said.

"I'm surprised they aren't just tearing the whole thing down."

"From what I can see, they're keeping with the character of the cottage, just modernizing it."

"I suppose Bessie must have had some family I didn't know about," James said. "Henry's cottage was further down the beach."

They walked past the old cottage and began to stroll along the beach. They'd only gone a few steps when James sighed.

"It's all vacation cottages now," he said. "Henry's house was about where the fourth or fifth cottage is."

"They look like nice cottages, anyway," Fenella said. "They seem to be in good repair."

"Maybe the next time I visit, I'll stay out here. I would love to wake up on Laxey Beach again just one more time. I didn't get to sleep over at Henry's very often, but it was always amazing when I did. The beach was perfect in the very early morning when no one else was around. We almost always ran into Bessie, though. She used to get up really early, too. When she knew Henry and I were at the cottage, she'd bring a few biscuits on her walk and share them with us when she found us."

"If you do decide to visit again, we'll have to find out about renting one of these cottages."

"I wonder if they would sell me one," James said. "Imagine living right on the beach like this, all year around. What are house prices like on the island? If I sold my house in Pennsylvania, could I afford a cottage on the beach?"

"House prices are pretty high here compared to the US. My neighbor's friend was looking for an apartment near mine and I was shocked when I first heard the prices they were asking. I can't even imagine what a house right on the beach would cost."

The pair continued their stroll along the sand. One or two of the vacation cottages looked occupied, but most of them seemed to be empty. Just past them, a dangerous-looking staircase climbed the cliff wall.

"I wonder where that goes," James said. "I don't remember it being there when I was a kid."

"Let's not find out. Those stairs don't look at all safe."

They walked for a while longer and then found a row of rocks and settled down to watch the tide come in.

"I feel as if I'm twelve years old again," James sighed. "And in some ways I'd love to be able to turn back the clock."

"Are you sorry that we moved to the US?"

"No, not at all. It was the right decision for the family at the time. I wasn't happy when it happened, but I settled in eventually."

"It's hard for me to imagine that I ever lived here before. I don't remember anything from the island at all."

"You were here, on Laxey Beach, about a week before we moved,"

James told her. "Henry and his mum had a little going-away party for me. They invited everyone from our class at school, but not many people came. One of my friends in Douglas had a party for me, too, and they all came to that one. Laxey was too far away, I suppose."

"And I was there?"

"You were there. The whole family came, Mum and Dad and all of our brothers. I remember watching you toddle up and down the beach and feeling sorry for you because you weren't going to get to grow up here. Of course, I felt as if I were nearly a grown-up already, and I knew that I was going to move back to the island as soon as I possibly could."

Fenella smiled at him. "And instead, I'm the one who's moved back."

"Yeah, and you probably don't want me moving over, do you? I'm sure you're quite happy to be far away from all four of your brothers."

"Not at all. I miss you guys. I'd be happiest if you all moved over here."

"You aren't thinking of coming back to the US, then?"

"No, I don't think so. Once the money is sorted out, I'll probably start visiting regularly, but I can't see myself moving back. I truly love it here. It feels like home in a way that nowhere else ever has."

"That's how I feel right now, sitting on this beach, staring at the same view that I barely noticed when I was a kid. There were too many things to explore. Sitting and watching the waves would have been boring."

"And now I find it fascinating."

"It's soothing. I needed this today."

"I'm sorry."

"So am I. Stephanie wasn't perfect and we weren't exactly madly in love, but she didn't deserve to die and she especially didn't deserve to get murdered. The police do think it was murder, don't they?"

"I'm not sure what the police think."

"I never did understand her, you know."

"No?"

"She had her own unique way of seeing the world, but sometimes she seemed to lose track of what was real and what was in her head."

"Don't we all do that sometimes? Especially when it comes to remembering our past."

"Yeah, I suppose so. I can remember so many things from my childhood as I sit here, but I couldn't prove that any of them actually happened. Some of them might just be things I wanted to happen rather than things that actually did happen, I suppose."

"Is that the sort of thing you mean about Stephanie, or was it something else?"

"I don't know. We used to have these long conversations that would start out perfectly normal and then turn into something else altogether."

"I'm not sure I know what you mean."

"We'd start out talking about the book. She'd give me an idea for a scene and then she'd tell me that it reminded her of something from her childhood. Then I'd have to hear all about the time her Aunt Mabel took her to Liverpool for the day and they got lost on their way back to the ferry. That all sounds reasonable, doesn't it?"

"Yes," Fenella said slowly.

"But then the story would get weird. They'd be wandering around and they'd run into one of the Beatles. He'd take them to a huge hotel and buy them dinner and sing to them before having his limousine take them back to the ferry."

"So you never knew where the true story stopped and the fantasy began."

"Exactly. That was one of the happier stories, actually, as well. Sometimes the stories got really grim. I remember one where she was lost on her own in Manchester and a gang of men started following her. She got really upset, telling me about running and running and not being able to get away from them until she finally ran into a restaurant and started screaming."

"My goodness."

"But was it true?"

"I don't suppose you'll ever know."

"No, I don't suppose I will," James sighed. "We were usually drinking, which didn't help, really. She liked to drink wine and talk about her past. She always said she didn't want to keep any secrets from me. I kept plenty from her, though."

"Really?"

"Oh, nothing serious, mostly things about other women that she didn't need to know. I didn't mention my inability to write to her, either. I didn't want her to think that she was wasting her time working with me. I'm still convinced that I can take her ideas and write a good solid story from them."

"Maybe she was just trying to impress you with her stories."

"That's probably it. I just wish I knew which ones to believe."

"Why?" Fenella asked, suddenly suspicious that there was more going on than James was admitting.

"I don't know. I feel as if I'm letting her down somehow. I should have taken the time to get to know her properly. I should have been able to tell when she was telling the truth and when she was creating fiction. I should have made sure that I knew the difference. She deserved a man who cared enough to know."

"You couldn't have known that it was going to matter," Fenella said. She moved over to sit closer to him, sliding her arm around him. "I know this is difficult for you. I wish there was something that I could say or do to make things better."

"I just want her back," James replied. "I'd listen more and try to understand her better. I'd be a proper partner to her. I was, I mean, I feel as if I was sort of using her for my own ends. I wanted to write another book and it seemed that she might be able to help me do that. I never once thought about it from her perspective, though."

"That's enough feeling sad for today," Fenella said briskly. "Let's walk back to the car and get out of here. It's nearly time for dinner, anyway."

"Is it that late? I didn't realize."

They walked back to Fenella's car, nodding politely at the family that had emerged from one of the vacation cottages along the way.

"I want to come back here again before I go home," James said as Fenella started back up the steep hill to the main road.

"We can do that," she promised. "Maybe I'll see if I can find another way down, though," she added as a car suddenly appeared in the road in front of her. She pulled into a small space by the side of the road and held her breath as the car inched past her. She felt as if she didn't start breathing again until they were halfway back to Douglas.

"I don't feel like much dinner," James said a short while later. "Maybe we could just hit a grocery store and I could get some snacks or something."

"We can do that if you want. Or we can buy something easy, like a frozen pizza, and I can make dinner for both of us."

James looked over at her and shrugged. "Would you mind terribly if I said I'd rather be alone? I'm feeling a bit overwhelmed about everything."

"I'm not sure I want you to be alone."

"The thing is, I live alone. I do everything alone. I'm not used to being around other people all the time. Stephanie understood that. I know I said she used to stay out with other men and I never complained. One of the main reasons I never complained was because I enjoyed having my house to myself while she was gone. And as much as I've enjoyed your company today, I really need some time tonight by myself."

"If that's what you really want," Fenella said, feeling slightly relieved. She loved her brother and she was enjoying having the chance to spend time with him, but she quite liked the idea of taking a break from him, as well. They had three weeks to spend together. Time apart would probably be good for both of them.

"It is what I really want. It's what I need, too. I have a lot to think about and I can't do that when I'm with other people. I need to go through the notes that Stephanie left with me and see if there's actually a story there, and I feel as if I need to start on that immediately. I feel that the book will honor her memory, if I can bring myself to write it."

"I thought you gave the police all of her things."

"Everything except the notebook we were using together for the book. It's just a bunch of notes for me to work from, nothing more. When I go through it tonight, I'll make sure of that, anyway."

"Do you want to go to the grocery store near your house or the one that was built on the land where we used to live?" Fenella asked.

"Oh, the one closest to the house where I'm staying," James said quickly. "I think I've spent enough time on memory lane today. Let's save something for tomorrow."

The store was quiet and it didn't take James long to find some snacks. "I haven't had any of these things since childhood," he told Fenella excitedly. "I didn't even think they'd still be available. I'm going to eat biscuits and chocolate until I explode."

"I don't think biscuits go with lager," Fenella told him, glancing at the packs of beer in his shopping cart.

"They totally do," he argued. "I have to wash them down with something."

When Fenella frowned at him, he sighed. "I lost my girlfriend today in the worst possible way. I think I've been holding myself together pretty well. If I want to have a few beers tonight to help numb the pain, I can't see why you care."

"I care because I worry about you."

"I know you do, but I can't get up to any trouble tucked up in the house with my beers and my biscuits. I'll have my snack and then drink myself to sleep. The hangover will be worth it."

"Hangovers are never worth it."

James took her hands and looked into her eyes. "Trust me on this, baby sister. I won't do anything stupid. I just want to have a few beers and try to forget about everything that's happened in the past twenty-four hours. Surely you can understand that."

Fenella nodded. "Okay, let's go." She insisted that he get a frozen pizza as well, and when they got back to the house, she put it in the oven for him.

"You will remember to get that out in twenty minutes, right?" she asked anxiously.

"As I don't really want it, I'm tempted to leave it in there," he replied. "But if I do, I'll turn the oven off, okay?"

"Eat the pizza. It will help soak up the beer."

"So will biscuits," he argued. As Fenella opened her mouth to reply, he held up his hand. "I'm only teasing, honestly. I will eat my pizza first, although maybe not all of it, and then I'll have a few beers and a few biscuits and an early night. I'm too old to do anything more ambitious than that, really."

Fenella gave him a hug. "I won't worry anymore, then," she lied. "What time do you want to get started tomorrow morning? Maybe we could visit a castle or something."

"How about if I call you when I get up? My body clock still isn't functioning correctly. If you don't hear from me by noon, come and pound on the door."

"You'd better call before noon," Fenella warned him, "or I'll send Inspector Hammersmith over to pound on your door."

James laughed. "I'll set an alarm," he promised.

Fenella had to force herself to concentrate on the drive home. Her thoughts were bouncing around in every direction, making it hard to focus on other cars and unexpected pedestrians. When she finally parked in the garage under her building, she felt fortunate that she'd made it home safely.

"What is going on?" Mona demanded as Fenella walked into her apartment.

"Meerooww," Katie said.

"Don't give me that. I know that Shelly fed you."

"I did," Shelly agreed as she walked out of the spare bedroom. "She had dinner not ten minutes ago. But what's going on?"

"I need some dinner," Fenella replied. "I'll tell you everything while I cook and eat."

James's pizza had smelled awfully good, so Fenella turned the oven on and found a similar one in her own freezer. "There's enough here for two, if you want to join me," she told Shelly.

"I wish I could, but Gordon is collecting me in half an hour. We're going to get something to eat and then see a movie."

"I'd better talk fast, then," Fenella sighed. She sat down at the counter. "I suppose I should start with when James called me this morning."

Fenella only stopped once, to get herself a cold drink, as she told Shelly and Mona all about her incredibly long day. They both gasped when she recounted opening the door to Mark Hammersmith, and Shelly gave her a quick hug when she told them about identifying the body. "And then I took James home, made him a pizza, and came back here," she concluded.

"I'm surprised Inspector Hammersmith didn't arrest you," Mona said.

Fenella opened her mouth to reply and then remembered just in time that Shelly couldn't see or hear the other woman. She snapped her mouth shut and then checked on her pizza. It was nearly ready.

"So the police are investigating and you're stuck in the middle again," Shelly concluded.

"I'm not, though, not really. James might be, but he's the one who brought her to the island. I'd never even met her before yesterday."

"Do you think that will get you off the list of suspects?" Shelly asked.

"No, of course not," Fenella sighed. "I'm really hoping that when they investigate further, they find that it was just a tragic accident."

"Nonsense, she was murdered by one of her old friends. I vote for Annie. She sounds disagreeable," Mona said.

"If it was murder, it must have been one of her friends that killed her, mustn't it?" Shelly wondered.

"We don't know who else she may have contacted while James was asleep. Maybe someone we know nothing about also had some sort of motive," Fenella replied.

"Do you have any idea which of her friends might have had a motive for killing her?" was Shelly's next question.

"Not at all. None of them seemed to be contemplating murder while I was at the pub with them, anyway."

"She probably stole Annie's boyfriend way back when they were both fifteen or something," Mona said. "And Annie has been waiting all this time for her chance to get her revenge."

"Not likely," Fenella said. When Shelly gave her a startled look, she laughed. "I was thinking out loud," she said, glaring at Mona. "I just meant none of the motives I can think of seem likely."

A knock on the door kept Shelly from responding. After a quick greeting from Gordon, he and Shelly left for their evening out. Fenella shut the door behind them and then sat down on the couch and stared out at the sea.

"Go on, then, let's talk about the suspects," Mona said.

"I don't want to talk about the suspects," Fenella protested.

"I never heard about last night. Tell me everything that happened at the pub."

Fenella sighed and then began yet another retelling of her evening at the pub. She was only just getting started when the phone rang.

"Hello?"

"Fen? It's James."

"Are you okay? You sound out of breath."

"I had to run home. And I fell down a few times."

"Run home? Fell down? What are you talking about?"

"I wanted some fresh air," he said, and then went silent.

"Yes, and?"

"Oh, I went for a walk around the neighborhood." Another long silence had Fenella nearly screaming.

"And then what happened?" she demanded.

"It was dark and there was this car. It nearly hit me when I crossed the road."

"Are you okay?" Fenella gasped.

"I thought it was an accident, but it kept following me. I started running, but I wasn't as fast as a car." This time Fenella used the silence to find her car keys and her handbag.

"I'm on my way to the house," she told James.

"I fell over a hedge and into someone's yard. I got pretty banged up. I ran home from there. My head hurts."

The phone went dead in Fenella's hand. She glanced at Mona and then headed for the door.

"What's going on?" Mona asked.

"It sounds as if someone tried to kill James," Fenella replied with tears streaming down her face.

9

Fenella tried to keep calm as she made her way out of the garage under her building. She hadn't been driving on the island long enough to be able to make the journey on automatic pilot. She had to focus. While she drove, she tried to decide whether she should have called for an ambulance or the police before she'd left home. If only Daniel were on the island. He lived right across the street from the house where James was staying. He could have walked over and checked on James for Fenella.

The neighborhood was dark and Fenella felt uneasy when she parked in the driveway. As she walked to the front door, a single car drove slowly down the street behind her. Fenella shivered and then knocked sharply. After a minute, she knocked again and then glanced around. There were lights on in a few houses, but most of them seemed to be dark. The evening had flown past, and as Fenella knocked again, she glanced at her watch. It was after ten o'clock, which surprised her. No doubt Shelly would be coming back to the apartment soon. Fenella realized she should have left her friend a note.

Somewhere in the bottom of her handbag, Fenella knew there was an extra key for the house. Doncan had given her two and she'd only given one of them to James. She dug around, pulling out seemingly everything but the house key. When she finally found it, she slid it into the lock and turned it. When she tried to open the door, it wouldn't budge. She turned the key again and then sighed. She'd been knocking all this time on a door that hadn't been locked.

"James? James? Where are you?" she called from the doorway. As she took a few steps into the house, she thought again about calling the police. "Hello?" she yelled again, digging back into her bag for her mobile phone. A loud groan answered her call. All thoughts of calling for help vanished as Fenella followed the sound into the kitchen.

"James!" she exclaimed. He was lying on the kitchen floor, holding his head and moaning softly. His clothes were all badly torn and Fenella could see blood seeping through in more than one place.

He looked up at her and sighed. "My head hurts," he said in a low voice.

Fenella bent over him and took a better look. There was a large lump on his forehead and she could see blood in his hair. "What happened to your head?"

"I tripped and I hit it on the curb," James replied. "It hurts a lot."

"I'm going to call for an ambulance."

"No, I don't need an ambulance. Help me sit up. I just need to get cleaned up and I'll be fine."

"You need a doctor. Head injuries can be very serious."

"Why are both of you shouting at me?" James asked, frowning.

"Both? You're seeing double?"

"I'm so very tired," James replied, lying back down on the floor.

"Right, I can't pick you up, so you can get up and walk out to my car or I can call for an ambulance. Which will it be?"

"I don't want to cause any trouble. I can walk. I'm sure of it."

James sat up again and then very slowly made his way onto his feet with Fenella's help. She supported him as he took a couple of very cautious steps.

"It isn't too bad," he said. "I'm only a little bit dizzy."

"We can rest for a while if you want."

"Maybe I could just sit down for a minute."

He dropped into the nearest chair and took a few shaky breaths. "I'm sorry. I shouldn't have gone out."

"Let's worry about that later. For now I just want to get you checked over."

"They're going to want to keep me overnight. I'll need clothes and things."

Fenella nodded. "Will you stay right there if I go and get your things?"

"Yeah."

Upstairs, Fenella simply threw just about everything she could find into the large suitcase that was in the corner of the bedroom. She left the pile of clothes in one corner, which she assumed were dirty, and a few spare T-shirts and pairs of jeans, but everything else went into the bag. Back in the kitchen, James had his head on the table.

"James? Wake up," she said loudly.

He jumped and then nodded. "I'm awake. Maybe you're right. Maybe I do need a doctor."

"Should I call an ambulance?"

"I'm not that bad. I can make it to the car."

He got back to his feet and then, with Fenella doing her best to keep him upright, the pair made their way through the house. In the living room, James stopped. "Maybe I could just sit again for a minute."

"Maybe you could keep going and then sit in the car," Fenella suggested. He was proving easier to move than to get going and she really didn't want to stop again.

"Yeah, okay," he muttered, gritting his teeth and taking another slow step. Time seemed to slow down as Fenella struggled to get him out the door and down the three steps outside. Once he was safely loaded into her car, she went back for his suitcase.

"Right, the hospital isn't far away," she told him as she put the car into gear. "I'm taking you to the emergency room."

"I've never been to an emergency room before," James replied before falling silent.

When Fenella pulled up at the hospital entrance a few minutes later, he appeared to be asleep again. She sighed and then put the car into park.

"You can't leave your car here," the hospital security guard told her.

"I won't. I just want to unload my brother before I move it," she replied.

He looked uncertain, but Fenella didn't wait for him to reply. She dashed around the car and opened the passenger door. James blinked several times when she shook him.

"Where am I?" he demanded.

"We're at the hospital. We need to get your head examined."

"I've always needed my head examining," he replied with a weak smile.

Fenella was grateful that he felt well enough to make a joke, even if she didn't find anything about the situation even remotely funny. "Come on," she said. "You need to get out of the car."

As Fenella did her best to help, James worked on sliding out of the car.

"Here," a voice said behind Fenella. "This may help."

She turned around and found the security guard standing there with a wheelchair.

"Thank you so much," she said, feeling overwhelmed by the entire situation.

With the guard's help, she managed to get James out of the car and into the wheelchair. Pushing it wasn't easy, but it was better than trying to get James to walk any further.

"I can't help you because I have to stay out here," the guard said in an apologetic tone. "I will keep an eye on your car for you, though. Get your brother registered at the desk and then come back and move it, okay?"

"Yes, that's great, thanks," Fenella said. She pushed the heavy chair with her very heavy brother up the short ramp and into the building. The woman behind the reception desk barely glanced at her.

"Fill out the entire form, front and back," she said as she handed Fenella a clipboard.

It didn't take long for Fenella to comply, mostly because she didn't know the answers to many of the questions. James had fallen asleep again, so he was no help at all.

"I did the best I could," she told the woman as she handed the clipboard back to her.

The woman glanced at the paper and then shrugged. "We'll call you shortly."

"I'm just going to move my car," Fenella replied. "You won't take him back before I return, will you?"

"I doubt it," the woman said.

Feeling as if that wasn't very helpful, Fenella pushed James into the small and empty waiting area and then rushed back outside.

The guard smiled at her. "I didn't think I'd see you again for hours," he said.

"I don't want to take advantage of your kindness. Now that James is settled, I'll move the car to a proper parking space."

"There should be spaces in the first car park that you'll drive past. It's marked as staff only, but that's only enforced between seven in the morning and seven at night. Anyone can park there after hours."

"Thank you," Fenella said. The lot was only a short distance away. Fenella slid into the first empty spot she saw and then rushed back into the building. James didn't appear to have moved. As Fenella dropped into a chair next to him, her mobile phone rang.

"Fenella? I hope I'm not interrupting something important, but I was surprised to get home and not find you here," Shelly said.

"James rang that he'd had an accident. I'm at the emergency room with him now."

"What sort of accident?"

"He wasn't totally clear on that," Fenella replied, not wanting to go into any detail until she knew more.

"I'll be there as soon as I can."

"Thank you, but that's not necessary. I suspect they're going to want to admit him, as he has a head injury. Once they do that, I'll be home."

"But surely you'd appreciate some company?"

Fenella blinked back tears. "I really would," she admitted in a low voice.

"I'm on my way," Shelly promised.

Now that she was sitting down waiting, Fenella began to think back through what James had said. Had someone in a car really chased him through the streets? It seemed impossible.

"Mr. Woods?" a voice called from a doorway near the back of the room.

James didn't move as Fenella pushed him toward the door. "This is James. I'm his sister."

The woman frowned and looked at the paper in front of her. "Sisters aren't usually permitted in the exam rooms with patients," she said.

"Well, I'm all he has on the island, so I'm afraid I'll have to do."

She nodded, but she still looked uncertain. "He is an adult. We'll need his permission if you want to come with him."

"James," Fenella said, tapping her brother on the shoulder. "Tell the woman yes."

James looked around and then frowned at Fenella. "What?"

"Just tell the woman that it's okay that I'm with you," she said. "Then we can see about your head injury."

"Is that why my head hurts?"

"Yes, dear."

The woman made a few notes on her clipboard and then nodded. "We'll take that as permission for now," she said. "If he objects later, you'll be escorted out."

"That's fine. If he's well enough to object, I'll go happily."

The woman led them into a small exam room. "He'll want to take off everything except his pants and put on the gown. It ties in the back. The nurse will be with you shortly."

There wasn't much that Fenella wouldn't do for her brothers, but helping them undress was a bit much. She shook James awake. "You need to take off your clothes and put on the gown," she told him. "I'll wait outside the door. You can leave your underwear on."

James nodded. Fenella waited until he'd risen to his feet before she stepped out of the room. She watched the second hand tick slowly around the clock on the wall for several minutes and then stuck her head back into the room. James was wearing the gown and his socks, and had climbed onto the examination table. He appeared to be asleep yet again.

"Good evening," a young man said as he pushed the exam room's door open a short while later. "What brings you in tonight?"

"My brother went out for a walk and nearly got run over," Fenella said. "He tripped and fell and hit his head on the curb trying to get away."

"Have you rung the police?" the man asked as he began to poke and prod James.

"No, I haven't. Do you think I should?"

"There was just a fatal hit and run yesterday. These things seem to be getting out of hand. I don't suppose there will be much the police can do, though. Your brother didn't happen to notice the license plate, did he?"

"I don't know. He hasn't been exactly coherent since I found him."

The man nodded. "Mr. Woods? Can you wake up for me, please?"

James opened one eye and then groaned. "I just want to sleep," he complained.

Fenella listened as the man asked James a series of questions. He knew his name and that he was in the hospital, at least.

"Who is the current prime minister?" the man asked.

James stared at him for a minute and then shrugged. "I didn't know that before I hit my head," he said. "I don't really keep up with British politics anymore. I don't keep up with US politics, either."

"None of his injuries seem too bad," the man told Fenella a moment later. "The doctor will be in shortly to take a look and if he concurs, then I'll dress a few of the more serious cuts on his legs and we'll probably keep him overnight for observation."

Fenella nodded. She'd been assuming that he was the doctor, but clearly she was mistaken. A few minutes later a much older man strode in.

"Good evening," he said. He checked that James knew his name, flashed a light in James's eyes and then shrugged. "He's given himself quite a bump on the head, along with some nasty cuts and bruises. I suggest you try to keep him from taking long walks when he's been drinking in the future. We'll keep him overnight. Head injuries can be serious."

The man swept out of the room before Fenella could reply. She looked over at James, but he seemed to be asleep again. Was it possible that the doctor was right and that James had simply tripped and fallen because he'd been drunk? An hour later, Fenella made her way back into the waiting area. James had been taken up to a room where he would be checked hourly. There was no reason for Fenella to stay.

"There you are," Shelly's voice cut through Fenella's thoughts.

"Shelly! I forgot you were coming up. I'm so sorry," Fenella exclaimed as Shelly pulled her into a hug.

"It's fine. I just assumed you'd gone back with James to see the doctor."

"Yes, I did. They've put him in a room for the night now. I was just heading home."

"Let's get out of here, then," Shelly replied. She followed Fenella home, which helped Fenella concentrate on her driving.

When Fenella opened her apartment door, Mona startled her.

"Is he okay?" she demanded.

Shelly was right behind Fenella, which made answering the question difficult.

"Anyway, as I said, James is being kept overnight, but they seem to think that he'll be fine," she said, repeating what she'd already told Shelly twice.

"Yes, you said that already," Shelly said gently. "I think you need some sleep."

"Yes, I'm sure I do."

"You can't just go to bed," Mona told her. "I need to know what happened to James. Did one of Stephanie's friends try to run him down? What do the police think?"

Fenella gave Shelly a hug and then went into her bedroom and shut the door. Mona followed a moment later.

"Tell me everything," she said as she sat on Fenella's bed.

"There's nothing to tell. James was barely coherent. I didn't ask him any questions. Hopefully I'll find out more tomorrow."

Mona looked angry for a moment and then shrugged. "Maybe I should go and visit him myself. We really should find out what happened while it's fresh in his mind."

"I don't think much of anything is fresh in his mind right now. I'll talk to him first thing tomorrow morning. That will be soon enough."

"What did Inspector Hammersmith think of it?"

"I didn't call the police."

"You didn't? Why not? They could find out where Stephanie's three friends were tonight and maybe solve Stephanie's murder. It must have been the same person who tried to kill James."

"Why?"

"It's the only thing that makes sense," Mona replied. "Stephanie must have been blackmailing one of her friends or something. Now that friend is worried that James knows her secret, too."

Fenella yawned. "You may be right, but I'm too tired to think it all through right now. I'll probably call Mark in the morning, after I talk to James again, maybe."

"I think you should call him right now. What if the killer tries to get to James at Noble's? The police should have a guard with him at all times."

"He's being monitored constantly right now. I'll talk to the police in the morning," Fenella said. She quickly brushed her teeth and took off her makeup and then crawled into bed. Katie was already asleep and it didn't take long for Fenella to follow suit.

"Mmerrreww," the voice said softly in her ear. "Mmerreww meerroowww."

Fenella frowned and looked at the clock. It was still a few minutes before seven. "You're early," she told Katie.

"Meeewwwwww," Katie replied.

Fenella sighed and squeezed her eyes tightly shut. A moment later, she heard a loud knock on the apartment's front door.

"Meeewww," Katie said, bouncing off the bed. She went and stood at the door, staring expectantly at Fenella.

"I could just ignore them, whoever they are," Fenella suggested.

A second knock, louder and longer than the first, put an end to that idea. As Fenella slid on her slippers and bathrobe, she thought of Shelly. Hopefully the person at the door hadn't woken her, too.

"Good morning," Mark Hammersmith said. His face was grim and he looked even more tired than Fenella felt.

"Good morning," she replied. "Is James okay?" she demanded as she suddenly realized the potential significance of the man's visit.

"He was fine when I left him a few minutes ago," the man replied.

"A few minutes ago?" Fenella shook her head. She felt very much like she'd walked into the middle of the conversation. "Did you want to come in?" she asked after a moment.

"Yes, please. And I'd love some coffee if you have any."

"I don't, as I wasn't out of bed yet," she replied, even though she was pretty sure that her pajamas and messy hair had already told the man that. "I can start some, if you'd like."

"If you can, I'd appreciate it. I didn't get nearly enough sleep last night, and then I was pulled out of bed at five."

Fenella filled the coffee maker without thinking. While it was brewing, she pulled out a loaf of bread. "Would you like some toast?"

"That would be good, too. I didn't get breakfast."

Fenella slid bread into the toaster and then found a jar of jam for the man. When the toast popped, she gave him both slices and started two more for herself. By that time the coffee was done and she happily filled two cups with the hot liquid. After a few sips, she started to feel almost awake.

"I'm sorry. I'm still half-asleep," she said. "What brings you here this early in the morning?"

"I understand you took your brother to Noble's late last night."

"Yes, that's right."

"My first question, then, is why didn't you ring me?"

Fenella had been mentally preparing herself for that very question. "I was going to call you after I talked to James. He wasn't making much sense last night. I didn't want to bother you if he'd simply had too much to drink and fallen over the curb."

"Even if that is what happened, I'd want to know about it. Your brother is a witness in a murder investigation. His being admitted to Noble's is important. I should have been informed."

"I'm sorry. I didn't realize."

"What did he tell you happened?"

Fenella frowned. "He wasn't making much sense when he rang," she said, trying to work out how much she wanted to tell the man. "He said he'd gone out for a walk and then fallen over into someone's yard. That was on the phone when he called me. Once I got to the house, he didn't tell me anything further, he just complained about how much his head hurt."

"He's still complaining this morning," Mark told her. "Do you have any reason to believe that this was anything other than an accident?"

"Until I talk to James, I simply don't know."

"And James doesn't want to talk to me," Mark sighed.

"He doesn't?"

"Oh, he was very polite and he answered all of my questions, but only with the vaguest answers I think I've ever received. I was hoping you might be more forthcoming."

"I probably will be, once I've spoken to James. I don't really know anything yet."

Mark nodded and then sipped his coffee. "Why was he taking a walk after dark last night?"

"He said something about wanting some fresh air."

"I'm surprised you left him on his own."

"I'm sorry now that I did. He wanted to be alone, though. He had food and a few cans of beer. He wanted to be alone to think things through, that's all. As I've always lived on my own, I could understand how he felt."

"How much beer did he drink?"

"I don't know. He had twelve cans when I left him. You'd have to count how many are left, I suppose."

Mark made a few notes in his phone and then got to his feet. "I'd appreciate it if you'd come with me now," he said. "I'd like you to talk to your brother and persuade him to answer my questions."

Fenella glanced down at her pajamas. "I need to take a shower and get dressed," she said.

"Meerroww," Katie interrupted.

"And I need to feed Katie," Fenella added.

"You may have ten minutes," Mark said. "Please be quick."

Fenella stared at him for a moment and then dashed away to her bedroom. She took the fastest shower she'd ever taken and then pulled on the first clothes she came to in her wardrobe. After doing the best she could with a light layer of makeup, she combed out her wet hair and headed for the door.

"You can't go out looking like that," Mona said sharply from behind her.

"Why not?" Fenella asked, glancing down at her clothes.

"There is a stain on the jeans and the T-shirt is far too big for you. At least put on a clean pair of jeans and a shirt that fits," Mona insisted. "People do know that we're related, you understand."

Fenella resisted the urge to sigh as she found a clean pair of jeans and a different shirt. Once she'd changed, she had to admit that Mona was right. She looked much more put together as she glanced at herself in the mirror.

"Okay, I'm ready," she said as she walked back into the living room. Mark was sitting on the couch with Katie on his lap. They were both staring out at the sea below them.

While they were distracted, Fenella filled Katie's bowls. Not completely sure what Smokey was meant to have for breakfast, she filled Smokey's water bowl but left her food bowl empty. After writing a quick note to Shelly, telling her where she'd gone and why, she tried again.

"Okay, I'm good to go," she told Mark.

He looked up at her and smiled. "I could sit here all day," he told her.

Fenella nodded. "Some days I feel as if that's all I do."

"But I have work to do, and I'm sure you're eager to talk to your brother. Let's go."

Fenella grabbed her handbag and followed the man to the door. "What did you want me to do exactly?" she asked as they boarded the elevator.

"I want you to persuade your brother to tell me exactly what happened last night," Mark replied. "He's being deliberately vague."

"He does have a large lump on his head. Maybe he doesn't remember what happened."

"The doctor didn't seem to think that the bump on his head should be causing him any memory issues."

"Maybe the doctor is wrong."

"Maybe, or maybe your brother has other reasons for not wanting to tell me what actually happened."

"If he does, I can't imagine what they are."

Mark's car was parked right outside the apartment building. "I'll make sure someone gets you home when we're done," he said.

Fenella climbed into the passenger seat and then sat back and shut her eyes. She nearly fell asleep even before Mark was behind the steering wheel.

"So, what did Stephanie's friends have to say for themselves?" she asked the man as he put the car into gear.

He gave her a surprised look. "Surely you don't really expect me to answer that question."

Fenella shook her head. "No, I suppose not. I was just wondering, that's all. Actually, I was hoping that two of them told you that they'd gone home right after I did and left the third with Stephanie. That would narrow down the possibilities for who might have killed her, wouldn't it?"

"It might have, if it had happened, but it didn't," Mark replied. "And before you start speculating on any other possibilities, I'm not going to keep answering your questions, so you can stop there."

"They were meant to be looking after Stephanie," Fenella said, mostly talking to herself, primarily to keep herself awake. "I don't understand why they didn't drop her off at the house when they left the pub."

"You'll have to ask them the next time you see them."

"Yes, I will, won't I?"

"No, you won't," Mark said quickly. "As in, I don't want you talking to them. I don't want you involved in the investigation. Leave the police work to the police. You concentrate on taking care of your brother."

"I think the police work would be easier."

Mark chuckled. "Having spent an hour with your brother this morning, you may be right. He seemed as if he might be difficult."

"He doesn't mean to be, really, but he's always been rather spoiled. He doesn't see it that way, of course."

"I've rung Daniel and filled him in on everything that's happening here, but you probably already know that. I'm sure he rang you straight away to get your side of the story."

"I haven't spoken to him since well before James arrived," Fenella replied, trying hard not to sound hurt or upset.

"Really? I suppose he's awfully busy with the course and his new friends and everything. No doubt he'll be in touch soon, though."

"Maybe," Fenella sighed. It was Mark who'd told her that Daniel had become involved with another woman. Surely he shouldn't be surprised that Daniel wasn't contacting her.

They parked in a special lot at Noble's and made their way inside. Fenella followed Mark through the building until he stopped in front of a closed door. He knocked twice and the door swung open.

The uniformed constable who'd opened the door nodded at Mark. "He hasn't said a word since you left," he reported. "He's been pretending to be asleep, but I don't think he truly is."

Mark nodded. "You can take a break," he said. "Go and get yourself a coffee or something. Be back in half an hour."

"Yes, sir. Thank you, sir," the man said. He walked out of the room, holding the door for Fenella and Mark to enter.

Fenella gasped when she saw her brother. His face was unnaturally pale and his head was covered in a thick bandage. He looked much worse now than he had when she'd left him the previous evening. As far as she could tell, he was fast asleep.

"James? Are you sleeping?" she asked as she crossed the room to his side. He stirred and then opened one eye.

"Fenella? Are the police gone?"

She shook her head. "I'm here with Inspector Hammersmith. You need to answer his questions."

"I did answer his questions," James replied. "I told him how I went for a walk and then tripped and fell over. I must have hit my head and blacked out for a bit. When I could, I walked back to the house and called you. That's about all I remember until I woke up here."

Fenella bit her lip. The story didn't match with what he'd told her last night. Was that because James couldn't remember what had really happened, or because he didn't want the police to know?

"You can't remember anything else?" she asked.

James shook his head. "One of the nurses was really pretty," he said after a moment.

Fenella sighed and looked over at the police inspector. "It seems as if he's suffering from some memory loss after all."

"Maybe. Can I talk to you outside for a minute?"

Fenella gave James's hand a squeeze and then followed Mark into the corridor.

"Look, whatever he's hiding, it would be much better if he shared it with me," Mark said. "I'm going to leave you two alone for a short while. You need to try to convince him to tell me everything."

"I'll do my best," Fenella promised. She didn't like the idea of keeping secrets from the police.

"If you can't talk him into telling me anything, I'm hoping you'll be able to convince him to tell you what's going on. I hope you'll be smart enough to pass along whatever he tells you."

Fenella flushed. She didn't like the idea of going behind her brother's back, but she knew Mark was right. "Let me see what he says when we're alone," she replied. "I won't keep anything from you that seems important."

Mark looked as if he wanted to argue, but after a moment he shrugged. "You have fifteen minutes," he said.

Fenella squared her shoulders and marched back into James's room. He looked to be asleep again, but as Fenella approached the bed, his eyes opened.

"Just you this time?" he asked.

"Yes, just me. What's going on?"

"Someone tried to kill me, and I'm pretty sure I know why," James replied.

10

"We need to tell the police," Fenella said.

James shook his head. "I'm not ready to talk to them about it yet. I have to get the whole story straight in my head first."

"Can you do that in the next fifteen minutes?"

"I don't know. It all feels unreal, and my head hurts a lot. Whenever I say that to anyone, they give me more drugs, which makes everything feel even more unreal. I'm starting to think that I'm crazy. Maybe Stephanie didn't even come to the island with me and this is all a bad dream."

"She definitely came to the island with you, and she's definitely dead," Fenella said flatly.

James winced. "Okay, then, so maybe this is just a horrible nightmare." He reached over and pinched Fenella.

"Ouch!" she exclaimed.

"Maybe it isn't a dream," he sighed.

"What really happened last night?" Fenella asked. "Start with what you did after I left."

"I ate my pizza. It was surprisingly good for a frozen pizza. And I drank a few beers. Not too many, maybe three. I felt really sad. I was missing Stephanie, and then I started to get homesick, which is silly as I've only just arrived for my vacation. All I wanted to do was be at home in my little cottage in the Poconos, away from everyone and everything."

"I can understand that," Fenella said, patting his arm.

"I decided that I needed to take a walk. The house felt really small and closed in, even though it's bigger than my house in Pennsylvania. Anyway, I found some shoes and a jacket and I went out for a walk."

"Was it dark by that time?"

"Yeah, really dark. I was surprised by how few streetlights there are around the place. I just started wandering around, not really paying attention to where I was going, and then I found myself outside the pub."

"The pub we visited with Stephanie?" Fenella checked.

"Yeah, that one. I really wanted another drink, but I didn't want to go inside that pub. I knew there was another one around somewhere, but I couldn't seem to remember how to get there. I started walking away, trying to think, when I heard a car engine. It seemed to be getting louder and louder, so I looked around and there was a car heading straight for me."

"You were on the sidewalk?"

"I was in the middle of the parking lot," he admitted sheepishly. "I wasn't really paying attention to my surroundings, if I'm honest. Anyway, when I saw it, I started running, but the car seemed to be chasing after me. I ran out of the parking lot and down the road, with the car right behind me. That's when I tripped and hit my head on the curb."

Fenella glanced at the thick bandages around his head. He was lucky he could remember anything at all, she thought.

"All I could think of was that I had to keep going. I stood back up and fell over immediately. This time I landed in someone's yard. I crushed a few of their plants, I'm sure, and I tore my clothes on their hedges. But I think that's what saved my life. I was out of sight behind the row of hedges and the person in the car wasn't sure where I'd gone."

"Did you stay hidden for long, then?"

"Not very long. I waited until the car's lights disappeared around a corner and then I started toward the house. My head was pounding and I wasn't thinking straight, of course. That was the last place I should have gone. I should have gone back to the pub or somewhere else with lots of people."

"But you headed for home. Then what happened?" Fenella asked when James lapsed into silence.

"Oh, I was nearly home before I heard the car engine again. When I saw it heading toward me, I ran as fast as I could to the house and locked myself inside. The car sat outside the house for what felt like a long time. When I could breathe again, I called you."

"Why didn't you call the police?"

"I don't know. You seemed like a better option."

Fenella rolled her eyes. "Whatever. Why haven't you told them all of this, then, now that they're involved?"

"They'll just think I'm making it all up," James replied. "They already think that I killed Stephanie, I'm sure of it. If I try to tell them about the car, they'll think that I'm making up stories to hide the fact that I killed her."

"I don't think you're being fair to Mark," Fenella told him. "He's a good investigator. He can probably find some evidence for what you're telling me. And anyway, why would he think that you had anything to do with Stephanie's death?"

"The romantic partner is always the number-one suspect. I know that from television and movies. You should know that, too."

"Even if that's sometimes true, it doesn't make sense this time. If you wanted to kill Stephanie, you could have done so back in the US. Why go to all of the trouble and expense of coming here just to kill her?"

"Maybe we fought after we arrived. Maybe a million other things. None of it matters, because I think I know why she was killed and why the killer is after me now."

"I'll get Mark."

"No, wait. Let me tell you the story first."

"I will, but you have to promise you'll tell Mark once you've told me."

"Maybe. Let's see if you think it's crazy or not, and then we'll decide," James said.

Fenella hesitated and then nodded. She pulled a chair closer to the bedside and sat down. Taking James's hand, she smiled encouragingly. "Go ahead, then."

"Do you remember what I said about never knowing if Stephanie was telling the truth or making things up?" he asked.

Fenella nodded. "You said her stories started out sounding believable, but then often wandered off into fantasy territory."

"Yeah, that's right. But now I'm starting to wonder if more of them were true than I ever realized. Do you remember what she said at the pub?"

"She said a lot at the pub."

"Yeah, but she told her friends that she didn't believe in regrets, lies, or secrets," he reminded her. "And she told them that she'd told me everything about her past."

"I do remember that, now that you mention it."

"She told me that she and her friends once killed a man," James blurted out.

"What?"

"I didn't mean for it to come out quite like that," he sighed, "but that's what she told me."

"Tell me the whole story."

"It wasn't long before she left the island, apparently. She and her friends were a little bit wild, running around and drinking a lot, or at least that's what she told me."

"Which friends?"

"The three from the pub the other night. Annie, Maureen, and Courtney."

"Oh, dear."

"Yeah, exactly. Anyway, they were out drinking and driving around late one Saturday night and they hit a man who was crossing the road."

"Who was driving the car?"

"Stephanie would never tell me that. She said that the responsibility for what happened was shared by all four of them equally, so who was actually driving didn't matter in the slightest."

"What did they tell the police?"

"That's just it. That's why I don't want to talk to the police. They didn't call them."

"It was a hit and run," Fenella sighed. "Just like Stephanie's death."

"No, not at all," James told her. "They hit the man, but he survived."

"I thought you said they killed him," Fenella said, feeling confused.

James took a deep breath. "The story would make more sense if I had been sober when Stephanie told it to me," he said, "and if I'd taken it seriously. I thought she was working on story ideas for our book while she was talking. It wasn't until last night, when I was lying here with my head throbbing, that I started to put it all together."

"Okay, so try to tell me what happened in some sort of logical order," Fenella suggested.

"The four of them were drunk and they hit this guy. He was badly injured, but not killed. They took him to an empty house that they knew about, somewhere they used to go to meet guys and drink and whatever, I believe. Stephanie said that the plan was to nurse him back to health and then let him go."

"But it didn't work out that way?"

James shrugged. "She was vague about exactly what happened. She spent a long time talking about the man. His name was Arthur Beck. It seemed as if they spent a lot of time getting to know one another. Again, though, I don't know how much of it was true or how much was fantasy."

"What did she say about him?"

"He was older, maybe forty, and on the island on his own. He'd come to the island to try to find a job, leaving his wife and their small child at home. Stephanie got quite emotional when she talked about the child, actually."

"So she spent some time with the man after the accident. I don't understand what happened to him."

"Neither do I. She told me all about Arthur and all about his family, and then she told me that he'd died. I asked her how it had happened, and she simply said that he'd stopped breathing one day and that she and her friends shared the blame equally, the same thing she'd said about the driving of the car."

"You think they killed him? That seems to be the only thing that makes sense."

"She wouldn't come right out and say that, not at the time, but sometimes when we'd be talking about other things, she slip it into the conversation. She'd say something like 'remember, I once killed a man,' or something like that. She always laughed after she said it, so I never took it particularly seriously, but what if she was telling the truth?"

"Then she and her friends committed murder and the police need to know about it."

"Except why should they believe me? I've no way to prove that anything she told me was true. What if we tell the police and they waste a bunch of time and energy looking into it and it was all made up?"

"What did they do with the body?"

"According to Stephanie, they buried it behind the empty house they had used to hold the man while he was alive."

"I don't suppose she told you where the house was? Or anything about it that might identify it?"

"Not really. She just said it was in Douglas and it was empty. That was over twenty years ago, though. It may have been torn down or renovated or goodness knows what in the years since then."

"Maybe the body was found," Fenella suggested. "If it has, your story would gain some credibility."

James shrugged. "I'm not interested in credibility. Mostly I just want to go home."

"Home to Poppy Drive or home to Pennsylvania?"

"Home to Pennsylvania. The island doesn't feel like home anymore, and it also doesn't feel safe to me."

"It will be a lot safer once you tell the police everything that Stephanie told you about Arthur Beck."

"I don't know about that."

"Think about it, James. The killer must have killed Stephanie because she told you about Arthur, right? Now the killer is after you.

Once you tell the police everything you know, the killer won't have any reason to kill you anymore."

James frowned. "Unless Stephanie was killed for some other reason, maybe for something I know nothing about. That's a possibility, too."

"Yeah, it is, but the fact that she and her friends once killed a man, and that she was killed within a few hours of seeing them again for the first time in twenty-plus years seems pretty significant to me."

"What if she was lying to me? What if she made up the whole story just to impress me?"

"Then the police spend a bit of time trying to verify it and fail. They have to be told, though."

"I don't want to tell them," James said stubbornly. "They'll just think I'm trying to divert suspicion away from myself."

"Maybe they will, but so what? Mark will still have to investigate what you tell him, and if it is true, he suddenly has a very solid motive for all three of Stephanie's friends. If you won't tell him, I will."

James frowned. "Let me think about it."

"No, I won't let you think about it. You're being stupid and I won't let you get yourself killed because of it. I'm going to talk to Mark right now." Fenella stood up, ignoring James's plea for her to wait. At the door, she turned back to look at him. "You know I'm right," she said softly.

He stared at her for a minute and then nodded slowly. Fenella opened the door and looked up and down the corridor. Mark was leaning on the wall, sipping a cup of coffee. He straightened up and crossed to her.

"James is ready to tell you the whole story," she said, "and it's quite the story."

Mark sat and typed notes into his phone as James told him all about the previous evening.

"You genuinely think that you were being chased by this vehicle?" he asked when James was finished.

"I'm positive. It was terrifying."

Mark nodded. "And can you think of any reason why anyone would want to kill you?" he asked.

"At the pub the other night, Stephanie told her friends that she didn't have any secrets from me," James replied. "I think her friends realized that she'd told me about the time they'd killed a man."

Fenella gave Mark a lot of credit. He blinked a few times, but otherwise he didn't really react to James's words. After a moment, he nodded. "Tell me the story that Stephanie told you, please."

Now that James had told the story once, it seemed to flow more easily for him. He told Mark everything that he'd told Fenella earlier.

"So in spite of telling her friends that she didn't keep any secrets from you, she never told you who was driving the car or what exactly happened to this Arthur Beck?" he checked when James was finished.

"No, she didn't," he agreed.

"That's unfortunate. If there's any truth to the story, I would think the driver of the car would have had the best motive for killing Stephanie," Mark said thoughtfully.

"Unless one of the others actually killed him some other way," Fenella said softly. "If he was able to talk to Stephanie about his family and his life, then it sounds as if he wasn't all that badly injured. I can't help but wonder how he died." She shivered as a few gruesome possibilities flashed through her mind.

"Yes, that may be the key to working out what happened to her," Mark agreed. "Assuming any of this is true, of course."

"I can't believe Arthur's wife didn't file a missing person report when he didn't come home," Fenella said.

"Unless he made her and his child up," James suggested. "If I woke up, badly injured and clearly being held a prisoner somewhere, I would probably tell my captors that I had a wife and a baby at home. Anything to make them feel sorry for me and let me go."

"I'll have to hope that Arthur Beck didn't have much of an imagination, then," Mark said. "Did Stephanie tell you anything else about her life on the island that you think could have led to her murder?" he asked James.

"Not really. She didn't talk much about her past really, except once in a while, when she'd had a few drinks. She had a lot more stories about her life in California than her life here, but they were all more ordinary stories, about drinking too much and sleeping with famous people. I can't believe anyone would have followed her here from California, anyway."

Mark stared at his phone for several minutes, swiping along what looked like a very long page of notes, and then nodded and stood up. "I'm going to leave a constable here to keep visitors out. Your sister can come and go as she pleases, but no one else."

James nodded. "I don't want to see anyone else anyway."

"The doctor has said that you'll be able to go home tomorrow unless your condition changes. Where will you be going?"

"He can stay in my apartment. Shelly can move home or to a hotel for a few days, until James is feeling better and is ready to go back to the borrowed house," Fenella said.

Mark nodded. "I think that would probably be for the best," he said.

"I can look after myself," James protested.

"Yeah, look what a good job you've done thus far," Fenella snapped.

James glared at her. "It's hardly my fault that someone is trying to kill me," he retorted.

"They wouldn't be trying to kill you if you'd told Mark everything yesterday," Fenella replied.

"Yesterday I still thought Stephanie had been making everything up," James said.

Mark held up his hand. "You can argue with one another after I've gone," he said. "I'll tell you one thing before I go, though. I expected James to come up with some story to suggest that he was being targeted by the killer. I even expected him to find a way to implicate the three women from the pub evening in his story. I didn't expect him to come up with anything quite this shocking, however."

"It's true," Fenella said softly.

Mark shrugged. "It just may be. I've just been sent a copy of Stephanie's will. She left everything she had to Andrew Beck, only son of Arthur Beck, formerly of Liverpool."

Fenella felt her jaw drop. "Arthur's son," she whispered.

"I really hope Arthur wasn't just making him up," James said.

"So do I," Mark told him. "I'm going to want to talk to you again. I'd really like to know where to look for that house, for one thing, but before that I have three women that I need to speak to rather urgently. First I will be looking for a missing person report, though."

He turned and left the room as Fenella sat back in her chair and looked at her brother. "She and her friends killed a man," she said in a low voice.

"It's starting to look that way," James said. "Of course, the other three will all deny it. I hope Inspector Hammersmith can find some evidence to support my story."

"He already has," Fenella reminded him."

"Yeah, but not enough," James sighed. "It's difficult, as I don't really believe the story myself. Teenaged girls don't just kill a man, hide the body, and then carry on with life as if nothing has happened, do they?"

"I certainly hope not. We should let Mark worry about that, though. You need to worry about getting better."

"I feel better now that I've talked to Mark. Although I hate to admit it, you were right, baby sister."

"Ha, remember that later, when you're staying in my apartment and we're making each other crazy."

James grinned. "I'll deny I ever said it."

"You will, too, won't you?"

"Pardon me, but Mr. Woods has had enough visitors for now," the frowning nurse in the doorway said. "He has a serious head injury. He needs rest and peace and quiet."

Fenella nodded and got to her feet. "I should get out of the way, then," she said. She gave James an awkward hug. "Do you want me to come back later today?" she asked.

The nurse shook her head. "Leave him to us for the rest of today. The doctor will be around shortly to check him over and then we'll have tests to run. Come back in the morning, around ten, and he may be ready to go home."

Fenella looked at James, who shrugged. "She's the boss," he said. "You'd better listen to her."

The nurse gave him a half-smile. "Remember that later," she told him.

Fenella followed the woman back to the nurses' station. "Is he going to be okay?" she asked.

"He seems to be recovering well," the woman replied. "Head injuries are always worrying, but I've seen quite a few in my day and he seems to be progressing nicely. If the doctor lets him go home tomorrow, I would suggest that he should be fine. You shouldn't worry overly much if the doctor keeps him for a while longer though, either. Sometimes, especially with our older patients, that's the safest option."

Fenella nodded and then headed for the elevators. The nurse hadn't actually told her anything, but she still felt better about her brother's condition. When she got outside, she suddenly realized that she didn't have her car. Mark had promised to get her home safely, but he was long gone. She sighed as she headed for the nearby taxi rank. Before she got there, she dug around in her handbag. She had exactly three pounds and eight pence on her. That wasn't going to pay for a taxi.

"Shelly? It's me. I've just left James and discovered that Mark has abandoned me, and I don't have enough money with me for a taxi anywhere."

Shelly laughed. "I'll be there in five minutes," she promised.

Fenella checked her wallet again while she waited. She always kept an emergency twenty-pound note tucked behind her credit card. It wasn't there. She must have used it and forgotten to replace it, she decided.

"Thank you so much," she told Shelly as she settled into the passenger seat of her friend's car.

"You're very welcome. I'm glad I could help. How is James?"

"He's recovering," she replied, "but wait until you hear what happened and why." She told Shelly the entire story. "You mustn't tell anyone any of this, though," she concluded. "Not until the investigation is complete."

"I'm too shocked to say anything to anyone," Shelly told her. "What did those girls do to that poor man?"

"I'm really hoping that Stephanie made the whole story up," Fenella told her. "Even though the story does move James way down the list of possible suspects."

Back at Fenella's apartment, Shelly helped her put together a quick lunch. "And now I'll move back into my own flat," she said as they loaded up the dishwasher. "It might even be nice for you to have James here."

"James is coming here?" Mona asked.

Fenella sighed. Once Shelly was gone, she was going to have to repeat the entire story to Mona, who'd only just appeared.

Smokey put up a token protest as Shelly picked her up to take her home. "Aww, she doesn't want to leave Katie," Shelly said.

"She's welcome to stay for as long as she likes," Fenella said.

Shelly grabbed her suitcase and headed for the door. Before she'd reached it, Smokey was standing in front of it.

"And now she's ready to leave Katie," Fenella laughed. She helped Shelly carry the cat's bowls next door and then pushed the door shut behind her friend. The apartment suddenly felt incredibly empty.

"What is going on?" Mona demanded. The words were only just out of her mouth when the phone rang.

"What is going on?" Daniel demanded.

Fenella sat down on the nearest couch and burst into tears.

"I didn't mean to make you cry," Daniel said quickly.

"It isn't your fault," Fenella told him, sniffling loudly. "It's all just been rather overwhelming."

"Yes, that's what Mark said, as well," he replied. "I'd appreciate it if you'd simply start at the beginning and tell me everything."

"Everything?" Fenella asked.

"If you don't mind."

She did mind, a great deal, really, but she was also eager to talk to Daniel. She had great faith in his abilities as an investigator and she'd sleep better knowing that he was helping Mark with the case.

"It all started when my brother decided to pay me a visit," she began.

Halfway through her recital, she stopped to get herself a cold drink. By the time she was done talking, she'd finished it and opened another. Mona sat and listened to the whole conversation with her eyes closed. As Fenella concluded telling Daniel everything that James had told Mark about Arthur Beck, Mona sat up.

"How exactly do you keep getting yourself mixed up in these things?" Daniel asked when Fenella was done.

"It isn't my fault," Fenella replied, feeling as if she might cry again.

"Yes, I know that it isn't your fault, but you do seem to find yourself in the middle of the strangest of things," he replied. "Mark rang me when Stephanie died, when he still thought it was just an accident, so I didn't ring you. I thought you'd probably appreciate not having to repeat the same story all over again. When he rang me this afternoon, though, I knew I'd have to ring you. Are you okay?"

"Me? I'm fine," Fenella said automatically.

"Yes, I'm sure you are, but how are you really?"

Fenella took a deep breath and tried to think. "I'm worried about James, badly shaken by the story that Stephanie told him, and terrified that it might actually be true."

"That's what I thought."

"But how are you?" she asked. "How is the course going?"

"I'm doing okay, better than you are, anyway. The course continues to be challenging, but interesting. I've learned a great deal. I don't think any of it will be helpful to your current circumstances, but you never know."

"I really hope this is the last murder I'm ever involved in," Fenella said, "and it wouldn't be a bad thing if there weren't any more murders on the island for the rest of your career, either."

"It would be a terrible waste of all of my new training, but I wouldn't complain," Daniel told her. "How are all of our mutual friends? Shelly? Peter?"

"Shelly is doing well. She was staying with me for a few days, but she's gone home now. James is going to be staying here once he gets out of the hospital."

"Are you okay with that?"

"I don't have much choice, but anyway, I want him here. I'd worry about him too much if he were back at the house."

"How did you find the house he was staying in, by the way?"

"Oh, it's one that Mona used to own," Fenella replied, flushing. "She had a lot of properties all over the island, it seems."

"So now you have a lot of properties all over the island?"

"Yeah, something like that,"

"I see. Which reminds me. How is Donald?"

"He's in New York. His daughter was in a car accident. Apparently she's recovering, but slowly."

"I didn't realize. I've missed quite a lot while I've been away, haven't I?"

"I suppose so. It will be nice to have you home."

Mona made a face at her as the words escaped Fenella's lips. Fenella frowned at herself. Mark had said that Daniel was involved with someone. She shouldn't have been saying such things.

"Well, I'll be back on the island in a few days. I'm bringing some of my new friends back with me, though. I'm not going to be back at work for another week or more. Mark has everything in hand. I'm sure of that."

"That's good to know," Fenella replied.

"You probably should know that he found a missing person report for an Arthur Beck," he added. "It was filed in Liverpool. If a copy was sent to the island, it's probably been lost for years."

"So he really did disappear?"

"He did, but his wife thought he was still in the Liverpool area. Mark said that the report read as if the pair had been having problems. The wife didn't seem too worried about the man, really. His parents seem to have been the driving force behind having him officially listed as missing."

"And he was never found?"

"The case is still open in Liverpool, but that doesn't mean he wasn't found. Sometimes people turn up years later and no one thinks to notify the police that they've returned or been found or whatever. Mark is checking that next."

"Did Arthur and his wife have a son?" Fenella had to ask.

"They did. A little boy called Andrew. Mark is trying to track him down, as well."

Fenella sighed. "I was really hoping that the whole story was made up."

"It may not all be true," Daniel said. "But it seems as if some parts of it are, anyway."

"I suppose it's too much to hope for that Stephanie made up the rest of the story," Fenella said.

"Daniel? Are you finished yet?" a female voice called from somewhere.

Fenella frowned. "It sounds as if you need to go," she said quickly.

"I'm meeting some of the other students for a drink," he told her. "I should probably go."

Fenella put the phone down and looked at Mona. "It's been a terrible day and it's only three o'clock. It's too early to start drinking, isn't it?"

"Yes, it is, rather," Mona said. "So let's talk about the suspects."

11

Fenella sighed. "You aren't going to be happy until we do, are you?"

"I'm always happy, darling. But I do think that your friend Inspector Hammersmith is going to need a little bit of help with this case. Whoever killed Stephanie must have been very clever about it."

"Clever or lucky," Fenella suggested. "Anyway, we don't have any idea who the suspects are, aside from the three women who were at the pub. Maybe Stephanie left the pub with someone else or something."

"We mustn't waste our time worrying about remote possibilities. Let's talk about Stephanie's friends. Together, they murdered a man. Maybe they worked together to kill Stephanie as well."

"If they did, they'll be able to tell Mark whatever they like about what happened after James and I left the pub."

"True, so we must work out what really did happen."

"How can we do that?"

"You must go and talk to the three women, of course."

"First of all, I'm not going to stick my nose into a police investigation. Secondly, I don't even know where to find the women."

"What do they do for work?"

Fenella shrugged. "They may have said, but I wasn't paying attention."

"James must have a memorial service for Stephanie. That would give you a chance to talk to them, and it would be a nice thing to do, as well."

"I'm not sure Mark would agree with that."

"Surely you don't need the man's permission? Schedule it for Saturday and put a notice in the local paper about it. No doubt dozens of nosy people will turn up simply because Stephanie was murdered, but I'm sure her friends will attend as well. They'll be afraid not to, in case it makes them look guilty."

"They could just say they never saw the notice, if anyone asks," Fenella pointed out. "I don't know. I'll think about it."

"Tell me again about Annie Lawrence," Mona said. "She was single and bitter, wasn't she?"

"I suppose you could say that. She had been in an abusive relationship that ended badly and hasn't dated since. I remember now, she works at the hospital, in the records department."

"You should have looked her up when you were there visiting James."

"Sure, because I'm sure she would have had plenty of time for a chat."

"You could have arranged to meet on her break."

"I could have, but I didn't. Anyway, I don't think she killed Stephanie. By the time I left the pub, she was nearly too drunk to move."

"Maybe she was exaggerating her level of drunkenness as a cover."

"Maybe. I wish we knew more about what actually happened. Mark said Stephanie was hit by a car. I'm not sure why they think it was murder. I do know that Annie wasn't in any fit state to drive when I left the pub."

"If they stayed for two or three more hours, she would have had time to recover, at least somewhat. And maybe she was counting on using her drunkenness as an excuse if she got caught driving away from the accident."

GUESTS AND GUILT

"The killer used a stolen car," Fenella reminded Mona. "He or she had to be sober enough to work out how to steal it in the first place."

"The keys may have been in it. People on the island can be incredibly casual about such things sometimes."

"Really? I was hoping that the stolen car was significant. I couldn't steal a car. I wouldn't even know where to start. I can't really imagine any of Stephanie's friends being capable of doing so, either."

"You may be right, but for the sake of argument, let's just assume the keys were in the vehicle, shall we? That suggests that everyone on the island had access to the means to kill Stephanie."

"And we have what seems like a fairly strong motive for Stephanie's three friends," Fenella said.

"Unfortunately, we don't know anything about opportunity for them. When you left, they were planning to get a taxi together to get home, right?"

"Yes, Courtney offered to pay for a taxi and for someone to drive Annie's car home, as well."

"And they were going to bring Stephanie home as well?"

"Courtney told her that she could share their taxi. She was going to have Stephanie dropped off first."

"So we need to find out what happened after you left that led to Stephanie being out on the street on foot," Mona mused. "Maybe the killer deliberately started a fight with her to get her to leave."

"And then what? Rushed after her, stole a car, and then ran her down before returning to the pub to get a ride home with the others?"

"We simply don't know enough. Did the others all leave together, or did something else happen? This was easier when Daniel was here. He could be persuaded to share information. Inspector Hammersmith isn't as forthcoming."

"I doubt Daniel will be, now that he has a girlfriend," Fenella sighed, "but I really don't want to talk about that right now."

"Let's talk about Maureen and Courtney, then. If you had to pick one of them as the killer, which one would it be?"

"Probably Courtney," Fenella said after a moment. "Mostly because she was the most sober of the group, though, not for any other reason."

"Maureen sounded dull, wanting babies and getting engaged all the time, but never married. I can't see why she'd want to kill Stephanie. Doing so won't have made her boring life any better."

"We have to assume that the killer wanted to make sure that Stephanie didn't tell anyone about Arthur Beck," Fenella said. "Surely none of the women want that story to come out."

"Including Stephanie, I would argue. She didn't tell James the whole story, only bits and pieces of it. I can't imagine that she was planning on repeating it to anyone else, can you?"

"I don't know. I'm not sure why she told James, but I can see all three women feeling threatened when they found out that she'd done so."

"Maybe they did all work together to kill Stephanie, then."

"From what I could see at the pub, they didn't seem to be getting along very well, though. I'm not sure they could have worked together, especially after the amount of drinking that they were doing."

"All except for Courtney?"

"She was drinking, just not as heavily as the others."

"If I were Inspector Hammersmith, I'd be taking a really good look at Annie," Mona said.

"Annie? Why?"

"She sounded very bitter about the way her life has turned out. Some of the things you said made me think that she might even blame Stephanie for her unhappiness. You did say that they were very close as children. I'm sure she must have felt abandoned when Stephanie left."

"She did say something along those lines."

"So maybe Stephanie's murder has nothing to do with Arthur Beck. Maybe Annie was just angry at her for leaving the island. When she saw her again, she was so upset that she killed her."

"Maybe," Fenella sighed. "There's just too much we don't know."

"So find out," Mona told her. "Have a memorial service or go and visit Annie when you next visit James. You could try tracking down Courtney, as well. Didn't you say she works for one of the banks? There aren't that many of them, really."

"I'm not going to start calling random banks, asking for her. I don't even know her married name."

"That shouldn't be too difficult to find out. She married a wealthy man about a year ago. I'm sure there are plenty of women on the island who'll be happy to gossip about her. I could name half a dozen who probably know the whole story."

"I can hardly call up any of your old friends and start asking, though, can I? They don't even know who I am."

"Oh, they know. Make no mistake about that. You'll be one of the island's favorite topics for gossip, or skeet, as they call it here."

"Why would anyone want to gossip about me?"

"Your nights out with Donald, for one thing, and then there's your tendency to get tangled up in murder investigations. Beyond that, you are my niece, after all."

Fenella sighed. "Now I'm getting depressed. I think I need to go for a long walk or something."

"While you do that, I'm going to see if I can track down Arthur Beck. If he was murdered on the island, he may well be haunting it somewhere. It might be interesting to have a word with him."

"Can you really..." Fenella began. She trailed off as Mona disappeared.

The bedding in the spare bedroom needed to be changed, and the room needed to be prepared for James. She had laundry that needed washing, dishes in the dishwasher, and a million other household chores that didn't appeal in the slightest.

"I'm going for a walk," she told Katie. The kitten didn't look impressed.

Fenella marched from one end of the promenade to the other, breathing deeply and trying to clear her head. Mona was right. They didn't have nearly enough information to even begin to try to work out what had happened to Stephanie. Maybe the police should be focusing on what had happened to James, instead. The only person who had any sort of motive for killing James had to be Stephanie's killer. Wondering what alibis Stephanie's three friends might have for the night of the attack on James, Fenella made her way home. The light was flashing on her answering machine when she got there.

"Ah, Ms. Woods? Fenella? I hope I have the right number. This is Annie Lawrence. The girls and I were talking and we were wondering if your brother was planning to have any sort of memorial service for Stephanie? We'd really like a chance to pay our last respects, as it were, and if he isn't planning anything, we'd like to do something ourselves. Can you ring me back?"

The message concluded with the woman's telephone number. Fenella quickly wrote it down and then frowned at it. "I don't know what James wants to do," she said, "and I don't know where the police investigation is at, either. You might not feel like honoring your friend's memory so much once you find out that James has told the police about Arthur Beck."

Katie had been staring at her all while she'd been talking. Now she shrugged and left the room. Fenella watched her go and then chuckled.

"I'm not losing my mind," she called after the animal. Katie didn't bother to reply. Fenella paced around the apartment for several minutes, trying to decide whether to call Annie back or not. When she finally did pick up the phone, she called James's mobile phone instead.

"What?" he said when he answered the call.

"That's not a very nice way to answer," Fenella told him.

"I didn't know it was you," he replied. "I've had three wrong numbers in the past hour and I'm afraid the nurses are going to take my phone away if it keeps ringing. I'm probably not allowed to have it."

"Three wrong numbers in an hour? That is odd."

"It's someone calling from somewhere overseas. I suspect they've written the number down wrong or something, but I can't seem to make them understand that. They don't seem to speak any English."

"Oh, dear."

"It's a good thing I paid extra for international calling before we left the US," James said. "Otherwise the calls would be costing me a fortune. But what can I do for you? Are you coming back to visit again? If so, bring food and something for me to do. I'm bored to tears in here."

"You're meant to be resting," Fenella reminded him.

"I've been resting. Now I'm bored. I don't suppose you can break me out of here tonight?"

"I thought you weren't getting released until tomorrow?"

"That's why I said break me out. I'm fine. I don't need constant monitoring and I don't need to be here. You said I could stay at your apartment, so I won't be going back to an empty house. They need to let me go."

"You need to wait until the doctor is sure you're okay. I'll come and get you in the morning. You'll just have to rest and watch television for tonight."

"I've been watching television. I've no idea what's happening on any of the programs, though. And I can't understand half of them, either. There are a lot more regional accents than I remember and some of them are unintelligible."

"I know what you mean, but it's only a few more hours. I'll be there in the morning."

"If you aren't going to rescue me, why did you call?"

"Annie called me. She and the other women were talking about having some sort of memorial service for Stephanie. She was wondering if you were going to have one or if they should start planning something."

"I was going to have something, but not here. I was going to do something when I got home. Stephanie made a few friends in the small village near my house. They'll all want to pay their respects, I assume."

"So should I tell Annie that she and the others should plan something on their own?"

"That might be for the best. They'll know who else on the island to invite, won't they? I'd like to attend, of course, but that might be awkward, as I'm the one who told the police about Arthur Beck."

"She didn't say anything about that, so I don't plan to mention it, either," Fenella replied. "I'll let her know your thoughts and see what she says. I think we should both attend the service, but I suppose that will be up to Annie and the others."

"Call me back if there are any issues," James said, "or just to chat. I can't begin to tell you how bored I am."

"Ask the nurse for some paper and a pen and write a book," Fenella suggested, "or at least start a rough outline for one."

"Very funny. You know I can't do that without the right inspiration. I had such high hopes for my collaboration with Stephanie. Now I'm right back where I started from, unless she left really good notes for me."

"Try not to worry about any of that for now. Focus on your recovery. I'll let you know what Annie says when I see you tomorrow."

"Yeah, okay," James said with a sigh.

Fenella put the phone down. She was worried about calling Annie back. After pacing for a while longer, she looked at Katie. "I have to call her," she told the cat.

"Meerreewww," Katie replied.

"Yes, I'll get your dinner as soon as I'm done on the phone," Fenella promised.

Katie nodded and then curled up in a ball and watched her owner. Feeling as if this might be easier without an audience, Fenella picked up the phone.

"This is Annie Lawrence. I'm probably at work, as that's the only place I go. If you leave a message and you aren't trying to sell me anything, I'll ring you back when I get home."

"Hi, Annie, it's Fenella Woods. I spoke to James, and he's going to have a memorial service for Stephanie back in the US. He would like to attend anything that you and the others have here, though, if that's okay. Thanks."

She put the phone down and shook her head. She should have just asked the woman to call her back, but she really didn't want to talk to her. As she mentally replayed what she'd said, though, she sighed. It sounded incredibly stupid to her now. "I should have practiced before I called," she told Katie as she filled up her food bowl. "That would have been the smart thing to do."

Katie didn't bother to reply. After Fenella was done fixing Katie's dinner, she decided to have some of her own. She had a short debate with herself on the relative merits of frozen dinners over fresh before she threw something into the microwave and ate it at the kitchen counter. When the phone rang, she hesitated before she answered it.

"Good evening, my darling," Donald Donaldson's voice came down the receiver. "How are you?"

Fenella felt relieved as she dropped into a chair. While she didn't really feel like talking to Donald, that was better than talking to Annie. "I'm fine," she replied.

"Are you? What's been happening on the island since I've been away, then? Didn't you say something about your brother coming for a visit? I'm disappointed I won't have a chance to meet him."

"He's here, although he's at Noble's at the moment."

"Noble's? What's wrong?"

Fenella took a deep breath and then told Donald a very abbreviated version of the things that had happened since James had arrived. She glossed over Stephanie's death, calling it a tragic accident, and told him only that James has taken a bad fall.

"My goodness, I am sorry I'm not there to help you through all of this," Donald said. "Is there anything I can do from here?"

"I don't think so," Fenella replied. "Unless you can tell me anything more about Stephanie's friends?"

"Stephanie's friends? Don't tell me her death was in any way suspicious?"

"I'm just trying to find out more about them. They might be having a memorial service for Stephanie."

"What were the names again?"

Fenella told him.

"The only one I know is Courtney Bridges, although she's Courtney Fleming now. I know her husband, Sam, quite well."

"Tell me about him."

"What would you like to know?"

"I don't know. Is he nice? Are he and Courtney madly in love? What are his children like?"

"Are you sure this isn't a murder investigation?"

"It might be. That's Mark's problem. I'm just nosy."

Donald laughed. "That's okay, then. Sam is very nice, if a little bit naïve. He is probably madly in love with Courtney, but I'm not sure I would say the same of her. His children are smart and deeply resentful of Courtney and the part she played in breaking up their parents' marriage."

"Oh, dear."

"Don't misunderstand, Sam and his wife were already having problems before Courtney came on the scene, but I'm sure Courtney helped hasten the inevitable, if you see what I mean."

"Someone said that he was a customer at the bank where she works."

"He was, and probably still is. They'd have known each other, slightly, for years before they ever got involved. If I'm remembering everything correctly, Courtney was promoted into the business banking department and put in charge of a number of important accounts a few years back. That's when she and Sam would have started spending more time together."

"What do you think of her?"

"I think she's very clever and incredibly opportunistic. Before she got involved with Sam, it was said that she was involved with one of the bank's senior vice presidents. If that was true, the man in question was never going to leave his wife for her. Sam was a better option."

"I didn't really like her when I met her. Now I like her even less."

"I find her charming, actually, but completely unable to be spontaneous. That probably serves her well in her career, but I wonder if she enjoys life very much."

"I'm not sure what you mean."

"She's a meticulous planner. I'm sure when she set her sights on Sam she planned exactly how their relationship was going to go, from first kiss to wedding night and beyond. I've never seen her really let her hair down, ever, and I've seen her at a number of parties were alcohol was flowing everywhere."

"She didn't seem to drink very much at the pub."

"I don't think she ever drinks very much," Donald replied. "She hates the idea of not being in control."

"But how are things there?" Fenella changed the subject. She would think about Courtney later.

"Things are slowly improving, and I'm cautiously optimistic," he told her. "I'm actually starting to believe that my Phoebe is going to recover eventually."

"That is good news."

GUESTS AND GUILT

"It's going to be a long process, though. I'm working with her doctors on a plan now. I'm hoping that I'll be able to bring her back to the island once she's stable enough to travel, but that will only work if I can find the right people to help with her rehabilitation once she gets there."

"If there's anything you can think of that I can do to help, just ask."

"That's kind of you. I wish there were, actually, but at the moment I'm mostly just waiting for other people. The good thing is that I have plenty of money to throw at the problem. Unfortunately, no amount of money is going to help if the right sort of specialist treatment simply isn't available on the island. I'm still working out whether or not that's the case, however."

"All I can do is wish you luck, then," Fenella said.

"If you really want to help, you could always come to New York and keep me company here," Donald suggested. "I'm probably going to be here for another month or more."

"Right now, I have James visiting," Fenella reminded him. "He's here for three weeks, but maybe after he's gone, I could think about it. I haven't been to New York City in years."

"We could take in a few Broadway shows, have expensive dinners at all the best places, and you could meet Phoebe."

"You make it all sound very tempting, but I still have to get through another two and a half weeks with my brother before I can even think about it."

"Maybe you could give it a little bit of thought while James is still there. I do miss you rather desperately."

Fenella frowned. "I'm not sure..." she began.

"No, no, don't say it," Donald interrupted. "I know. I'm pushing you again and I promised you that I wouldn't do that anymore. The problem is, I'd only just realized how much I was starting to care about you when I had to come to New York. That isn't your fault, though. You enjoy your brother's visit and don't give me another thought. Just know that I'll be thinking of you."

"I'll be thinking of you, too," Fenella replied, "and of Phoebe."

"Thank you," he said.

Fenella set the phone back down and wiped a stray tear from her eye. Her feelings for Donald were far too complicated to even think about in the middle of a murder investigation, she told herself. When the phone rang again, she answered it without thinking.

"Ah, Ms. Woods? It's Annie, Annie Lawrence. Thank you for ringing me back. I wasn't sure I had the right number, but you were the only F. Woods in the phone book."

"Annie, how are you?" Fenella asked.

"If I'm honest, I'm really shaken up about Stephanie," the other woman replied. "I mean, she was the closest thing I ever had to a sister and I'd missed her terribly while she'd been away. I was so happy to see her again, and I was really looking forward to spending lots of time with her while she was here."

"I'm sorry for your loss."

"Ah, thanks. The worst part is, it was all my fault, you know."

"It was?"

"You didn't know? I thought the police would have told you the whole story. If not them, then someone, anyway. I thought you and James were avoiding me because you blamed me."

"We aren't avoiding you. We simply didn't have a number where we could reach you."

"I never thought of that," Annie said. "So you aren't blaming me for Stephanie's death?"

"Maybe you should tell me what happened," Fenella suggested. "I don't know anything about it."

"I'll tell you, but only because you need to know before you make any decision about the memorial service. It really was all my fault."

"I'm sure that isn't true," Fenella lied.

"We had a fight, you see," Annie said. "Not long after you left, actually. I was drunk and I got too emotional about, well, about everything. I said horrible things to Stephanie about her leaving. I was sorry immediately, but too stubborn to admit to it."

"I can understand why you were upset," Fenella said.

"I know I shouldn't drink. I was never good at it, and I stopped for a few years, but I keep going back to it. Anyway, we argued. We were both crying. Stephanie finally stormed out. Maureen went after her, but she couldn't catch her. Stephanie never should have been walking home alone after dark. She must have looked the wrong way when she was crossing the road. It was my fault she was even out there."

"It was still just an accident,' Fenella said soothingly. She could tell that Annie was crying.

"I know. That's what the police told me, but I can't help but feel that it was my fault. I shouldn't have shouted at her. I should have gone after her. I don't know."

"It was a difficult evening. Emotions were running high while I was there, for sure. You hadn't seen Stephanie in over twenty years. When you add alcohol, it's hardly surprising that things blew up."

"Courtney was always the one who kept us under control," Annie told her. "She never gets emotional about anything, really, but after you and James left, she started drinking a lot, too. By the time Stephanie and I started arguing, she wasn't in any fit state to calm us down."

"As I said, it was a terrible accident, but that's all it was. You mustn't blame yourself or anyone else."

"Thank you for seeing it that way. As I said, I thought you and James probably blamed me for what happened."

"We didn't and we don't, and you mustn't blame yourself, either."

"I can't promise I won't do that. We did try to find her, though. When Maureen came back and said that she'd disappeared, we went after her. We walked around for a short while, looking for her, and then we got a taxi and drove around looking for her for ages. We didn't have the address for the house where James was staying, or we would have gone there to make sure she was okay."

"I'm sure you did everything you could."

"We did our best."

"And now you want to have a memorial service for her."

"Yes, we do. We were talking about it last night. We met here to talk about Stephanie and, well, celebrate her life, I suppose. Someone suggested that we should do something to honor her memory. There are other people on the island who knew her. They'll want to pay their respects, I'm sure."

"James and I would very much like to attend the service when you have it."

"Oh, yes, of course. We were talking about trying to arrange something for this Saturday, if that isn't too soon. I know James is in Noble's, but I don't know why. Is he okay?"

"He's going to be fine. He went out for a walk and tripped over a curb, that's all. He banged his head pretty badly, which is why they're keeping him at Noble's for the moment."

"Oh, dear. I should pop up to see him during my break tomorrow. He'd probably like to see a friendly face."

"They're talking about releasing him tomorrow morning, so I wouldn't bother," Fenella told her.

"That is good news. I'll ring you back when we've set a time and a place for the service, then. I don't suppose you know if Stephanie was particularly religious?"

"I don't know for sure, but I doubt it."

"Yeah, me, too. Maybe we'll just do something at one of the community centers rather than at a church, then."

"That may be for the best."

"I'll let you know what we decide. Thank you for being so understanding about everything. I was terrified to talk to you, you know."

"You shouldn't have been. It was an accident," Fenella said, wondering if it was possible that she was right. Maybe Mark had changed his mind and written the whole thing off as an accident after all.

"Talk to you soon, then," Annie said before the call disconnected.

Fenella put the phone down and looked at Katie. "That's quite enough phone calls for today," she said.

The phone rang as soon as the words were out of her mouth.

"It's Shelly. I was wondering if you'd like to go to the pub."

Fenella laughed. "Finally a phone call that I'm happy I answered," she said. "I'll be ready in ten minutes."

She gave Katie a few treats and refilled her water bowl before changing into a pretty flowery shirt. After combing her hair, she touched up her makeup and splashed on some perfume. A trip to the pub was exactly what she needed after what had been a very long day.

She grabbed her handbag and checked that she had everything she needed.

"I won't be long," she told Katie as she headed for the door.

"Merrew," Katie replied.

Fenella let herself out and locked the door behind her. A moment later, she tapped on Shelly's door.

12

"I suppose it makes sense that the police haven't mentioned that they're investigating the story that James told them," Shelly said after Fenella had brought her up to date on everything that had happened since she'd last seen her. "They're probably keeping it quiet until they know for certain whether it's true or not."

"I understand that, but I'd be less worried about James if the three women knew that he'd told them Stephanie's secret," Fenella replied.

"I can see that. Maybe you should tell them yourself."

"I don't think that's a very good idea."

"I don't mean confront them about Arthur Beck, I mean say something about how James spent hours with the police, telling them every single thing that Stephanie ever said to him, or something like that."

Fenella took a sip of wine and leaned her head against the nearest bookshelf. "That might be a good idea, but I'd really rather avoid talking to them at all. I really hope that Stephanie's death was just an accident and that the police find Arthur Beck happily living out his golden years in Liverpool or somewhere."

"What's really bothering you?" Shelly asked.

"Daniel seems to think that I'm doing this on purpose or something," Fenella complained, "and he's found someone else, as well."

"He has? I know Mark said something about him going to Scotland for a visit, but that doesn't mean it has to be romantic, does it?"

"There was a woman with him when he called me. I heard her urging him to get off the phone. That's the second time that's happened, and I'm pretty sure it was the same woman both times."

"Maybe they're just friends. They're on a course together, after all. Didn't you ever become friendly with someone at a conference or anything like that?"

"Not really. I usually went to conferences with Jack, though."

"Why don't you wait until Daniel is back before you start worrying about what he's doing in Milton Keynes? I'm sure he'll tell you everything. He isn't the sort to lie about it."

"And I've been seeing Donald while he's been away, so I can't complain if he has found another woman. It just seems as if he's a lot less patient with me now when it comes to this murder investigation."

"If it is a murder investigation," Shelly said.

"Mark and Daniel both seem to be treating it like one," Fenella sighed. "I don't suppose you'd like to come to the memorial service with me on Saturday? Obviously, I'll be taking James as well."

"I'm not sure that I want to come, but I will come if you need the moral support."

"That's very kind of you, but I should be okay. I just thought you might be interested in meeting the three suspects, that's all."

Shelly frowned. "Now that you mention it, I am. What time is the service? I'm meant to be having lunch with Gordon on Saturday."

"I don't know yet. Annie is supposed to call me back to let me know. I'm planning on letting the machine answer all of my calls for the next week."

"And James is being released tomorrow?"

"Hopefully in the morning. He'll have to stay with me for a short while. The doctor said he shouldn't be alone."

"If he starts making you crazy, you can always come and visit me."

"He's been surprisingly easy to get along with thus far," Fenella told her. "He hasn't said much about his money troubles or hinted that I should give him some of my inheritance. We've actually been getting along surprisingly well. That may all change when he sees Mona's apartment, of course."

"Maybe the shock of being mixed up in a murder investigation will keep him from pestering you about money."

"I'd rather he were pestering me."

Shelly laughed. "I know what you mean, but surely it won't take Mark long to work out what happened, with only three suspects."

"There could be others that we know nothing about."

"Who else even knew the woman was on the island?"

"I have no idea. James was taking a nap when Stephanie called Annie to set up the meeting at the pub. We've no idea who else she might have spoken to at that time, or what other arrangements she might have made."

"So she could have arranged to meet someone later in the evening and that someone might have killed her," Shelly said.

"Exactly. Although that brings up the question of motive."

"We do have a pretty compelling motive for the three women, at least."

"If the story about Arthur Beck is true."

"Well, yes, there is that," Shelly sighed. "Let's keep things simple, then. Which of the three women do you think killed Stephanie?"

"My first inclination is to say Annie. She's incredibly bitter about Stephanie leaving, not that I blame her, but that could have given her a motive beyond Arthur Beck. She also admitted to having fought with Stephanie after I left. Maybe she got home and started feeling even more upset. She could have driven back to the pub and found Stephanie still wandering around lost."

"And then stolen a car and run her down," Shelly finished the story as Fenella swallowed the last of her wine.

"The stolen car feels like a complication," Fenella admitted. "I could almost see Annie running Stephanie over in a fit of anger, fuelled by far too much alcohol, but stealing a car requires some level of planning or premeditation, and I'm not sure I can see Annie managing that."

"Are you ruling Annie out?"

"I'm moving her down the list and thinking about Courtney. She absolutely seemed capable of planning to murder someone. And she was the least drunk of the trio when I was at the pub. Annie said she started drinking heavily after I left, though."

"Can you see her knowing how to steal a car?"

"Someone suggested the keys might have been left inside. It doesn't take any specialist knowledge to steal a car if the keys are inside it."

"Does that mean Courtney is your number-one suspect?"

"Maybe. If the Arthur Beck story is true, she has a motive, but beyond that I can't see any reason for her to kill Stephanie."

"We need to find out if the story is true or not," Shelly sighed.

"Daniel said that they'd found a missing person report on the man, which suggests it might be, but just because a man went missing doesn't mean he was killed by four teenaged girls twenty-something years ago."

"I can't believe that they've all kept the secret for this long. I'm surprised none of them told a partner or their mothers or someone."

"Maybe one of them did tell someone else, but that other person is also keeping things quiet," Fenella replied.

"We haven't talked about Maureen. What about her as a suspect?"

"I feel as if I didn't really get to know her, not as much as the other two, which makes me suspicious of her, probably unfairly."

"You said she's been engaged six times?"

"It was something like that. She was, I don't know, slightly flighty, or maybe she had something on her mind. She didn't talk that much, really."

"Maybe because she was busy plotting how to kill Stephanie."

"I suppose that's one possibility."

"She is the one who went after her, right? Maybe she caught up with her and told her to meet her later somewhere. Then she went back and told the others that Stephanie was gone. Once she got home, she only had to get in her car and drive back to wherever she'd told Stephanie to meet her."

"But where was Stephanie for the hour when the three women were looking for her?"

"I don't know. Maybe she just hid in the loo."

Fenella nodded slowly. "No one has said that they checked the bathroom, but I assume they must have. She could have hidden in a stall, I suppose."

"Maybe you should ask Annie for more details."

"Or maybe I should just let the police do their job," Fenella retorted. "If it was all perfectly straightforward, Mark would have arrested someone by now."

"From where was the car stolen? Do you know that?"

"Mark said it had been taken off someone's driveway. I got the feeling that it was somewhere in the area near the pub, but I don't know that for sure."

"It was too much to hope that it had been stolen from Courtney's next-door neighbor, I suppose."

Fenella nodded. "As I said, if it were that easy, Mark would have arrested someone by now."

They finished their drinks and then made their way back to their apartment building.

"Are you going to be okay on your own tonight?" Shelly asked as they rode the elevator to the top floor. "I could stay tonight, if you need company."

"I'm fine. It will be nice having my apartment all to myself for tonight, what with James moving in tomorrow."

They hugged in the corridor and then went to their respective apartments. Once in bed, Fenella tossed and turned for a few minutes before falling into a restless sleep.

"I'm sorry, but you've reached your limit," Mark Hammersmith said. "We have no choice."

"But none of it was my fault," Fenella told him.

"That may be the case, but we can't afford to take any chances. If we lock you up, we expect the murder rate on the island to plummet," Mark replied.

"But I didn't kill anyone. I would never kill anyone. Ask Daniel. He's the one who involved me in those cold cases. He'll tell you."

"Daniel has moved to Scotland now. He's going to be getting married in a few days and settling on some remote Scottish island. I'm afraid he can't help you anymore."

"You can't arrest me for being in the wrong place at the wrong time."

"We let you off the first few times, but it's becoming too much of a habit with you. We're prepared to let you keep your kitten in your cell with you, though. That seems a reasonable concession."

"Reasonable concession? You can't just throw someone into prison like this. What about my trial? What about my lawyer? I want to talk to Doncan Quayle right now."

"You'll be allowed to ring your advocate next month. In the meantime, I suggest you settle in and make yourself at home."

Mark slid the thick metal door into place and then turned and walked away from the small cell. Fenella sank down onto the rock-hard bed and grabbed Katie. "This isn't fair," she said, tears streaming down her face.

"Meerrooww," Katie said softly. "Meeroooooowwwww."

As the kitten got louder, Fenella could only stare at her.

"MMMEEERRROOW!" Katie shouted.

Fenella blinked several times and then woke up with a start. Katie was standing on her chest, glaring at her. Fenella found that she was holding the small animal tightly.

"Oh, my goodness. I am sorry," she told Katie. "I was having the most horrible nightmare. Thank goodness we aren't in prison."

Katie shook her head and then jumped off the bed and sauntered away without a backward glance. Fenella checked the clock. It wasn't quite six, which meant she probably could get another hour of sleep in before Katie would start demanding her breakfast.

She rolled over and plumped up her pillow. Squeezing her eyes tightly shut, she told herself to go to sleep, but her brain refused to cooperate. The dream kept replaying itself over and over again in her head.

"Daniel is not getting married and moving to Scotland," she said loudly, "and even if he is, it's not any of my business."

After fifteen minutes of tossing and turning, she gave up and got out of bed. After a long shower, she took her time putting her makeup on and fixing her hair. By the time she was ready for the day, Katie was ready for breakfast.

"What do I do now?" she asked the animal as she filled her bowls. "It's far too early to head to Noble's."

The sun was doing its best to break through some high clouds, so Fenella pulled on a jacket and headed out for a walk. She'd only just crossed the road to the promenade when she heard loud barking from behind her.

"Good morning," Harvey Garus called as he and his dogs joined Fenella. "How are you this morning?"

"Much better now," she replied, showering first Winston and then Fiona with affection. She'd looked after both dogs some months ago under unusual circumstances. While she didn't exactly miss having them around all the time, she greatly enjoyed getting to see them again whenever possible.

"They're happy to see you," Harvey said.

"I'm happy to see them, too."

"Happy enough to want to take them off my hands for a few days?" Harvey asked.

Fenella stopped herself before she said yes immediately. "Are you going away?" she asked.

"I'm meant to be going to a music festival. I'm sure someone told you that I used to manage bands back in the seventies and eighties. One of the festivals in the US wants to give me some sort of award. I think it's just for being the last one still alive or some such thing, but they're really pushing me to come over and accept it in person."

"Congratulations. You should definitely go," Fenella told him.

"Yes, I suppose I should. It isn't as if I'm likely to get any other awards, not in this lifetime, anyway. But I can't take the dogs with me, you see. And I've never left Winston with anyone, not ever, not until, well, until I didn't have a choice. I know Mr. Stone would keep them both, but I don't think they'd enjoy that."

"No, they won't want to be stuck in the vet's office while you're away," Fenalla agreed. "When would you be going?"

"Next month. I don't remember the exact dates, but I can ring you and let you know if you think you might be able to help."

"Definitely ring me," Fenella said. "I have my brother staying with me now, but once he's gone, I could probably accommodate these two monsters."

Harvey laughed. "They aren't so bad, as long as you keep them well away from the sea."

"I think we both live in the wrong place for that," Fenella laughed. "But have you just come out for your walk now? I can take one of them for you, if you'd like."

"Maybe you could take Winston for a run," Harvey suggested. "I can't run with him when I have Fiona, so he doesn't get nearly as much running in as he used to before Fiona came into our lives."

Fenella took the big dog's leash and began to walk at a rapid pace. Winston walked for a few minutes and then gave Fenella a mischievous grin. As he picked up his pace, Fenella increased her own speed. When she finally got back to where Harvey and Fiona were resting on a bench, Fenella was dripping with sweat and breathing hard.

"I should take him out more often," she said when she'd caught her breath. "I'm more out of shape than I realized."

Harvey chuckled. "You can take him every day, if you'd like. I know Winston would love it."

Fenella petted Winston and Fiona for several more minutes before she glanced at her watch. "I need to go," she told Harvey. "Let me know about next month."

"I will do," he promised.

Fenella took another quick shower and gave Katie her lunch before she left for Noble's. "Now don't eat this until later," she told her pet. "I'm just not sure how long I'll be, and I don't want you to starve."

Katie shrugged and took a few bites before wandering into the living room and settling in on one of the couches. "You're going to eat it all before I get to the elevator, aren't you?" Fenella asked her.

Katie didn't even bother to reply. Fenella was temped to walk to the elevator and then sneak back and try to catch Katie gobbling up her lunch early, but she really didn't have time for games. James would get grumpy if he had to wait for her.

"Maybe we could have dinner together one night while I'm here." Fenella heard James's voice as she pushed the door to his room open.

"I'm not meant to get involved with patients," the pretty brunette nurse replied.

"But I won't be a patient in another hour," James replied. "You can't expect me to eat dinner with my sister every night for the next twenty nights, surely."

The woman looked at Fenella and chuckled. "He's charming, your brother."

"Really?" Fenella replied. "That's news to me."

James frowned. "Hey, watch it, baby sister."

Fenella grinned. "You're the one trying to get away from me."

The nurse shook her head. "Siblings," she said. She handed James a slip of paper. "Ring me once you're well and truly out of here. If I'm not busy, maybe I'll let you buy me dinner."

James took the paper and tucked it into a pocket. "I'll be in touch," he promised.

"Did he really write a book?" the nurse asked Fenella as she headed for the door.

"Yes, he did. It's won a number of awards and it's very popular with college professors. They keep assigning it to unsuspecting undergraduates year after year."

The woman laughed. "I thought maybe he was lying to me. Now I'm intrigued. I will have to look him up online when I get home tonight."

"Don't believe the negative reviews," James told her. "They were all put there by jealous competitors."

The woman nodded and then left the room, chuckling to herself.

"I take it you're feeling better," Fenella said.

"Much better, and I really want to get out of here now. I'm sure I could simply go back to the house, as well. I don't need looking after."

"The doctor said you shouldn't be left alone for a few days. I'm not going to leave you alone, therefore."

"Would it do me any good to argue?"

"No, none at all. It will only be for a few days, and if you're very good, I'll even drive you to and from your date with that nurse."

"What about the other three?" James asked, his eyes twinkling.

GUESTS AND GUILT

Fenella shook her head. "Maybe you should be seen to be missing Stephanie, at least for a few days," she suggested.

"I told you how it was between me and Stephanie. We had more of a working relationship than a romance. I mean, I do miss her, but that doesn't mean I can't notice other women."

The door behind Fenella swung open and a middle-aged man with what looked like a permanent scowl on his face strode in. "Ah, Mr. Woods, I hope you're feeling better today," he said.

"I'm feeling great and ready to go home."

The man nodded and then made a few notes on the sheets on his clipboard. "I was going to keep you for another day or two," he said, "but in order to feel truly justified, I'd have to keep you for three months, and that would be a stretch."

"I'm sorry?" James replied.

"When I was at university, I thought it would be a good idea to do a semester at a university in the US. I took a few classes there, including one on American literature," the doctor said.

Fenella hid a smile as she realized where the story was going. James sighed deeply. "You've read my book," he guessed.

"Oh, no, I didn't just read your book. That's far too simple. I studied your book, analyzed your book, scrutinized every single word of your book. I wrote a ten-page essay on why your main character had eggs for breakfast every morning. It was symbolic and just one of the many hidden meanings buried in that stupid book."

James flushed. "I'm sorry," he said. "I never intended for my book to be studied at all. It was just something I wrote because I had to get the words out of my head."

The doctor nodded. "So tell me. Why did your main character eat eggs for breakfast every day?"

"Because I like eggs," James said softly.

The doctor stared at him for a minute and then began to laugh. He laughed until tears ran down his face. Fenella looked over at James, but he wouldn't let her catch his eye.

"I'm sorely tempted to write to my American literature professor and tell her that she can disregard the ten pages of pointless analysis that I wrote," the doctor said once he'd composed himself. "I could have simply written 'the author likes eggs' and been one hundred percent correct."

James shrugged. "I dropped out of college to avoid having to write those sorts of papers."

The doctor laughed again. "I'd love to tell her that as well, but she probably wouldn't believe me. Actually, she's probably passed away by now. I'm sure she was sixty when I had her and that was twenty years ago."

"I am sorry," James told him.

"Then I'll let you go," the man replied. "The nurse will be in shortly with a list of instructions for you. You need to pay attention to your body very carefully for the next few days. Head injuries aren't to be taken lightly."

"I'll make sure he takes it easy," Fenella assured the man.

"What did you think of his book?" the doctor asked.

"Ah, he won't let me read it," Fenella replied.

"Lucky you," the man said, laughing again.

A few minutes later a nurse stuck her head in the doorway. "Knock, knock. Are you ready for your instructions?"

Fenella paid careful attention to everything the woman said while James yawned and seemingly ignored her. When she was done, she handed Fenella a pile of papers.

"Everything I've just gone over is also in this packet," she said. "I just have one question for you before you go."

"What's that?" Fenella asked.

"What did you say to Dr. Shaw? I've been working with him for fifteen years and I've never even seen him smile. He was laughing when he came out of here, laughing and muttering something about eggs."

Fenella looked over at James, who sighed. "He has a strange sense of humor, your Dr. Shaw," he said.

The nurse insisted that James be taken out of the hospital in a wheelchair. Fenella went and got her car, driving it right up to the main hospital entrance. As soon as she stopped, the nurse helped James into the passenger seat.

"Ring us if you have any questions or concerns," she told Fenella.

"The number is on the paperwork I gave you. Someone is always available."

"Thank you," Fenella replied.

The drive back to the promenade didn't take long. James was silent on the journey and Fenella didn't push him to chat. They were going to be together a lot over the next few days. There was plenty of time for conversation later.

Fenella slid her car into one of her assigned spaces in the garage under the building and then took James's bags out of her trunk. He was standing next to Mona's little red sports car when she shut the trunk.

"This is gorgeous," he said. "Who does it belong to, and do you think they'd let me take it for a spin?"

"You don't have a valid driver's license," Fenella said.

"I can drive on my US license," he replied. "I checked that before I left home, just in case Stephanie and I wanted to get away, just the two of us, sometimes. I even looked into renting a car, but the forms online wouldn't take my US address."

"Let's make sure you're fully recovered from your head injury before we worry about you driving anywhere. The nurse said you could still lose consciousness unexpectedly."

"I'm fine," he snapped, "and I won't be treated like a baby."

"Grab your bags and follow me, then," Fenella told him, spinning on her heel and striding across the garage as quickly as she could. When she reached the elevator, she pushed the call button and then turned around. James was struggling toward her, pulling one bag and trying to carry the other two in his other hand.

"Would you like me take one?" she offered, feeling guilty about leaving him with all three, even if he was being annoying.

"I've got it," he snarled.

The ride up to the sixth floor was a tense one. James put the bags down and spent most of the journey shifting them around, muttering under his breath. When the elevator stopped, Fenella stepped off and then waited while James gathered his things.

"This is me," she said brightly as she opened the door to her apartment.

James followed her inside and then whistled loudly. "Wow, this is something else. Mona must have done really well for herself to have been able to afford this place. What did she do, anyway?"

"Tell him I was an undertaker," Mona suggested from her seat near the windows. "Or better yet, tell him that I wrote erotic fiction under several pen names. That would be fun."

Fenella ignored both of them as she opened the door to the spare bedroom. "This is your room," she told James. "I hope you'll find it comfortable."

He dragged his bags into the room and glanced around. "Yeah, it looks great, actually. Thanks."

"Meerroow," Katie said in an inquisitive tone.

"This is James, my older brother," Fenella replied. "James, this is Katie."

James looked over at the cat and then sat down on the bed. "Come here, then, Katie," he said.

Katie jumped up on the bed and then climbed into James's lap. She curled up under his hand and began to purr loudly as he stroked her back.

"She's lovely," he said after a moment. "If I'd known about her, I would have asked to stay here from the start."

"I didn't know you liked cats," Fenella said.

"I like all animals. I've always wanted to have pets, but I've never felt ready for the responsibility." He looked at her and then shook his head. "I'm sixty years old. If I'm not ready now, when will I be? I should get a dog."

"Yooowwlllll," Katie protested.

James chuckled. "Maybe a cat would be a better idea."

"Mmmeeewww," Katie told him.

"I'd take you home with me if I thought I could," he added.

"That's not happening," Fenella said firmly.

James nodded. "She is a lovely little thing, though. I'm quite jealous."

"Well, you can enjoy her company for the next two and a half weeks, anyway. Maybe she'll keep you from getting so restless while you're recovering."

"I'm sure she's already lowering my blood pressure."

"How about some lunch?"

"That would be great. The food in the hospital was not very good. Oh, I ate it anyway. I'll eat anything that I don't have to make myself, but it will be nice to have something other than hospital food."

"I'm afraid I wasn't planning on anything extravagant for lunch. I thought maybe cold sandwiches and some salad would do."

"Even that sounds good, if I can make my own sandwich the way I want it. They gave me something yesterday that was like a sandwich, but I didn't recognize any of the fillings and the bread was stale."

"I have fresh bread and your choice of fillings," Fenella assured him.

Fenella spread everything out along the kitchen counter and they made themselves sandwiches before they sat down at the table together.

"The view from here is incredible," James said. "I could sit and watch the water all day."

"As your doctor wants you to rest, I suggest that's what you do for the next week or so."

"Yeah, yeah, I know. Lots of rest, no physical activity, no alcohol. It's like being eight with chicken pox again, but with aches and pains."

Fenella laughed. "I'm sorry, and I'll do my best to keep you entertained."

"I'd love to do some more sightseeing, but mostly I want to find out what happened to Stephanie. I don't suppose you've heard anything new?"

"Annie is planning a memorial service for Saturday," Fenella began. She told her brother everything that Annie had said during their phone conversation.

"But that doesn't even make sense. If they all left together and Stephanie was already gone, how did one of them kill her? They must have all been in on it together. That's the only thing that makes sense."

"Let's let the police worry about that," Fenella suggested. "I wonder if they know about the memorial service. Maybe I should call Mark and tell him about it."

A knock on the door kept James from replying. Fenella crossed the room and pulled the door open.

"Good afternoon," Mark Hammersmith said. "I understand your brother has been released from Noble's. Is he here?"

"Yes, he is. We were just having lunch. Would you like to join us?"

"I probably shouldn't, but I do need to speak to James. I have a number of questions for him."

"Questions? About what?"

"About a number of things," Mark replied vaguely. "Can I come in?"

Fenella stepped back to let the man into the apartment. "We're in the kitchen," she said.

Mark followed her across the room. "Good afternoon," he said to James. "I hope you're feeling better."

"I am, thanks," James replied. "But what can I do for you?"

"You can start by telling me why Stephanie asked her friends to help her find a way to get away from you," Mark replied.

13

James shook his head. "What?"

"Perhaps you could tell me again about your relationship with Stephanie. Tell me again how you met," Mark asked.

"She wrote to me to tell me that she'd enjoyed my book," James replied.

"Do you always correspond with your fans?" Mark wanted to know.

"My publisher has a form letter that he sends to most of them. I never even see those letters. Stephanie wrote to me at my home address, rather than in care of my publisher, though."

"How did she get your home address?" was Mark's next question.

James frowned. "I'm not actually sure. It isn't a huge secret or anything, though. Probably anyone could find it if they tried hard enough. It's only a post office box, actually, not my real street address, anyway."

"You never asked her how she found you?"

"No, it never came up. Like I said, she wasn't the first person to track down the box number, and she wasn't the last, either. I probably get at least one letter a month in my box."

"And do you reply to them all?"

James shrugged. "It depends on my mood. Most of them I ship off to my publisher and let him deal with them. I give threatening ones to the police. Occasionally there will be something interesting in one of them that gets me to reply in person, but it's pretty rare."

"So why did you reply to Stephanie?"

"She sent me like five pages of nonsense. Some of it talked about the Isle of Man and some of it was about how she wanted to be a writer herself. I found it, well, amusing, I suppose. I went through the first two pages with a red pen, correcting all of her grammar and punctuation, and then sent it back to her. I didn't expect to hear from her again."

"I can see why," Mark said dryly, "but she did get in touch again, didn't she?"

"Yes, she sent another letter, one that had been carefully edited. She wanted writing advice. She told me she had millions of ideas but no way to put them on paper. I've been struggling for ideas for years, so I suggested maybe we could work together on something. It was a crazy idea and I never truly expected her to take me up on it. She didn't write back, but then one day she turned up on my doorstep."

"And you started a relationship?"

James flushed. "She was far more attractive than I'd expected from her letters. I told you before that she'd sent me some photos, but I wasn't sure that the photos she'd sent were really her, you know? It was probably a mistake to get romantically involved with her when I was hoping to work with her, but I found her charms somewhat impossible to resist."

"Did you want a drink?" Fenella asked Mark, wanting to give James a break from the rapid-fire questions.

"Pardon? Oh, sure, something cold would be good," he replied.

"You're welcome to make yourself a sandwich as well," she offered, gesturing toward the counter where everything was still spread out.

"I will, if you don't mind. I didn't get time for lunch yet, and I doubt I will later."

Fenella handed him a can of soda after he'd put together a sandwich. James made himself another sandwich as well and then the three of them sat back down together.

"Right, so where were we?" Mark asked. He tapped on his phone for a moment and then looked at James. "Were you and Stephanie working on a book, then?"

"We were starting to put ideas together, but we hadn't actually done any real work yet," James replied.

"Can you be more specific?"

James shrugged. "Stephanie was trying to make an outline for a story, something that I could work from as I wrote. She was also going to give me detailed character profiles, but I don't think she'd started them yet."

"So she was providing the plot and the characters, and you were going to actually write the book?"

"Something like that. We hadn't worked out all of the details yet. She may have done some of the writing as we went along. I really don't know."

"But she hadn't written anything yet?"

"She hadn't even finished the outline yet," James told him.

"Can you think of any reason why she might have told her friends that she'd already written the book?" Mark asked.

"Maybe she was just showing off," James suggested.

"Maybe," Mark replied, making a note on his phone. "Would you be prepared to let me search your belongings for the draft manuscript that Stephanie told her friends you have?"

"Draft manuscript? I don't know what you're talking about," James said. "I don't want you searching my things, either. Even if I do have a draft manuscript, which I don't, why does that matter to the police?"

"It matters if it provided a motive for murder," Mark replied.

"You think I killed Stephanie so that I could steal the manuscript?" James asked.

"It's one possibility," Mark said.

"It's a crazy idea. First of all, there is no manuscript. Second of all, Stephanie and I were working together. If there were a manuscript, it would already belong to me, or half to me, anyway."

"Unless you didn't want to admit that you'd used a ghost writer," Mark suggested. "Maybe you wanted to publish the book under your name and cut Stephanie out entirely."

"Is that what her friends told you? They all got together and murdered her to keep her from telling anyone about Arthur Beck. Now they're trying to pass the blame off to me with this crazy story," James scoffed.

"But you won't let me search your things?" Mark asked.

"If it will help get the focus of your investigation back onto the three women who killed Stephanie, then you can search my things," James said. "Fenella, did you pack up the papers in my room when you packed my bags?"

"No, I just brought your clothes and personal items," Fenella replied. "I thought I could go back for the paperwork if you wanted it."

"So everything you want to look at is at the house where I was staying," James said. "I already gave you everything of Stephanie's, so you know there wasn't any manuscript there. You'll have to go and search the house, I suppose. I'm meant to be resting, so I'll stay here, if you don't mind."

"Perhaps Fenella would like to accompany me?" Mark said.

"I could do that," she replied.

"You'll find some sheets with the story outline. They may even look like the beginnings of a story, but they're really just rough notes. That's truly as far as we ever got," James said.

Mark didn't look as if he were in any hurry to get to the house to start searching. He took another bite of his sandwich and then swiped something in his phone. "How were you and Stephanie getting along lately?" he asked.

"I won't lie to you; traveling together was, well, difficult. We were forced together in fairly tight spaces for much too long. We were both snapping at one another by the time we arrived on the island. The fact that I was badly jet lagged when Stephanie wasn't didn't help."

"How important was it to you to have her help with the book?"

"I was looking forward to working with her, as I thought some of her ideas were interesting, but if she'd decided she was no longer interested, I would have understood. I know I'm not the easiest person to live with and I've never tried collaborating with another person on a book before. I have no idea if it would have worked or not, and now I suppose I'll never know."

"Do you think you were putting pressure on Stephanie to stay with you for the sake of the book project?"

"Not even a little bit. The thing is, I'm the well-known author. If Stephanie wanted to be published, she knew her best chance was to work with me. Once our book hit the market, if it was a success, she'd have a foot in the door, not to mention a source of income that she didn't currently have."

"And she was happy with your plans for how you were going to publish, I mean, in just your name?"

"We weren't necessarily going to publish in just my name. We were still working that part out, but she was going to get credit in some way. And yes, as far as I know, she was happy with the arrangements, at least as far as they'd gone. If I ever do decide to try something like this again, I'm going to have a lawyer work out every detail before we begin, though."

Mark nodded. "That's probably a wise idea." He finished his sandwich and typed a bit more into his phone before looking at Fenella. "If we could, I'd like to go and search the house now."

Fenella stood up. "Are you going to be okay on your own?" she asked James.

He shrugged. "I'll be fine. I'll watch the sea for a while and then take a nap, probably."

"Call my mobile if you need me," she told him. "Do you want to double-check the things I packed and brought here before we go?" she asked Mark. "I'm sure you want to be thorough."

He nodded. "If no one minds."

It only took him a few minutes to glance through the suitcases that Fenella had packed. It was clear there wasn't any paper in any of them.

The trip to the house on Poppy Lane took only a little bit longer. Mark was silent on the drive over. Once inside, he checked every room, not just the one that James had been using.

"Of course, with today's technology, the entire manuscript could be on a flash drive or even in the cloud," he remarked as Fenella locked the house behind them.

"You didn't find any flash drives, either here or at my apartment," she pointed out. "I don't have any cloud accounts, but I don't know how you would check that. James doesn't even have a computer, but again, I suppose you can't just take my word for that."

"I probably should have his house in the US searched," Mark said as they drove back to the promenade. "I'd rather not take things that far yet, though."

"Have you found Arthur Beck?" Fenella asked.

"We're working on that and many other things."

"Did you know there's going to be a memorial service on Saturday for Stephanie? Annie told me about it. James and I are planning to attend."

"I didn't realize you'd spoken to Annie. Can you take me through the conversation, please?" he asked as he parked in front of Fenella's building.

She quickly recounted the telephone conversation that she'd had with the other woman, while Mark made notes on his phone. When she was done, he sighed.

"I don't suppose I can talk you into skipping the memorial service?"

"Why?"

"I'd rather keep James and Stephanie's friends apart, that's all."

"I can try talking to James, but I know he really wants to be there."

"I'll be there as well, so let him know that I will stop him from talking to the women if he tries anything."

"I'll tell him. I think he just wants to pay his respects to Stephanie, though. He's planning another service back in the US as well."

Mark nodded. "If I don't see you between now and then, I'll see you on Saturday."

Fenella climbed out of the car and made her way into her building. She stopped to check her mailbox, which was empty as usual, and then headed up to her apartment. As she opened the door, she could hear James's voice.

"What do you mean, who is this? That isn't any way to start a conversation. Who were you calling?"

Fenella raised an eyebrow at him. He was sitting on the couch, holding the phone and scowling.

"Maggie? Well, there, you see. You have the wrong number," he said after a moment.

"Wait," Fenella said. "That might be Jack."

"Jack? Is this Jack?" James asked the caller. He looked at Fenella. "Yeah, it's Jack. Do you want to talk to him?"

Fenella made a face. She didn't, really, but she couldn't exactly bring herself to tell her brother that. "Sure, I'll talk to him," she said.

"Who was that?" Jack demanded as soon as Fenella said hello.

"What do you want, Jack?" Fenella replied.

"I was calling to tell you that I miss you," Jack replied, "but it seems as if I'm wasting my time. You've moved another man into your apartment, I gather. It seems to me that you've moved on rather quickly. After being with me for ten years and never once suggesting that we should live together, you've been there, what, four or five months and you've already invited a man to live with you? I'm saddened and shocked, if I'm honest."

Fenella sighed deeply. "Not that it's any of your business, but that was my brother James who answered the phone."

"Your brother? Why didn't he simply say so?"

"I don't know. I'm sure your call took him by surprise. He may even have been asleep. He's recovering from an accident."

"What happened to James?"

"It's a long story, and not one that need worry you."

"Now I am worried, though. It does seem as if that island is a very dangerous place. Every time I call you it seems as if someone has just been murdered or some such thing. You really should come home."

"This is my home now," Fenella said firmly. "I am home and I don't anticipate returning to the US, at least not in the foreseeable future."

"That's the other reason why I called. I've been thinking a lot about your situation there and I've realized why you keep refusing to come back to me. It's money, isn't it?"

"Money? No, not even a little bit."

"You can be honest with me," Jack told her. "You sold up everything here and rushed over there without doing any checking into what you'd actually inherited. Now you're stuck in a tiny apartment in what's probably a bad neighborhood and you've no way to afford a ticket home, let alone to replace your house and everything else that you sold or gave away. I know you well enough to know that you've far too much pride to admit to any of that, though."

"I have plenty of money," Fenella told him, very conscious that her brother was paying close attention to her end of the conversation.

"You know you don't have to pretend with me. Anyway, I want to help. I was thinking that I might take early retirement. That would give me access to a large lump sum of money. I could come over there and help you settle your aunt's estate. I'm sure it will be difficult to sell her apartment, but with my financial backing, you won't have to worry about how much you actually get for it. Once everything is taken care of, we can move back to the US. I was thinking maybe we could try Florida. I think I've had enough of snow and ice, really."

In spite of how she felt about the man, Fenella couldn't help but be touched by the generous offer. "That's very kind of you, Jack, but I'm really okay. I'm not moving back to the US because I simply don't want to do so. Money is not an issue."

"But I miss you. We belong together. If you won't move back here, I will have to move there."

"No!" Fenella exclaimed. "You can't move here. You've no legal right to live in the UK."

"I've been checking into that. We'll just have to get married, as far as I can tell. Once we're married, I'll be able to live wherever you are."

"But I don't want to marry you," Fenella said softly.

Jack laughed. "You've always said that, but you don't really mean it. If I came over and got down on one knee, you'd say yes. I know you would."

"I might have once, but I wouldn't now," Fenella told him, trying to be gentle, but losing patience with the man. "I'm really happy here. I have new men in my life, and I'm finding that being single agrees with me. You're better off where you are, anyway. You'd miss teaching and you'd miss the American way of life."

"But I'd stop missing you," Jack replied sadly.

Fenella swallowed hard. "I'm sorry, Jack, but I have to go. James needs his next dose of antibiotics and he has to take them with food. I need to go and make him a snack. Please try to move on with your life. I'm not coming back, and I'm not marrying you."

"Then I shall have to find another way for us to be together," Jack said. "I won't give up on us, you know. It would be easier if you simply stopped pretending to fight me."

It would be easier to invite you here and then murder you in your sleep, Fenella thought. "Jack, I'm not pretending," she said.

"Yes, darling, you keep telling me that so that you don't feel guilty. I quite understand. It's asking a lot of me, asking me to move halfway around the world. I wouldn't do it for just anyone, you know, but I will for you. You're worth it."

"I'm really not. Please, just stay there. You've Hazel and Sue to think of, as well. They'd both miss you terribly if you left."

"Hazel has taken a six-month sabbatical to study the eighteenth-century history of Canada, a subject I can't believe will be at all interesting. And Sue has just become involved with one of the professors from the mathematics department. I can't imagine what she sees in him, but they seem very happy together."

"How nice for both of them," Fenella said. Hazel and Sue were two other professors in the history department where Jack worked. When Fenella had worked there as well, she'd always felt that the pair of them disliked her and thought that Jack could do better. From what Jack had told her, when she'd first moved to the island they'd each made a play for him, but Jack seemed to have misunderstood their friendly overtures. It seemed that now they'd both given up and moved on.

"I suppose so. Anyway, you think about my offer. I'll call you again in a few days and we can talk further. Why don't you ever call me, though? It seems as if I'm always calling you, and that means I'm the one paying for the incredibly expensive international calls."

"I don't call you because I've moved on with my life," Fenella snapped, "and you don't have to pay for any more calls. Simply stop calling."

"I can't do that. Not until I'm sure you're truly happy."

"What do I have to do to prove that I'm happy?"

"I don't know. Maybe I'd believe you if I could see you in person.

Maybe you should come back to Buffalo to visit me. Then I could see how you really feel."

"I'm not coming back to Buffalo. Please stop asking. I have to go." Fenella put the phone down before Jack could reply. After she'd done that, she banged her head on the wall in front of her.

"I never did like that guy," James said. "I only met him once or twice, but he always seemed like an idiot."

"He's a brilliant historian," Fenella replied, feeling foolish for defending the man but unable to stop herself.

"Yeah, but he's not a great human being," James said. "I should know what I'm talking about. I'm not a great human being, either."

"It's never too late to change," Fenella told him.

"Eh, I'm happy the way I am. It isn't like I want to get married or anything, not at this late date. Maybe if I were a nicer person I'd have found someone to collaborate with on my next book years ago, but that's all water under the bridge now. But why did Jack ask for Maggie?"

"I was always Fenella to the family, but outside of home I usually used Margaret, as it was easier for Americans," Fenella explained.

"Fenella isn't difficult."

"No, but it's unusual, which means it was often spelled incorrectly. I don't know. I suppose when I was younger I just wanted to feel as if I fit in more. Margaret was a more common name."

"And Jack calls you Maggie."

"Which I've always hated," Fenella sighed. "He's got it in his head that we belong together, and he keeps trying to find ways to get me to move back to Buffalo."

"You should have him come and visit. Once he saw your setup here, he'd stop talking about you moving back to Buffalo. This apartment is gorgeous."

"It is really nice, but having him come here might be worse. He seems to think that he should move here if I won't move there."

"And you don't want him here."

"I'd have to marry him in order for him to stay. I don't want to marry him, that's for sure."

"So stop answering his calls."

GUESTS AND GUILT

"I haven't been answering his calls. You're the one who answered him today."

James laughed. "I did, didn't I? I am sorry, baby sister. Do you want me to go and talk to him when I get home? I could probably convince him to leave you alone. Maybe I could take John with me. He can be pretty intimidating when he wants to be."

"Thanks for the offer, but Jack is my problem. One of these days he's going to start believing me. I keep hoping he'll meet someone else, but that doesn't seem to be happening."

"What about you? You told him that you have men in your life. When can I meet them?"

"Unfortunately, I may have been exaggerating slightly when I spoke to Jack," Fenella replied. She really didn't want to explain her love life to her brother, especially when it wasn't any of his business anyway.

"I assume the police inspector didn't find any secret manuscripts hidden in the house, then?"

"No, he didn't," Fenella replied as Mona wandered into the room.

She looked from Fenella to James and back again before walking closer to James. "He can't see me," she said after a moment.

Fenella shrugged.

"I thought he might be able to, as you can," Mona told her. "How very interesting. If he's staying in the spare bedroom, I shall have to chat with him while he's sleeping."

"Anyway," Fenella said. "I told Mark about the memorial service. He said we're not to speak to the three women when we're there."

"We have to speak to them," James argued. "It would be rude otherwise."

"Yes, well, I suppose he can't object to us saying a few words to them, but he doesn't want us mentioning murder or Arthur Beck to them," Fenella clarified.

"I hope he isn't going to be too angry with me, then," James said.

"What do you mean?"

"I mean I have every intention of discussing Stephanie's murder and Arthur Beck with those three women. I also plan to ask them why they're lying about the work that Stephanie was doing with me. I'm not going to let them accuse me of anything and I'm not going to let them get away with murder."

Fenella frowned. "Mark will be there. He will step in and cut the conversation short if you insist on talking about any of those things."

"But we can at least see the reaction that Arthur Beck's name gets," James argued. "That should be telling, anyway."

"And I'm sure Mark is hoping to see that reaction when he questions them about the man, but not at a public memorial service," Fenella said.

"James is right," Mona interrupted. "Confronting them could be the fastest way to solve Stephanie's murder."

"He's dragging his feet, not knowing what to believe," James said. "I have the advantage of knowing that I didn't kill her or even have any reason to do so. I know those three killed her, probably as a group."

"I'm not sure about that," Mona said. "It didn't sound as if they were getting along particularly well at the pub that night. I can't see them getting organized enough to kill as a group again."

"Except they weren't getting along very well at the pub," Fenella repeated what Mona had said.

"Maybe they were pretending to fight to disguise their intentions," James replied.

"Or maybe just one of them killed Stephanie," Fenella said. "Or maybe she really did have an accident. It doesn't really matter. Mark will work it all out eventually."

"But I don't want to wait for eventually. Do you know how I felt when your inspector friend was here today? Guilty. And I didn't do anything wrong. I hate feeling as if I'm being watched and judged. That man actually thinks that I might have murdered Stephanie. It's a horrible feeling."

"I know exactly how you feel, and I'm sorry, but if you start confronting those women on Saturday, Mark will probably arrest you."

"Then I can sit in jail and try to work out who killed Stephanie and who tried to run me down. Don't forget that. One of them tried to kill me, too. The sooner the police find out what happened, the safer I'll be."

"I was going to tell Annie that you've told the police everything that Stephanie ever told you, but I didn't get a chance."

"Tell her when she calls back with the time for the service," James suggested. "I'll feel better going if the three of them know I've told the police about Arthur Beck."

"Remind me when she calls," Fenella told him.

"Even if they know, someone might still try to get rid of James," Mona said. "I hope you're going to keep a very close eye on him at the service."

Fenella looked over at her and nodded slightly.

"I'm still not convinced that he didn't just trip over the curb when drunk," Mona added. "He looks thoroughly disreputable. I'm not very happy with him staying in my flat."

Biting her tongue to avoid responding to Mona, Fenella went into the kitchen to get a snack for Katie.

"What was all that about making me a snack?" James called across the room. "You told Jack you were going to make me a snack, didn't you?"

"I was just saying that so that I could get off the phone," Fenella replied. "You aren't on antibiotics."

"I know, but don't you feel guilty for lying to Jack? You should probably make me something to eat, just so you weren't totally lying to the poor man."

Fenella rolled her eyes and then sighed. She did feel badly about lying to Jack. She glanced through her cupboards and found a small bag of potato chips. After dumping them into a bowl, she walked back into the living room and handed the bowl to her brother. "There you are," she said.

James took the bowl and chuckled. "I'm not sure putting chips into a bowl counts as making me a snack, but I'm not going to complain."

"I should hope not," Fenella replied.

Annie finally called the next day, just as Fenella was heading out to do some grocery shopping. James had already eaten just about every bit of food that she'd had in the apartment.

"Hello?" she said when the phone on the table next to her rang.

"It's Annie. I just wanted to let you know that the service will be at two o'clock on Saturday. We're just having it at the community center in Onchan. I don't know that there will be anyone there besides the three of us, but we're putting a notice in the local paper."

"Thanks for letting me know. James and I will be there. He's been spending so much time with the police, I'm sure he'll be happy to speak to other people."

"The police? Why has he been talking to them?"

"I'm not sure why, but they've been asking him questions about the things that Stephanie told him about her life when she lived on the island. He's told them everything he can remember from the stories that she told him."

"Has he really? I'm going to be in trouble then, aren't I? There are a lot of stories from those days that I'd rather the police didn't know."

"There are?"

"Well, yeah, sure. I mean, we all drank too much, and we may have borrowed a few cars without permission. I'm sure you heard the story about the time we broke into the school to drink. We were a pretty wild bunch, the CAMS. I sure hope he didn't tell the police all of those stories."

"I believe he told the police everything that Stephanie had told him. I wouldn't be too worried, though. I'm sure they can't prosecute you for breaking and entering after all these years."

"Probably not," Annie agreed, "but I'll feel uncomfortable if I ever see that police inspector again. I'd rather he didn't know about my youthful indiscretions."

"I'm sure he's heard much worse," Fenella said. "James and I are both looking forward to seeing you all on Saturday."

"You don't happen to know what sort of stories Stephanie told James, do you?"

"Not at all. I just know that James passed them all on to Inspector Hammersmith."

"Okay, well, thanks. We'll see you on Saturday."

Fenella put the phone down and looked over at James, who was stretched out on one of the couches. "The service is at two. I hope I've told her enough to keep you safe."

"At this point, I'd almost relish another attempt on my life. I'm so bored I can barely stand it. I can't believe you aren't letting me out of the apartment."

"I've told you that you're welcome to come with me to the grocery store."

"That isn't what I mean."

"The doctor said no alcohol for a week. You know if you go to a pub that you'll have a drink, no matter what you promise me or yourself. Let's get through the memorial service and then have this argument, okay?"

James nodded, and Fenella had to be happy with that. Having him staying with her was proving challenging. Mona seemed to have disappeared, as well. Fenella could only hope that the police would hurry up and solve Stephanie's murder so that James could move back into the house on Poppy Drive.

14

Saturday morning dawned bright and sunny, but by the time Fenella made lunch it was raining and grey outside.

"The weather looks like I feel," James said as he ate.

"Yeah, me, too," Fenella replied. "Maybe we should skip the memorial service. They probably wouldn't even miss us."

"You don't have to come. You barely knew Stephanie. I'm going, though. I was her, well, significant other, and I need to be there."

"If you're going, I'm going."

"I wish I could go," Mona sighed. "It will be nice to have my flat to myself for an hour, though. James does seem to take up more than his fair share of space when he's here."

Fenella only just stopped herself from agreeing out loud. "You can load the dishwasher when you're done," she told her brother when she'd finished eating. "I'm going to go and find something to wear to the service."

"You know I don't know how to load the dishwasher," James replied. "You've shown me every day since I've been here, but I'm still not getting it."

"Do your best," Fenella told him. "I'm getting tired of waiting on you hand and foot. Try to help out a little bit, okay?"

"I'm sorry to be such a burden, baby sister. I didn't ask to come over here and get targeted by a serial killer."

Fenella rolled her eyes and then walked out of the room. James had grown increasingly demanding and difficult as the days had progressed. Now he seemed convinced that if he left the apartment he would be murdered by one of Stephanie's friends. Apparently, even that threat wasn't enough to keep him home from the memorial service, though.

"What should I wear?" Fenella asked Mona after she'd shut and locked her bedroom door.

"To a memorial service at a community center? I would think just about anything would be fine. People probably won't bother to wear black, even though they should."

"I want to wear black."

"Then try the set of dresses on the right side of the long hanging bar," Mona said, gesturing toward the huge wardrobe that was still packed full of her clothes. "That's my funeral collection."

"You had a special collection for funerals?" Fenella asked as she opened the wardrobe.

"In the last ten or so years of my life, I lost a great many of my friends," Mona told her. "I attended a lot of funerals."

Fenella pulled out a beautiful black dress. "This is gorgeous," she said.

"I'd rather you didn't wear that one, actually," Mona said in an odd tone.

Fenella looked over at her. "Are you crying?"

"No, of course not. It's just that I wore that to Max's funeral. It was a very difficult day for me, not least because Max's sister refused to speak to me."

"I am sorry."

Mona shrugged. "Max and his sister didn't get along very well, but that's a long story for another time. Let's worry about today."

"As much as I love this dress, it's far too formal and nice for where I'm going," Fenella said as she slid the dress back into the wardrobe. "What about this one?"

The next dress along was also lovely, but far less formal.

"It's probably too nice for where you're going as well, but if you really want to wear black, it may be your best option."

"I really want to wear black," Fenella said firmly. "I think Stephanie deserves that."

With the dress decided upon, Fenella did her hair and makeup before finding shoes and a handbag that she liked. When she was all ready, she turned slowly in front of the full-length mirror. "What do you think?" she asked Mona.

"I think you'll be the best-dressed woman there," Mona replied, "but then I'd expect nothing less from you."

James looked surprised when Fenella walked into the living room a moment later. "You look great," he said. "That dress looks like it cost a ton of money."

"It was one of Mona's."

"It fits you like it was made for you."

"Yes, we seem to have been the same size," Fenella replied. Mona laughed and then faded away.

"Where are we going, again?" James asked as they boarded the elevator.

"The Onchan Community Center. It's just like a hall that anyone can rent for any purpose," Fenella explained.

"Seems an odd place to have a memorial service."

"Take that up with Annie and the others."

"I already have a long list of things to discuss with them."

Fenella drove her car to the community center and parked next to the only other car that was there.

"Quite the turnout," James said sarcastically.

"We're a few minutes early. We can wait in the car for a little while, if you want."

"I'd rather not be the first ones in," James said. "I'm sure Annie and the others are waiting for me."

"No one else might be coming," Fenella reminded him.

"I'm sure there will be a few people who will turn up out of curiosity, if nothing else," James said.

Fenella wasn't sure if it was simply curiosity or something else, but while they waited, three other cars parked in the lot. She and James watched the people who exited them.

"Any idea who that is?" Fenella asked as an elderly man walked toward the community center

"None at all."

"What about those two?" The women who were talking together as they walked both appeared to be around Stephanie's age. They were both wearing black, but seemed to be chatting happily as they walked.

When the door to the third car opened, Fenella smiled. "I didn't recognize Shelly's car," she said as she opened her door.

"I didn't know you were coming," she said to Shelly as she gave her a hug.

"I thought about telling you, but I decided to just wait and see you here. I know you've been busy with James," the other woman replied.

"Yes, but that doesn't mean I don't want to see you," Fenella said.

"I didn't know how his recovery was coming, but if he's up to visitors, I'll start annoying you both immediately."

"We won't be annoyed," Fenella assured her, "or at least, I won't. And James will probably be moving back to the house soon, anyway."

Another car pulled into the parking lot and slid to a stop next to the women. Mark Hammersmith climbed out and nodded at them.

"Good afternoon."

"Good afternoon," Fenella replied.

As she spoke, James pulled open the passenger door on Fenella's car. "Now that the police are here, I feel safe," he said brightly.

Mark just gave him a blank look and then turned and walked toward the community center. James rushed to keep up with him, leaving Fenella and Shelly to follow.

"Are you okay?" Shelly whispered as they went.

"I'm fine, but I've had quite enough of James," she replied.

"I kept thinking about asking you to go down to the pub with me, but I knew James couldn't come and I didn't want to upset him."

"Let's go tonight," Fenella suggested. "I have a feeling I'm going to need a drink after this is over."

They all stopped right inside the door. The community center was basically just one large room with a few kitchen appliances along one wall. The basketball hoops at each end felt incredibly out of place for a memorial service. A number of folding chairs had been set up in rows, facing a small platform. Fenella could see plates of cookies on a long table against the back wall.

Stephanie's three friends were standing together, talking to the older man that Fenella had spotted in the parking lot. The other two women were standing together, looking around nervously. Annie suddenly seemed to notice the new arrivals.

"Ah, James and Fenella, you're here," she said loudly. She crossed the room toward them, leaving the others behind.

"How are you?" she asked James, staring at the still noticeable bruise on his forehead.

"I'm fine, mostly," he replied. "Just devastated to have lost Stephanie."

"We're all devastated," Courtney said as she and Maureen joined them. "It seems particularly cruel as we'd only just reconnected that night."

"Yes, the timing was particularly sad," James agreed.

"But you must meet Wilbur Rush," Courtney said. "He's Stephanie's third cousin on her father's side."

"It's nice to meet you," Fenella said to the older man as Courtney performed the necessary introductions.

"Likewise. I didn't really know Stephanie, but I'm the last one left on the island, so I thought I owed it to her to come. Everyone else either died or moved away, same as she did, really. I'm here now until the end, I suppose. It's not been a bad place to be, though."

"I'm sorry for your loss," Fenella said.

The man shrugged. "As I said, I didn't know her. If I'm honest, I don't even remember ever meeting her. Her father didn't get along with the rest of the family. We rarely saw any of them."

The other two women, who'd been standing on their own, walked over and gave everyone tentative smiles.

"You're Annie Lawrence, aren't you?" one of them said.

"Yes, I am," Annie agreed. "You both look really familiar, but I couldn't say why."

"I'm Susan Sinclair and this is Hannah Christian. We all went to school together, back in the day," the woman replied.

"Of course, now I remember you," Annie said. "You must remember Maureen Rhodes and Courtney Bridges, as well."

Susan looked at her friend and then nodded. "Yes, of course we do."

"I'm Courtney Fleming now. It was nice of you both to come to Stephanie's service," Courtney said.

"We both felt as if it was the right thing to do. We both remember her from school. She was in most of our classes, and I worked with her for a little while before her parents died and she left the island. She used to come over to my house on weekends to do homework sometimes."

"I didn't realize you two were such good friends," Annie said coolly.

Susan flushed. "We weren't great friends, but it was helpful to have someone to do homework with, that's all."

The tension that was building was broken when the door behind Fenella opened and an older woman walked in, leaning heavily on the arm of her companion. He looked to be about twenty-five.

"Mrs. Harrison?" Annie gasped. "Is that you?"

The woman frowned and then narrowed her eyes. "Annie Lawrence? Can that really be you? You've grown old since the last time I saw you."

"You haven't seen me since primary school," Annie shot back. "That was over thirty years ago."

"Was it really? Where has the time gone?" the woman sighed.

"Mrs. Harrison? It's so good to see you again," Susan said. She stepped forward and held out a hand. "I'm Susan Sinclair. I went to school with Annie and Stephanie."

The woman stared at her for a minute and then shrugged. "I don't really remember you. You must have been well behaved and quiet."

"I suppose I was both of those things," Susan agreed.

"I only remember the troublemakers," the woman said. "I remember Stephanie very well indeed."

Annie and her friends laughed. "I'm surprised you don't remember Maureen or Courtney, then," Annie said.

"I didn't move to the island until after primary school," Courtney reminded Annie.

"And I was well behaved in school," Maureen added.

Mrs. Harrison shook her head. "I do remember you, Maureen Rhodes, don't think that I don't. You weren't as naughty as Annie or Stephanie, but that doesn't mean I don't remember you. You were in trouble in my class fairly regularly."

Maureen laughed. "I'm glad I'm too old to get into trouble with you anymore."

"You're never too old, young lady," the woman snapped.

Maureen's smile faded and she looked around at her friends.

"Maybe we should get started," she muttered.

"I was hoping that we'd have a few more people than this," Courtney said, "but it's ten past two. We should get started. If everyone could take a seat, we'll begin."

Fenella looked at James, and he shrugged. No one seemed to know where to sit, so for a minute no one moved. Finally Mark crossed over to the rows of chairs and took a seat in the very back row. Mrs. Harrison's companion walked her over to the chairs and helped her settle into a seat in the next row forward. Shelly sat in the same row, with a few seats between herself and Mrs. Harrison.

"James, sit in the front," Annie suggested as Susan and Hannah slid into seats in front of Shelly.

"I don't think so. You three should get the front seats," he replied.

"There's plenty of room for you and your sister and us," Maureen said, "and you were her, well, her boyfriend, after all."

"Yes, but you were her family," he argued. "I'll sit in the second row."

Wilbur Rush had taken the seat next to Shelly, and Fenella could see them talking quietly as she and James took seats in the second row. The three remaining CAMS took seats at the front and then whispered amongst themselves for a minute.

"Thank you all for coming," Courtney said from the small platform a minute later. "We're grateful that you were willing to take time out of your busy day to help honor the memory of our dear friend, Stephanie."

James glanced at Fenella, and she suddenly began to worry that he intended to start shouting out questions about Arthur Beck during the service. She shook her head at him and he winked, which didn't reassure her in the slightest.

"I moved to the island when I was fourteen. My parents were in the middle of an ugly divorce and the Isle of Man was the last place I wanted to be. I'll be forever grateful to Stephanie for befriending me and making me feel as if I belonged here. When I first arrived, I swore I'd leave as soon as I turned eighteen. Now I can't imagine living anywhere else. I'm sorry that I lost touch with Stephanie over the years, and I'm grateful to have had a chance to spend at least a little bit of time with her before her unfortunate accident."

Fenella shot James a warning glance as he opened his mouth. He sighed and settled back in his seat.

"I met Stephanie at school, when I was all of five," Maureen said. "She was smart and funny and clever and I could never quite believe that she was willing to be friends with me. I missed her every day when she was away, and I was so happy when she came back. I'll miss her every day from now on for the rest of my life." She wiped away a few tears and then sat back down.

"Yeah, Stephanie was the closest thing I ever had to a sister. She lived next door to me from the time I was three until her parents died, and we were pretty much inseparable when we were younger. I was really happy when she came back to the island, but now I wish she'd never come back. At least when she was away, she was alive and well. I know I'll never get over losing her," Annie told them all before dissolving into tears. Maureen stood back up and pulled her back into her chair.

"We'd like to invite anyone else who'd like to say a few words to do so," Courtney said over Annie's sobs.

Susan stood up. "We all knew Stephanie as part of the CAMS. You four were always together, always having more fun than anyone else. All of the guys wanted to be with you. All of the girls wanted to join your gang, Annie's gang. But once in a while, when Stephanie was on her own, she'd take the time to talk to other people. I was one of those other people, and I liked Stephanie very much. I was sorry when she left the island and I'm desperately sorry that she's gone."

She sat down, and everyone looked around the room. James cleared his throat and stood up. Mark sat up straighter in his seat and stared hard at James as James gave everyone a nervous smile.

"I'm not a public speaker. I'm a writer. I should probably have written something to say today and then just read it out. Stephanie and I weren't together for long, but we were really happy together. She was an inspiration to me and I truly believe that we would have done something incredible together if we'd been able to write that book we had planned. I'm going to miss a million little things about her, from her smile to her laugh to the way she'd argue with me about anything and everything."

Everyone in the room chuckled. "She could argue with anyone," Annie said.

"Yeah, and she could talk like no one else I knew," James replied. "I was used to living alone, and there were days when she'd just start talking at breakfast time and not stop until past time for bed. When we first met, I used to listen to every word, but I soon learned to tune her out, at least some of the time. I would have been driven crazy otherwise."

Another general chuckle went around the room.

"She loved to tell me stories about her life on the island," James continued, "and from what she told me, a lot of very interesting things happened to her here."

Fenella saw Mark getting to his feet. "I think that's probably enough," he said in a low voice.

"I'm only just getting started," James retorted. "I thought Stephanie's friends might like to hear a few of the stories she shared with me."

"I don't think this is the time or the place," Mark said.

"It's the perfect time and place," James argued. "She told me that she and her friends once broke into their high school and got drunk in the gym."

Annie laughed. "That was a wild night. We had a really good time until the police came. Then we had to sneak out and we only just managed to get away."

"She also told me a story about the four of you breaking into Peel

GUESTS AND GUILT

Castle one night," James continued. "She said Annie tried to climb up the tower and that you all got spooked by the ghost dog."

Annie nodded. "The Moddey Dhoo was there, barking at us. It was terrifying."

James grinned. "I thought maybe she made that story up."

"Oh, no, it really happened," Maureen said. "We were very young and very stupid in those days."

"I'll assume you were also young and stupid that time you stole a car and accidently ran over Arthur Beck, then," James said in a conversational tone.

All three of Stephanie's friends turned pale, and Mark put his hand on James's arm.

"I told you that was not open to discussion today," he said firmly.

"I don't know what Stephanie told you," Courtney said, "but clearly that story was a fantasy."

"Was it?" James shot back. "Because you've all just confirmed her other stories were real."

"We did a little bit of breaking and entering," Courtney admitted, "but that's very different to stealing a car."

"I wasn't all that bothered about the stolen car," James said. "It was the man you killed that upset me about the story."

Annie had tears streaming down her face as she stood up. "It wasn't true. It wasn't like that. Not at all."

"Perhaps you'd like to tell me how it was, then," James suggested. "Because the way that Stephanie told it, you four murdered the man."

"It was an accident," Annie sobbed, "and Stephanie knew that."

"Annie, that's quite enough," Courtney said firmly. "None of us know anything about this story you're telling," she told James. "Clearly Stephanie told you all sorts of fanciful things. It certainly isn't our fault if you chose to believe her."

"You know what's really interesting?" James replied. "I didn't believe her, not until right now."

"I need to speak to each of you," Mark said, "and I'd appreciate it if you didn't talk amongst yourselves for the moment."

"We've no need to talk to one another," Courtney said. "Maureen and Annie know that the whole story is a complete fabrication. We've never even heard of Arthur Beck, or whatever his name was."

"You have the name right, which is pretty impressive since you only heard it once," Mark said.

Courtney flushed. "I was paying attention," she snapped. "It isn't every day that I get accused of murder, after all."

"We didn't kill him," Annie said. "It was an accident."

"Annie, stop," Courtney snarled. "We didn't know the man. He was a figment of Stephanie's imagination."

"Except his wife filed a missing person report on him," James said. "And his son, his baby son, never knew what happened to his father."

"He didn't really have a baby son," Annie said. "That was just a story he told us so that we'd let him go."

"He did have a son," James replied. "His name was Andrew, and Stephanie left everything she had to him."

Annie gasped and looked at the other two women. "He wasn't lying," she whispered softly.

"I don't believe this," Courtney said loudly. "Stephanie made up some crazy story and now even you are starting to believe it."

Annie shook her head. "I've been lying for too many years," she said, "but it wasn't even lying, was it? No one ever asked. No one ever came looking for the man. We all thought we were safe."

"We were safe," Maureen said, "until Stephanie came home."

"She wasn't really going to go to the police," Annie said. "She was just talking."

"If she told James, maybe she was going to go to the police," Maureen said. "She wasn't meant to tell anyone. We made a pact. We all promised."

"Has it escaped your notice that the man standing there is a police inspector?" Courtney said through gritted teeth. "I suggest you two get your story straight."

"No more stories," Annie said. "It's time to tell the truth. Maybe Stephanie was right. Maybe we'll all feel better if we tell the police what happened."

"No, we won't," Courtney said. "None of this is official. Keep your mouth's shut from now on and my advocate will be able to fix this. Just shut up now."

"What did Stephanie tell you?" Maureen asked James.

James took a deep breath. "She told me that you four were drunk and stole a car. While you were driving around the island, you ran over a man called Arthur Beck, but he wasn't killed outright. You took him to a house somewhere and looked after him for a while until he died."

"That's right," Courtney said quickly. "We didn't realize that he had a heart condition. He was recovering just fine from his minor injuries, and then one day when we went to check on him, he was dead. We can't possibly be blamed for that."

"I think we'll have to let the courts decide about that," Mark said. "Let's move this conversation down to the station. You'll be able to ring for advocates there if you want them."

"How did you know he had a heart condition?" James asked.

Courtney blinked a few times. "He must have. He was fine one day and dead the next."

"How long did you keep him as a prisoner?" James wanted to know.

"He wasn't a prisoner," Maureen said desperately. "He was our guest. We didn't want to take him to Noble's because we knew we'd be in trouble, but we were taking good care of him. He was happy because we took better care of him than they would have in hospital, anyway."

"Until he died," James said.

Maureen flushed. "But that wasn't our fault. It was like Courtney said, he must have had a heart condition or something."

"I don't know that we'll ever find out what happened to poor Arthur Beck," James said, "but I'm much more interested in what happened to Stephanie, anyway."

"She had a terrible accident," Annie said. "It was weirdly similar to what happened all those years ago. I wonder if she was thinking about Arthur when she stepped out in front of the car."

"I wonder if she was conscious when she was run over," James said, "or maybe someone hit her over the head and then put her in the middle of the road and ran her over."

Annie gasped and Maureen began to sob. "That isn't true," Annie said. "No one wanted to hurt Stephanie."

"Except maybe someone who wanted to keep the past a secret," James suggested. He looked over at Courtney, who chuckled.

"Am I being accused of murder for a second time in five minutes? My advocate is going to love this," she said.

"We all went home together," Annie said, "and that was after Stephanie left."

"I'm sure the police will be able to work out exactly what happened," James said, "but I have a pretty good imagination. Maybe it went something like this. Everyone was getting drunk and starting to get argumentative. Stephanie had said she wanted to go to the police about Arthur Beck and none of you wanted that to happen. I'm guessing one of you made arrangements to meet Stephanie later, maybe suggested that she get away from the others who were clearly angry. Stephanie could have hidden herself in the bathrooms or just about anywhere while you were looking for her, and she would have done that if she felt threatened by any one of you."

"But surely if she felt threatened, she would have just gone home?" Annie suggested.

"The killer must have convinced her that she'd be safe with her, somehow," James said, "and then the three of you went to your homes. Then one of you went back, met Stephanie, and killed her."

"I was too drunk to do any such thing," Annie said.

"We all were," Courtney said. "Even me, and I don't normally drink."

"Annie, she'd have trusted you the most," James said. "Don't you agree?"

Annie shrugged. "Probably, but I didn't have any reason to kill her. I wasn't fighting with her about Arthur Beck. I didn't really care if she told the police about it or not. I'm broke and alone. I've nothing to lose if the truth comes out. Yeah, I was in a car when a man was accidently run over and I didn't report it to the police. That we tried to help the man recover can't be held against us, surely. Anyway, as I said, I've nothing to lose. If I end up in prison, well, at least I won't have to worry about my electricity bill anymore."

Fenella frowned. Annie's words rang true. She didn't have much to lose if the story came out. That left Maureen or Courtney as suspects. Courtney clearly had the most to lose. She turned and looked at the woman. Courtney looked slightly uncomfortable, but still in control.

"By that standard, I must be the prime suspect," she said lightly. "Too bad I was too drunk to kill anyone."

"Were you, though?" James asked.

"The others will tell you that I started drinking heavily after you and your sister left. I was upset by the idea that Stephanie might go to the police about the Beck incident, I'll admit to that. But as Annie says, being a passenger in a car that was in an accident all those years ago isn't that big a deal."

"Except you were driving," Annie said quietly.

Courtney flushed. "It will be your word against mine on that one," she snapped. "Anyway, it was dark and it was a complete accident. We should have reported it, of course, and we should have taken that man to Noble's, but he didn't want to go to hospital. He wasn't even meant to be on the island. We did him a favor, finding him a place to hide while he recovered."

"Let's go," Mark said. The door behind him opened and four uniformed constables walked into the room. Mark nodded at them. "Please escort the three ladies in the front row down to the station," he said. "Take them in separate cars and put them in separate interview rooms."

"This is completely unnecessary," Courtney said. "Do you know who my husband is?"

"I do, yes," Mark replied. "You can ring him from the station if you'd like."

"She was driving," Annie said, "and she was the most upset when Stephanie said she was going to the police. She followed Stephanie to the loo, and then when she came back to the table she told us that Stephanie was gone. Maureen tried to catch up with her, but she couldn't find her. None of us could find her."

"That's hardly my fault," Courtney said.

"And that's where we end things for now," Mark said. He took Courtney's arm and led her out of the room. Annie and Maureen followed, each being escorted by a uniformed constable. Everyone else sat in silence as they went. A moment later, the door swung open again.

"Mr. Woods? I'll be at your sister's flat later today to get your statement. We're also going to have a long talk," Mark Hammersmith said from the doorway. The door banged shut behind him. For several minutes everyone sat in stunned silence.

"Maybe we should all have biscuits," Mrs. Harrison suggested. "It would be a shame to see them go to waste."

15

Fenella still felt as if she was in shock as she drove herself and James back to her apartment a short while later. She waited until they were in her kitchen with coffee in front of them before she spoke. Mona was sitting at the counter, obviously eager to find out what had happened.

"Courtney killed Stephanie," she said slowly.

"It certainly looks that way," James agreed.

"Courtney?" Mona asked. "Well, she was on my short list, but I still thought Annie was more likely."

"And she was driving when Arthur Beck was hit," Fenella continued.

"Again, that's the way it looks, anyway," James said.

"I wonder if she did something else to him," Fenella said. "It seems odd that he was recovering and then suddenly died."

"I doubt the police will ever be able to prove anything, not after all these years. First they'd have to find the body," James said.

"I suspect Annie and Maureen will tell Mark everything they know," Fenella said. "I'll be happy if they can put Courtney away for Stephanie's murder, at least."

"Yes, me too. I'm sorry about Arthur Beck, but I loved Stephanie," James replied. After a minute he laughed. "Who am I kidding? I liked the woman, but I didn't love her. I'm not sure I'm capable of actually loving anyone. I'm incredibly shallow, you know. What I did love was the idea of writing a book with her, and I may still try to make that happen."

When Mark arrived a few hours later he was far gentler with James than Fenella had been expecting. After taking a statement from James, he accepted the offer of coffee and biscuits from Fenella.

"I may as well tell you a few things," he said as he ate. "The local paper will be full of all of it anyway. It seems Wilbur Rush used to work for the *Isle of Man Times* and he was quick to ring in with every last detail from the memorial service."

"Oh, dear, I didn't think about that," James frowned.

"It was bound to hit the papers eventually. It's a small island. Anyway, Annie and Maureen have both told me the entire story, and their stories match so closely that I have to believe them. Courtney's story isn't at all the same, but her story also changes every time she tells it as she tries to work out exactly what to tell me to best help her advocate get her off."

"Will he get her off?" Fenella asked.

"We'll see. He'll have better luck with what happened with Arthur Beck than with Stephanie. The other two women have told me where to find the body, though, so we'll have to see what we find," Mark said.

"What about the attack on me?" James asked.

"Courtney doesn't have an alibi, but that's all I can say at the moment," Mark replied.

"I still don't see how she managed to get Stephanie to agree to meet with her later that night," Fenella said. "Stephanie must have known that Courtney was upset."

"I don't think she arranged to meet with her later," Mark said. "Here's the way I think it happened, although I can't prove it yet. I think Stephanie and Courtney went into the loo. Courtney hit Stephanie over the head with something. We're still looking for that something. Then she hid Stephanie somewhere and went out to pretend to look for her with the others. After they all went home, she went back to the pub, moved Stephanie into the road, stole the car, ran her over, and then made her way home."

"How did she get back to the pub?" James asked.

"Another car was stolen from a house not that far from Courtney's home," Mark said. "It was abandoned in the pub's car park as well."

"And how did she get home?" was James's next question.

"We aren't sure about that, but we're working on it. She must have taken another taxi," Mark said.

"Annie's car," Mona and Fenella said together.

"Pardon?" Mark asked.

"Courtney had Annie's keys and she promised to have Annie's car brought home for her. Maybe she drove herself home in Annie's car. I'm sure they said they don't live that far away from one another."

"They don't, actually, even though the streets are very different. She could have walked home from Annie's fairly easily," Mark replied, "and that might answer another question, too, actually."

"What question?"

"Where she left Stephanie while they were looking for her," Mark replied. "She could have hit Stephanie over the head and then put the body in the boot of Annie's car. Even if Stephanie wasn't already dead, she was unlikely to wake up and find a way out of there before Courtney returned."

Fenella shivered. "What a horrible thought."

With Courtney safely behind bars, Fenella was able to take James back to the house on Poppy Drive the next day. After James put his bags in his room, he joined Fenella in the house's living room.

"I appreciate everything you've done for me while I've been here," he said, "but when Inspector Hammersmith said I could leave the island whenever I'm ready, I realized that I'm really ready to go now. I'm sorry, but I'm going to cut my vacation short and go back to Pennsylvania where I belong."

Fenella nodded. "Maybe you could visit again one day, after you've had time to recover from everything that happened on this visit."

"Maybe," he said, "but you know what? Ever since Stephanie died,

I've had these voices in my head, talking to me, telling me a story. I really want to get home and write the story down. It might be terrible, but at least it's something."

James called the airport and managed to arrange flights for later that same day. He quickly gathered up his bags and loaded them into Fenella's car. As he was doing that, Fenella noticed a car pulling into the driveway across the street. She held her breath as Daniel emerged from the car. A moment later a very pretty blonde, who looked no more than twenty-five, climbed out of the passenger seat. They both removed suitcases from the back of the car and then Daniel opened the house's front door and they went inside together.

"I'm ready," James said.

Fenella blinked back tears and then climbed into the car and started the engine. For several minutes, she focused on driving and tried to put what she'd seen out of her mind.

"I came over planning to ask you for money," James broke the silence. "Aunty Mona left you quite a fortune, didn't she?"

"I won't have to worry about money as long as I'm reasonably careful," Fenella admitted, knowing that she could even be somewhat unreasonable and be okay.

James nodded. "That's what she told me," he said, "but she also told me that I wasn't to ask you for anything. She said that she'd left you the money because you deserved it and I didn't."

"Who told you?" Fenella asked, feeling confused.

"Aunty Mona. She came and talked me every night while I was staying with you. I didn't really remember her, but she was incredible when she visited. She didn't look a day over thirty and she was, well, amazing. That's why I'm not asking you for any money. Because she'd be disappointed in me if I did. I'm going to go home and write the book that's brewing in my head, and when that's done, I might just write another one. Maybe I'll even look at the notes that Stephanie left and try to do something with them. It seems the least I can do for her."

Fenella wasn't sure how to reply to that, so she was grateful that they were at the airport as James finished speaking. She helped him with his luggage and then watched as he made his way through security and disappeared. She was surprised to find that she already missed him as she walked back to her car.

ACKNOWLEDGMENTS

My editor, Denise, has done another great job keeping me from embarrassing myself too much! Thank you.

I'm also grateful to Linda at Tell Tale Book Covers for another great cover and to my beta readers who help make these stories the best they can be.

Mostly, I want to thank everyone who is reading this note for spending time with Fenella and her friends. I have great fun with them and I hope you do, too.

HOP-TU-NAA AND HOMICIDE

AN ISLE OF MAN GHOSTLY COZY

RELEASE DATE: AUGUST 17, 2018

It's Hop-tu-Naa time on the Isle of Man and Fenella Woods is excited to learn more about this uniquely Manx celebration. When a day of fun at Cregneash village ends with Fenella finding a dead body, though, she finds herself tangled up in another murder investigation.

As the inspector in charge of the case calls on Daniel Robinson to help with the investigation, Fenella finds an uncomfortable distance has grown between herself and handsome Inspector Robinson. The distance is only reinforced by the ubiquitous presence of Tiffany Perkins, a pretty young police inspector who'd been on the same course as Daniel.

No one seems to have had a motive for killing young Phillip Pierce. He'd only been on the island for a short while. He was newly married and his beautiful widow seems suitably devastated.

Can Fenella work out why the man was killed? Will Daniel seek her help with this investigation or is he determined to keep her at arm's length? And if he is keeping his distance, is Tiffany the reason or is there something else going on?

ALSO BY DIANA XARISSA

Aunt Bessie Assumes
Aunt Bessie Believes
Aunt Bessie Considers
Aunt Bessie Decides
Aunt Bessie Enjoys
Aunt Bessie Finds
Aunt Bessie Goes
Aunt Bessie's Holiday
Aunt Bessie Invites
Aunt Bessie Joins
Aunt Bessie Knows
Aunt Bessie Likes
Aunt Bessie Meets
Aunt Bessie Needs
Aunt Bessie Observes
Aunt Bessie Provides
Aunt Bessie Questions
Aunt Bessie Remembers
Aunt Bessie Solves
Aunt Bessie Tries
Aunt Bessie Understands
Aunt Bessie Volunteers
Aunt Bessie Wonders

The Isle of Man Ghostly Cozy Mysteries
Arrivals and Arrests
Boats and Bad Guys

Cars and Cold Cases

Dogs and Danger

Encounters and Enemies

Friends and Frauds

Guests and Guilt

Hop-tu-Naa and Homicide

Invitations and Investigations

Joy and Jealousy

Kittens and Killers

Letters and Lawsuits

The Markham Sisters Cozy Mystery Novellas

The Appleton Case

The Bennett Case

The Chalmers Case

The Donaldson Case

The Ellsworth Case

The Fenton Case

The Green Case

The Hampton Case

The Irwin Case

The Jackson Case

The Kingston Case

The Lawley Case

The Moody Case

The Norman Case

The Osborne Case

The Patrone Case

The Quinton Case

The Rhodes Case

The Isle of Man Romance Series

Island Escape

Island Inheritance

Island Heritage

Island Christmas

ABOUT THE AUTHOR

Diana grew up in Northwestern Pennsylvania and moved to Washington, DC after college. There she met a wonderful Englishman who was visiting the city. After a whirlwind romance, they got married and Diana moved to the Chesterfield area of Derbyshire to begin a new life with her husband. A short time later, they relocated to the Isle of Man.

After over ten years on the island, it was time for a change. With their two children in tow, Diana and her husband moved to suburbs of Buffalo, New York. Diana now spends her days writing about the island she loves.

She also writes mystery/thrillers set in the not-too-distant future as Diana X. Dunn and middle grade and YA books as D.X. Dunn.

Diana is always happy to hear from readers. You can write to her at:

Diana Xarissa Dunn
PO Box 72
Clarence, NY 14031.

Find Diana at: DianaXarissa.com
E-mail: Diana@dianaxarissa.com

Printed in Great Britain
by Amazon